FIVE TO ONE

**Winner of the Wink Publishing
Debut Novel competition**

**Nominated for the
Polari First Book Award**

'Funny, painfully honest and moving … Recalls Armistead Maupin's Tales of the City.' Penny Hancock, novelist

'A charming novel. Cleverly structured and consistently engaging.' Matt Cain, Editor-in-Chief, Attitude magazine

'A poignant study of genuine love in a big and fantastically diverse city.' Bytethebook.com

Five-star praise for *Five To One* on Amazon:

'Rare to find a book that makes you laugh out loud. Brilliantly observed with cracking one-liners, Five to One *is a supremely enjoyable vignette of the lives of our times, with a serving or two of pathos that holds up a mirror to us all.'* Webbie

'A gripping and witty novel. I was intrigued how the different strands would be drawn together ... Chalmers succeeds with an admirable denouement.' Otleytipped

'He writes with precision both in his lapidary (occasionally snort-inducing) prose, and his character studies of lonely Londoners and their lives, in settings as diverse as New Zealand, the Galápagos Islands and Loch Ness.' Avidreader

'Chris Chalmers has a great ear for dialogue and his characters are well drawn, flaws and all. This is a book about the people you see every day, the struggles they face and the strength required to overcome them. The stuff that makes ordinary people extraordinary.' Caro Gold

'I read 50% of the book in the space of an afternoon. Perfect holiday book – download it before you hit the airport.' Doc

'Enormously witty – the Houseboat on Loch Ness made me laugh uproariously.' JaynieR

'A gorgeously written book. Intelligent, insightful, funny and charmingly accessible.' Erminiafaith

'I found it hard not to read this book in one go. The fascinating mix of characters and sense of suspense gripped me from the first chapter. Fast-paced, well-written and witty throughout.' Mightier Than The Sword

'A highly engaging, impeccably observant read.' Mbee1

'I found the characters compelling, funny and touchingly sad in equal measure. I didn't see the ending coming. Off-the-wall, but at the same time completely satisfying.' Crokey

'Beautifully written, fabulously crafted and a jolly good tale. Fast moving with characters that leap off the page – all with a wonderful turn of phrase.' BMcB

'Utterly hooked from the beginning. One of the finest opening chapters I've read in a long while.' A.B. Pearl

By the same author

Light From Other Windows

And for children

Gillian Vermillion – Dream Detective

FIVE TO ONE

Chris Chalmers

J.Mendel Books

This edition published in the UK in 2017 by J.Mendel Books, London

First published 2012 by Wink Publishing

Cover design by Mecob Design

ISBN: 978-0-9933239-6-6

For R.H. with love

PROLOGUE

Ninety metres beneath his feet, the wake from a dredger unzipped the murky satin of the Thames.

The cockpit of the little red AS350 reverberated to the juddering rotor, visible through the skylight as a bowl of blur. With a gentle tilt on the cyclic control he checked downstream. Past the Power Station. Past the London Eye, stark as a pram wheel against the blue. To the winking obelisk of Canary Wharf and beyond …

Money, money, greed and money. All the way to the Barrier!

But the sights weren't on his schedule today. Today was strictly a two-hop stop: one hardly worth buckling up for, the other so long he'd need a refuel at Carlisle. Still, it was a change from ferrying the nobs to their crumpet-and-croquet weekends at Cliveden.

Left hand up a bit ...

He gave the collective a gentle tug, turning tail on the river and Chelsea Embankment, all laid out like a picnic. Took the chopper to a safe height without going full pelt; Battersea Heliport to Clapham Common was all of seventy seconds. He sincerely hoped someone had clearance for this; it was highly irregular, flying over anything but the water.

A tap on the pedal, a twist on the tail and he was over those ugly new flats on Falcon Road.

Afternoon, folks!

He waved to Mr and Mrs City Slicker, partaking of a light lunch on their overpriced balcony. Could join them for pud if he wasn't in a rush. Strawberries by the look – his favourite.

A double-pip in his headphones; he flipped the switch.

'Can't leave me alone, can you, Joyce?'

'Got Ol' Blue Eyes for you again, love. Urgent as ever ...'

'Get away. Patch him through.'

The trouble with flying charter was that you sometimes got clients like this one. Name of Sinatra, if you could believe it.

'Wotcha, mate!'

'Afternoon, squire ...' He eased the cans away from his lucky yellow helmet. A shouter too, this one, as he'd discovered taking him and his lady friend up to Scotland. Couldn't grasp the intercom to save their lives.

'Just fort I'd check we're all systems go an' that ... ETA as is, yeah?'

'Sorry, sir?'

'Landing on the Common oh-twelve fifty-five hours?'

'Five to one, sir. Yes.'

'And you've got the package? For your mystery passenger?'

The plastic wallet was in the pocket beside him.

'Ready and waiting, sir.'

'Cool ... Listen, where shall I say you'll be?'

'Probably best you tell him to keep an eye out, sir. Strictly speaking we're not supposed to—'

'Understood, mate! Leave the legals to me, yeah? Right, I'll see you both in free hours ... Roger Wilco, over and-'

Out. Tosser.

Far below through the glass, the train lines of Clapham Junction bunched like sinews. He settled back and let her breeze, smooth as smooth. Beyond a certain point, London blended to a uniform grey – like someone had emptied a Hoover bag over the horizon. Not quite Dubai, where he'd meant to end his career: sun, sand and healthy savings plan.

Hey-ho. Not to be.

And there was the Common, dead ahead. Wide open spaces and broccoli trees; two hundred acres if memory served, as close to a triangle as you got with Victorian town planning ... Now where the hell was he going to land?

Nice one, Mr Sinatra. But then, you would have it your *way.*

He hoped his next passenger had his eyes peeled, so they could take off before the Parks Police rolled up in their motorised wheelbarrows. Hoped he wasn't starving either; it was a long old haul to Inverness, even with a stop, and he'd only a sandwich in the back. Mints too, somewhere ...

Café, bandstand, pond. Nothing else to avoid. Hardly anyone about, even on a lovely day like this. Just a Land Rover over to starboard, mowing the grass – another jobsworth, no doubt … All the more reason to get down and get up again, sharpish.

Oh look – that's where they kept 'em; oval bit, all fenced off, with two more Land Rovers and a couple of sheds. Nice open space beside it too. That'll do nicely …

He scanned the instruments. Quick three-sixty visual: sun-kissed lady taking the rays; couple of joggers; the usual likely lads fishing for Jaws in that dirty old pond ... No one who looked like they'd got a kilt in an overnight bag.

He brought her level and settled into descent. Could do with one of those mints now, as a matter of fact-

Hang on, what the hell's that?!

Bloody tramp on the grass, lying right on his patch! Singing away to himself, waving it all about like a dying fly … *Go on, sling your hook!*

There was another Charlie down there, too. On his phone with his fingers in his ears. Gawd, they were all out today!

He put her into hover. The noise usually drove them off. That was another thing about Dubai – at least the sheikh kept an AK47 under the front seat.

Stubborn old sod wasn't shifting. *Un-be-bleeding-lievable!* And the chaps at base wondered why he wanted to hang up his helmet! If someone got a camera out now, he'd never hear the end from Health & Safety.

Nothing else for it.

He pulled up and swung her round, banking over Parky's lockup. Decent-sized spot by the pond. (Sorry lads, I'm going to scare your fish …)

As he did, a tube of Extra Strong Mints rolled out from under the seat.

There they are!

Another visual: all clear, bar a traffic cone some smart alec had plonked on the grass. Soon blow that away.

Light on the throttle, bit of left pedal. Nice and square … Perfect! All he had to do now was keep the tail clear of those trees.

'Course, it was different for the young lads. They still got a buzz from flying boys' toys, plus it did no harm with the ladies. He'd been the same at their age, but now all he wanted was to be near his daughter and little Ben. Finally get round to building his grandson that—

Steady! Eye on the ball, old son … Don't want to end up like Nobby Curtis in the Forest of Dean!

He could kill for one of those mints.

He put her into settle; thirty metres and counting. If he leant over carefully he could just – about – reach …

That was another Health & Safety no-no: loose items in the cockpit. Get something stuck under the pedal at the wrong moment and you were as good as—

BUGGER!

He didn't feel the tail hit the branches.

Didn't hear the rotor shred them to a blizzard of splinters.

Didn't see the four upturned faces, open-mouthed, aghast, as the fuselage slumped into a spiral.

As he braced for impact, the litany of safety drills tumbling through his head fell short of his hands. And his last thought was for all the ribbing he'd taken from the chaps at the base about his lucky yellow helmet.

If he was going to see little Ben again, it had better do its stuff ...

FIVE

I

'I like your radishes. They are werry nice.'

Ian looked up from the compost. He hadn't heard the back door open. It was Agnes, the nanny to the child of the house, standing on the garden path.

He wiped his hands on his vest. As he shaded his eyes from the fading sunlight, his fingers framed her in an aura that seemed entirely appropriate. It reminded him of tales of shepherd boys on lonely hillsides, visited by visions of the Virgin Mary and / or a very bright light. Except that the way this particular maiden was looking him over was less than virginal.

He'd seen her before: through the window preparing the child's tea, and hanging out the washing in that lacy T-shirt that exposed her belly button to the breeze. But this was the first time he'd ever heard her speak.

'Sparkler White-Tips,' he said, breaking a foolish silence. 'Top variety for the soil around here.'

Agnes nodded her mane of reddish curls as she opened her hand. Inside were two healthy round roots, cleaned and trimmed and ready to eat. She rolled them deftly, one over the other, like a tennis pro preparing to serve.

'And they are *werry* good for childrens. They have a lot of *witamins* and also iron.'

Her flat, Polish tones pronounced it *eye-ron,* which to Ian's surprise he found spectacularly arousing. As if her natural cleavage and the hipbones peeping saucily over her jeans weren't enough. He leant on his spade to disguise a sudden awkwardness in his all-weather shorts. Watched, as she cradled the pinky-red balls a moment longer. Popped one in her mouth, and crunched.

Ian Newton was forty-seven. He had run his own gardening business for eleven years, since a long-forgotten drop in the FTSE lost him the City job he hated. He preferred fresh air and being his own boss to watching screens and fielding calls from Tokyo. His friends joked about the temptations of bored, immaculate housewives, with nothing to do between school runs but sip espresso and wait for the gardener to get his shirt off. But the fact was, he had never strayed. As a professional, a pessimist and a coward, he automatically assumed any husband would have hit-squad connections if he so much as left a boot-print on the stair carpet. So in all his years of marriage he had never seriously considered being unfaithful. Even when Carla was at her most bloodyminded.

Until now.

On a late May afternoon in the Wallaces' back garden, when Agnes Skirowska smiled and chewed a second radish in the sunlight.

Half an hour later, with Jasper at his heels, Ian knocked the earth from his spade and tossed it in the van. Followed by one welly, then the other, swapping them for the moccasins he wore for driving. Another of Carla's little rules – though God knows why he was sticking to it now ...

'In you go, fella!'

The little West Highland terrier made a mountain of climbing in the passenger door, settling for base camp in the footwell rather than striking out for the summit. By the end of an afternoon the dog was more tired than he was. Even the earthworms that once whipped him into a snuffling frenzy had lost their allure.

Not many summers left for the old team now, thought Ian, driving with one eye on the furry bundle. Jasper was highly impractical as a gardener's dog. His white fur showed every sticky bud and bloodied raspberry that clung beyond the canine radar. On one occasion they had narrowly avoided a collision when Ian caught sight of that noble muzzle accessorised by a jaunty feather.

But on this day he looked without seeing. His fingers quivered and his armpits gave off an aroma a little like fear. They were the signs of anticipation; of a man about to break new ground without working through the consequences. As they pulled out of Luther Road, Ian ran through his imminent schedule:

Feed dog. Shower. Get changed. Set Sky Plus.

After every glance at Jasper, his eyes trailed back via the dashboard clock. Nine minutes to seven; just sixty-nine minutes to go.

They opened a fraction wider.

*

Glory spotted the roadworks as soon as she stepped off the bus.

Laying new electric cable evidently took a dozen men and an awful lot of machinery. Not to mention closing the road until August, according to the notice on the lamp post. It also meant that her bus stopped short of the Hall, so from now on she'd be finishing her journey on foot.

Mechanical diggers were no substitute for the dawn chorus, she thought, as she crossed on the zebra by the estate agents. But it pleased her that some people had to be at work even earlier than she did. And there were worse ways to start the day than strolling across Clapham Common.

As she reached the other side, the changing sound of her footsteps – from pavement to grass to gravel – reminded her of walking to the Pentecostal service as a little girl. Of making Ma drag her along, all for the fun of feeling the ground change beneath the soles of her T-bar sandals – black with proper heels! How Glory had coveted those shoes, till her first pair appeared on her sixth birthday, making her feel as grown-up as her sister and all her sister's friends.

Glory slid through the gap in the car-park fence that no one ever mended. Sodden troughs had formed in the gravel overnight where the rain collected. She wiped her feet on the edge of the grass. She wasn't about to let Mrs Molyneux say she trod dirt about the place. (Why give her the pleasure?)

Across the road the gates of Cedars Hall were already open. The lounge curtains had been drawn but the room was empty, as it would be till after breakfast. She let herself in through the first door, punching the security code into the second. It was meant to change every month, but no one ever did that either.

'Morning, Glory!' pealed an insolent voice behind her.

Lord! If she had a pound for every time she'd heard that one!

It was the foolish caretaker's boy. Too big for his boots, too skinny for his jeans, and not worth so much as a look back through the frosted glass.

Dennis was awake. Dennis woke at six-thirty every morning, with a consistency that sent Glory scurrying upstairs the one and only time his high-pitched cry had been wanting. She had caught her breath – composed herself, before she opened the door of his room – to find Dennis propped up on the pillows, bedspread to his chin and mouthing furiously.

Laryngitis!

This morning his moan was there as usual, to be repeated at thirty-second intervals throughout the day. It reached every floor, like the cloying smell of disinfectant that acted as a distraction from the Hall's other, less floral odours.

Down in the basement Glory changed into her uniform. She was stowing her things in the locker when Jan came off the night shift.

'How was it?' she asked, patting down the Velcro fastenings of her tabard.

'Nothing to report,' said Jan. She yanked off the rubber band that held her ginger bob in a bunch. ''Cept for Pearl. She's been battling the Vietcong again. Single-handed, right up to breakfast! No wonder she's got such an appetite.'

Glory shook her head and laughed. Pearl was one of her favourites. She tried to treat all the residents equally, but she was only human. Some of them touched your heart more than others.

Jan sniffed her blue work shirt and stuffed it in her bag. She shut the locker with a jingle of keys. 'Off till Thursday now, I am. See you later.'

'Doin' anything nice?' asked Glory.

'With my lot? You must be joking. My eldest's on daily report, and if I don't watch the other two they're sagging off down Borough Market. Skived football last week. Came home with two pineapples and a mini DVD player.'

Glory tutted consolingly.

'I don't ask,' said Jan. 'What's the point?'

*

Tony was still muzzy with jet lag, which probably explained the randomness of the thought. It was a bit bloody bizarre, he knew, to walk into a beauty parlour and immediately think of *Star Wars*.

It wasn't like he was about to blow away on the breeze

himself; but the girl on reception had to be a hundred and twenty kilos if she was a day. And something about that tiny head on a pyramidal body …

Got it: Jabba the Hutt!

Or was that in *The Empire Strikes Back*?

He couldn't help thinking that Pippa (her badge said **PIPPA**) was a strange choice to work in a place like this. But fair dos – she had good skin, if the tiny proportion on display was anything to go by.

'Can I help you?'

Her voice was high and achingly nasal. Polystyrene on a wet window.

'Erm, yeah. I've got a two o'clock appointment. With Latasha?'

'Name?'

'Tony Torrence.'

Pippa ran a sausage down the desk ledger. Her fingernails were so immaculate, Tony thought she could have been a hand model. For those high-calorie energy bars they made for mountaineers.

'Back facial today, is it?'

Or bath lifts.

'Yeah, if that's what you call it over here.'

Pippa applied a tick to his name with a cocktail-stick of a pen. 'Take a seat,' she squeaked. 'Latasha will be with you in five …'

He wondered if Pippa did the treatments too; maybe some women would prefer to be primped by a girl who didn't look like a Chanel model? One thing for sure, she didn't lack confidence. Pippa ran her fingers through her well-groomed hair as she rummaged in a drawer; pushed a hank behind each ear while she filled the stapler, drawing attention to the golden hoops that swung from her lobes like a budgie toys.

But any further south and you were in very different terrain: the zipper on that shiny white coverall deserved an award for endeavour – and as she swivelled to replace the staples, her upholstered back made him yearn for a toboggan.

And to think, he used to worry how *he* would ever get a boyfriend!

A buzzer curtailed the thought.

'Go through, Tony,' said Pippa. 'Suite Three. Door's a bit dicky, so give it a shove.'

He had no idea what she was talking about but it sounded intriguing. As he slid past the sun creams that were half the price back home, Tony's elbow jogged a display of pygmy superglue.

'*Mind out!*' squealed Pippa.

Crystalline tubes cascaded to the floor. She didn't move from the counter as Tony crouched to retrieve them.

'Oopsy,' she shrugged gelatinously.

He slotted the tubes of Youth Release Signature Eye Dew back in their stand.

'Corridor's a bit tight there, isn't it?' sympathised Pippa.

Or was that *empathised*?

Tony shot her a look.

Now he thought of it, Jabba the Hutt was in *Return of the Jedi*. Not a movie he'd ever really taken to …

*

Mari knew Adam was hiding something in the pocket of his shorts. She avoided asking what, for fear of one of his favourite, unoriginal jokes. He was still fiddling as he slipped his other arm around her shoulders. Mari ignored it and followed his eyes to the beach.

'We had an animal encyclopedia when I was a kid,' said Adam. 'With this picture in it I've never forgotten ...'

She wondered if he was about to whip the page out now, six thousand miles and twenty years from the bedroom he shared with his brother in Altrincham.

'It was a beach like this. Sea lions and iguanas basking in the sun. And a blue-footed booby, puking up fish for its chicks – just like that one!'

Mari looked away. She waved a fly from her sunglasses and smiled as a baby sea lion twitched a flipper in much the same way. Like all the finches and the little green lizards, it seemed oblivious to her, even a metre or two from her toes.

'I always thought it was a trick photo – cos how could they get all of them in one shot? But it wasn't.' His voice ebbed away on a wave. 'It was here ...'

'Punta Espinosa, auf der Insel von Fernandina!'

The voice behind them was Heike-with-the-eyebrows, speaking into the mic of her camcorder. She was standing on a boulder, scoping the bay in a sweep.

'Magic, innit?' whispered Adam.

Fernandina was their fourth island in as many days, but even Mari had to agree. There wasn't another beach in the world where you could see all these animals, side by side. Like Noah had pressed the fire alarm on the Ark.

She watched as a white bird sailed overhead, tail plumes trailing. When she looked down again, Adam's hand was out of his pocket.

II

Ian crossed the pub car park with a nonchalance he did not feel. As he bipped the Peugeot's central locking, a memory intruded:

Driving out to a country pub aged seventeen, in his best cords and new Wrangler jacket. His first-ever date with Jessica Gidley.

The car so muggy with the great smell of Brut, it almost masks the reek of his dad's fags. He turns up the stereo full blast – a compilation tape he's made for her specially. The new Gary Numan single drowns out the rush of blood in his ears.

Here in his car, he feels safest of all ...

It's a relief to be out of the house. And away from that phone, when every ring is a heart attack: Jessica, bound to be, calling to cancel.

But now he's alone, on the open road to his destiny. Will she turn up – is she already there – or has he sneaked the keys to the Capri for nothing?

Inside the Windmill, no horse brasses hung in an eerie silence. It was thick with student types, slotted around tables and yelling to their mates at the bar. The tang of beer and garlic butter replaced the wood smoke of his memory. And tonight was different for another reason, too.

Thirty years ago, it wasn't Jessica Gidley who'd asked *him* out on a date.

The Windmill was a sprawling pub with stairs and nooks and rooms leading off rooms. The only one on Clapham Common, and as much a landmark as its namesake. Ian rarely came here now that Jasper had lost his appetite for walkies. And Carla preferred restaurants to pubs, though she could be persuaded to the gastro type –

all folded napkins and scrubbed-up surfer boys waiting table.

The big front room was congested. He felt conspicuous as he made his way to the bar (… *Might as well get himself a T-shirt and be done with it: MARRIED MAN, MEETING GIRL HALF HIS AGE.)*

'Hell-o,' said a voice behind him.

Agnes had changed her top. And she'd done something with those corkscrew curls.

'Hello,' he said. 'Can I—'

The kiss on his cheek cut him short and left it blooming like a prize radish.

'I already got drink,' she said in delectably imprecise English. 'I am sit through there.' She nodded to an arch and smiled, disappearing back through the knot of bodies.

By the time he fought his way to the annexe, Ian's blushes had subsided. She was on a banquette by the fruit machine, an empty space beside her. As he opted for a chair instead she launched brightly into conversation.

'I think this is *werry* nice pub.' She nodded to the giant TV playing music videos on mute. 'I came here when was the football, one year ago. England play Poland. Rasiomski score the – *hatt-er-ick*, no?'

'Probably,' said Ian. 'Must have missed it.'

He was more of a cricket man, and not at all sure he was blokey enough for this. It was quieter in here and, while less people meant fewer eyes, it also meant a distinct lack of cover if anyone he knew walked in.

He stopped looking around.

'So, how do you find the Wallace boy?'

Agnes looked blank. 'How do I … ?'

'I mean, do you like him? Friendly lad, isn't he? Likes helping me with the mowing.'

He was treading carefully: Sebastian Wallace was three foot six of obnoxious little runt. He treated Ian like a serf who had turned up at the Big House with a begging bowl and the raging pox.

Agnes sipped her vodka and tonic. She studied him carefully, as if trying to see behind his eyes.

'Actually, I think Sebastian is a little bastard.'

Her laughter broke the tension. They were on common ground.

'My bedroom is in the roof of the house,' she explained. 'The loaf – *loaft*, no?'

'Loft, yes.'

'Yes. And I got my own bathroom. With shower.'

Ian's mind was racing.

'Well, on the first day I start to work at the Wallace house, Sebastian hide behind the curtain with his toothbrush – *and jump out when I am sit on toilet!'*

Her eyes were wide. Ian was a-quiver with responses. Until a second gale of laughter signalled the right one.

He shook his head. 'Kids, eh? Who'd have 'em?'

This Guinness was slipping down a treat. He had worried he might rediscover the joys of boozing while he only had Jasper for company, but this was his first drink in a fortnight. Bringing the car had been a ruse to make sure he stuck to Coke after this.

'And you,' said Agnes, 'you don't have childrens?'

The question halted his glass in midair. Partly for not being: *And you – you don't have wife?*

As the white coronet of foam sank down inside the glass he wondered if his bonhomie was about to follow.

'No.'

Agnes nodded. 'Better.'

She sipped her drink. 'I think childrens are *werry* good

for peoples who have empty lives. Peoples who want to fit in like everybody else. You understand?'

Ian nodded. Whatever he'd expected from drinks with a twenty-two-year-old Pole with come-hither eyes and tits to die for, it wasn't philosophy.

'But some peoples, they are more independent, no? Whole, *as themselves*.'

She stood abruptly. Pushed back the table with her well-toned thighs. For a moment he thought she was off, seminar dismissed. But it was the only way she could reach into the hip pocket of her jeans. From where he sat, Ian's nose was inches from the fastening – an enamel button in the shape of a daisy. As she fumbled for something millimetres from her groin, he glimpsed the fleeting white waistband of her panties, rising from the blue of her jeans like a sunlit wave, then plunging out of sight.

With a conjurer's flourish, a crinkled ten-pound note appeared on the table.

'So. Is my round.'

And before he could object Agnes was off with her meagre wages to buy a drink for a man old enough to be her father. A man with his own business, a solid City pension and no mortgage on a highly desirable house a few hundred yards from Clapham Common.

A man who wondered: *Does it get any better than this?*

*

Upstairs in the staff room Glory checked her rota.

Clear breakfasts on First Floor East. Change beds. Load laundry. All before the coffee run at eleven-fifteen, followed by cleaning bedrooms East 7 to 13.

'Good morning, Glory!'

This time the voice was Mrs Molyneux, the senior manager in charge of the day-to-day running of Cedars Hall. She was a small woman, white and proper, like someone from the Second World War. Glory knew she was looking at her shoes even before she turned round.

'Nice to see you looking smart today! First Floor East for you, isn't it?'

When Mrs Molyneux spoke, her chin jutted out as if she was peering from an invisible lectern. Glory nodded.

'Good. We've got the inspectors in this afternoon. Unannounced visit. I'll be checking the bedrooms myself before lunch, so let's make sure they're done properly ...'

Her high heels ticked away down the corridor. Shoes that Glory thought would look tarty on a taller woman; on her they just looked remedial.

She wondered how Mrs Molyneux knew about the inspection. Unannounced visits were meant to be a surprise, to catch poorly run care homes off guard. But then, that woman probably knew the Lottery numbers before the programme had even started.

Glory sighed ... You could say what you liked about Mrs Molyneux; she might be short of inches, but she wasn't short of balls.

East 9 was Pearl's room. When Glory knocked there was no reply. Though that meant nothing.

The door dragged on the heavy pile of the carpet.

Empty.

She plugged the Hoover into the socket by the wardrobe. After all these years, Glory could tell most of the residents by the state of their carpet. Hairgrips for Daisy. Pink wafer crumbs for Alma. Mint imperials for Archie, half sucked and two feet from the bin. But old Pearl was tidy as a soldier; not that she had much to make a mess with. She had moved into the Hall with very few knick-knacks from her old life. Just a couple of vases, a box meant for sewing things, and one or two books Glory had never seen her read.

And then there were her photographs. Two, framed on the wall. A portrait of Pearl as a young woman, with a baby on her knee and her late husband behind her; and the same pose forty years later, this time with her grown-up son sitting at her feet, cross-legged and a little cross-faced.

As she was swilling away the suds in the basin there was a thud on the other side of the door. The footplate of Pearl's wheelchair slid into view, mounted by tartan-slippered feet.

'There,' said the podgy girl pushing. 'All done.'

She was one of the new care assistants. Too new for a proper name badge, which read *Trainee*.

'She's been toileted,' said the girl, as if she was returning a dog.

And with that she disappeared, leaving Pearl parked in front of the wardrobe to study her reflection in the lacquer.

Glory tutted. *These new girls had no idea!*

The thirty-one beds at Cedars Hall were occupied by fragile bodies and fragile minds; old souls who appreciated familiar hands and faces. The way staff came and went these days did them no good at all – but that was how it was since Mrs Molyneux arrived with her new broom, shifting everything about from top to bottom. And, just like in the old cartoon, when she was done that broom kept sweeping on its own, as more of the old staff left and new ones arrived. Foreigners; mostly East European. Now the only ones left from the old days were Jan and Glory herself.

She turned round the old lady's wheelchair and sat on the bed to face her.

'How you doin' today, Pearl?'

Pearl's eyes fixed on something over Glory's shoulder. She was wearing her favourite blouse and cardigan. Her eyelashes were matted with the gunk that came back no matter how many times you wiped it.

Pearl smiled, as if noticing Glory for the first time.

'I'm fine, thanking you. How are you?'

'Mustn't grumble, me darlin'. Now, where'd you like to sit? It's an hour till your lunch. How about by the window?'

Pearl appeared to mull this over. When no answer came Glory wheeled her to the window, where she could see the blue tits zeroing in on a hanging bag of peanuts.

'There,' she said. 'Your own private floor show. Wasn't it nice of your son to buy you that bird table?'

Pearl sniffed. 'That's Gerald all over,' she observed tartly. 'Pay someone else to entertain us before he'll do it himself.'

Glory smiled; with Pearl it wasn't the royal 'we'. In her world, her husband, Ernest, was still alive, kicking and often a cause of concern. Only the previous week she had confided in Glory that Ernest was having an affair *'with that flighty piece from the laundry!'*

Whoever that was.

It was a revelation that caused her remarkably little distress, and wouldn't necessarily be referred to again; because, at the ripe old age of eighty-four, Pearl's life had turned into her own personal soap opera. The plot was often far-fetched, with threads that were picked up and dropped too casually for the occasional viewer. And sometimes, the channel changed completely:

'Have they found that boy?' asked Pearl. 'The one that was kidnapped by the Vietcong?'

Glory filled the tooth mug from the jumbo bottle of ginger beer she kept in Pearl's wardrobe. 'I don't think I know about him, Pearl.'

The old woman flinched, swinging round as far as her safety harness would allow.

'*You must!* I had four of them in here last night! It wasn't me they were after, thank goodness. Slanty-eyed devils!'

Glory screwed the cap back on the bottle. 'Now that'll do, Pearl. Here, drink your pop.'

Political correctness had passed the old lady by; she was that generation. Glory found it disconcerting at first – until the day Pearl asked her, quite without irony, if she knew 'any coloured people. *Personally*, I mean.'

Other times she was right as rain, asking sensible questions about Glory's cousins in Jamaica. But that was how it was with folk like Pearl; you never knew how they were going to be today.

*

The door to Suite Three had a wobbly handle. Inside, it was hardly big enough to swing a receptionist's garter.

Latasha *(*LA'TASHA*)* took Tony's jacket and hung it up beside a funky number in purple suede. She was small with lots of makeup and a smooth, elaborate hairdo.

'Pop your top off for me, Tony. And lie face down, I'll be back in a tick ...'

She wafted out in a vapour trail of something foxy.

Every available surface was stacked with towels and clinically packaged products. Tony laid his T-shirt across the coat hook. The massage table very nearly filled the room, and was covered in paper from an industrial-sized roll on the wall. He climbed aboard, tearing a vent over the vinyl blowhole which took him back to his first-ever facial – with Greta, at a chi-chi little beauty parlour in Dunedin. It was the day of the Freshers' Ball at Otago Uni; they both had the hots for Mikey Huata, and one look at the massage table's strategically placed opening reduced them to hysterics. It was the same contraption they had seen in a porno movie, hired for a dare one giggly, girlie night in. It never occurred to either of them the hole had a legitimate purpose.

His smile was in the gap when La'Tasha reappeared and looked him over in all his furry glory.

'So … No back wax today, Tony?'

'Erm, no.'

'It's just some of my gentlemen prefer it in the summer. Cuts down the static.'

'Oh,' he said. 'Well, maybe another time, eh.' Some of *his* gentlemen liked his back just the way it was, thanks very much.

There was a sound of scraping and something mixing in a bowl. La'Tasha set to with her rituals in silence, upholding the tranquility of the sanctum. When she slathered on the results, Tony focused on the toes of her lilac winkle pickers as his skin surrendered to the therapeutic equivalent of a bicycle chaining. Exfoliator: one part walnut shells to three parts cat litter.

More mixing followed, accompanied by faint odours of clay, vanilla and ylang ylang, which suggested a purifying mask. This time the concoction went on like melted toffee. But once applied, La'Tasha was off again, leaving the poultice to do its work.

Tony luxuriated in the moment and tried not to flex his back. Low-budget pornos aside, he couldn't think of a nicer reason to have his face wedged in a very small toilet seat. The room was warm; the ambient soundtrack was mercifully free of whale song, and to cap it all he wasn't paying. How his mate Geoff could call himself a gay man and be too busy to use a free treatment voucher was way beyond him.

Five minutes later, an irresistible twitch caused a crackling sensation down his spine. The winkle pickers reappeared, and hands sloughed off the mask, along with enough skin cells to reconstitute a baby rhino. It was total bliss; and they hadn't even got to the best bit.

A fluffy towel alighted, covering his exposed skin but for a hand-width at the top of his shoulders. There was a respectful pause, and Tony wondered if La'Tasha was saying a prayer. Then she set to work on his blackheads.

As the towel moved slowly down, her fingertips swept his back almost imperceptibly, as if coaxing a note from a wine glass. The dual downdrafts from her nostrils skimmed an inch behind as her fingers lifted, then touched down again enveloped in tissue. It signified they had found a target.

Extraction was quick and remarkably painless. Tony winced, but only at the memory of letting Greta loose on his teenage pores. It was his best friend's callous gusto that had taken them to the Dunedin beauty parlour in the first place, saving him the agony of martyrdom as every extrusion brought him closer to dermatological piety.

Too quickly, La'Tasha's attentions reached the small of his back.

'All clear!' she chirped. 'You've got very nice skin, Tony.'

A mixed blessing; he wanted to get Geoff's mum's money's worth.

'We'll just finish off with a tone and light massage,' she

said, chilling his serenity with something misty from a greenfly gun. And with that, the curfew lifted.

'So, are you living here or just visiting?'

'I'm here for a few months,' said Tony reluctantly. 'Staying with a mate round the corner.'

'That's nice. You're from Australia, aren't you – Sydney?'

'Auckland.'

'Thought so!' La'Tasha's fingers swept in waves across the top of his back. 'I can tell you're from Down Under. Not being horrible or anything, but you've got a bit of sun damage on the tops of your shoulders.'

'Yeah?'

'Mmm, bit blotchy. Must be all those years skipping round your barbie!' She tittered abruptly. 'Barbecue, I mean. Not the dolly …'

Tony tittered back. Silly cow.

'Mind you, I'm surprised the sun got through all that hair. What are you doing in London?'

(Jeez – how come it was always their business?)

'Just hanging out. Might take a trip down to a few places in Europe.'

'Oh – not working, then? That's nice.'

'Have to see how the money goes. And how long I can hog my mate's spare room.'

'Lovely ...'

La'Tasha tittered again. And with a flourish, she was done.

'Whoops!'

Tony winced a second time as she grazed a potential melanoma with her French manicure.

She handed him his clothes.

'Anyway, pop back if you want us to sort out your back,

won't you? Only £28, and Monday to Wednesday we throw in a complimentary Gentleman's Sports Wax.'

He hardly dared ask.

'You know, your downstairs bits. Very popular with the joggers.' She stripped off the paper tablecloth and scrunched. 'Do you jog?'

'No.'

'*No* ...'

That tone again!

'Nice jacket. I tried to get my bruvver one of those. Big sizes go first though, don't they?'

Tony tipped her a pound less than he intended. He crept back through reception, carefully negotiating the narrow passage. Pippa was on the phone, receiver to her ear like a very small croissant. He held out the voucher in lieu of cash. She took it and shot him a lukewarm smile that missed.

As Tony let himself out, the 'Open' sign caught his eye:

Welcome to PLUSH
Haven of Holistic Well-Being

Yeah, right! Was that their idea of making him feel good – bloody Jabba-of-the-Larder and Miss Fuck-Me-Heels? Weren't Brits supposed to be reserved about making personal remarks? Then again, maybe Geoff wasn't being an odious English queen after all when he asked Tony how many kilos he'd put on.

He was about to cross the street when he caught his reflection in the salon's tinted glass.

Yep; no two ways about it. It was time to lose weight.

*

At first Mari thought Adam was holding a giant Quality Street. But if he'd brought that all the way to the equator in his pocket, it would be liquid by now.

What lay on his palm was a purple dome-topped box. The kind that—

'I bought it in Quito,' he said, flicking off a thread of khaki lint.

A seagull keened overhead. Before she could take it, Adam prised up the lid and cleared his throat.

'Marry – will you Mari me. *Oh shit!*'

They both snorted with laughter. It was a snapshot moment, to be framed in hilarity and passed around at family gatherings for eternity: *'Our Adam! Waits seven years to pop the question, then gets his lass's name wrong!'*

The stone was sparkling blue. He was still shaking as he slipped the ring from the box. Mari felt the hard slide of it over her knuckle; it was a snug fit.

'Phew,' said Adam.

He kissed her; then they both looked round.

But the rest of their party were too absorbed in the tableau of Punta Espinosa … Paloma, their squat Ecuadorian guide, was by the shore, a respectful distance from the beach master sea lion; she was explaining the hierarchy of his harem to the other English couple, who were listening with a high degree of nudging. The elderly Americans were birdwatching from a sand hill – a Galápagos hawk, coming into land beside its mate in a straggly tree. And Klaus was twiddling his Nikon, composing a group shot of iguanas as they lolled in a flinty cauldron. Which only left-

'Congratulations! So charming, no?'

Heike trotted up behind them with her camcorder. She had one eye to the viewfinder like an assassin as she zoomed in on Mari's finger with a lurid lack of tact.

'Wait, I have magnification ...' She pulled back, motioning to Adam. 'Come, ask her again and this time I will film!'

Mari froze. Adam backed away, grinning weakly. 'I don't think we—'

'*Yes, yes!*' insisted Heike. 'Into the microphone, please. Everybody – *Klaus!* – come and see! Adam and Mari are proposing to marry, isn't it wonderful? All these beautiful creatures and now two lovebirds. Ha ha!'

She gave Adam a shove. 'Over here, yes? Then down on the knee, like so ... Perfect! And now the words again ... Smile – *oh, but mind the lizard!*'

They had booked the cruise after two months in Quito, living out of backpacks in a room on the appropriately named Calle Rabida.

'We deserve a treat after this shithole,' cajoled Adam. 'And we can't leave South America without seeing the Galápagos Islands!' Which meant he couldn't.

Since the *Beluga* was due to sail two days before the end of term, it meant doing a runner on their students at the *colegio*. Being unprofessional went against the grain with Mari, but she could live with it. They had done Teaching English as a Foreign Language as far as she was concerned. Done the whole, daring trip of a lifetime they never got round to at university. She was ready to go home.

Even a mile above sea level, the Ecuadorian capital had brought her down to earth. Jitters which weren't helped by the gun-toting security guards in every shop doorway, most of them no older than her pupils. Each morning, as she and Adam walked to class, the same inky crew cuts and MTV pouts turned to her from every bank and chemist. At least the school was fitted with security scanners. She knew her students weren't armed, yet the sullen stares from the back of the classroom made her just as uneasy – from teenagers, only there because their parents bribed or threatened them. The modules of the TEFL course had prepared her for the intricacies of teaching English grammar; but not for Javier and his omnipresent toothpick. The warped, pitted thing idled at one corner of his mouth like an everlasting roll-up, before swivelling to the other side in appreciation of his own cockiness.

If Adam had problems with his own students, he never let on. Hardly mentioned them in fact, even as he sat up marking homework beneath a shadeless bulb. He might be five foot eight with an early-onset paunch, but Mari was quite sure some of the girls would have fallen for his English charms. One day, as they queued in the supermarket for bread and chorizo, she even asked him.

'God knows!' said Adam.

Which would have been suspicious in another man, but it was just like him not to notice. The same way he missed that little smile the checkout girl slipped in with his change.

Good old Adam; he might not be the most exciting boyfriend in the world, but Mari knew he wouldn't look at another woman if she scored for Man United in a push-up bra. Plus he treated her like a proverbial princess; stood up when she walked into the pub, held the door open when she walked out again. He wanted babies and so did she; wanted to move to the country and so did she.

It was just that he wanted it sooner. Which was why, every time Adam told her he'd be there for her for the rest of his life, a gnawing voice inside Mari's head asked: *Does that mean for the rest of mine?*

It was a voice she had intended to confront on this trip, while she was free of her job at the estate agents and the skein of everyday life – the congestion charges and parking tickets, the calls to her freeholder about the communal carpets. All things Adam didn't understand, because Adam didn't drive and Adam still rented.

He ignored the property specs she brought him from work: floorplans of nice little studios and one-beds that lay around the wasteland of his bedroom until they ended up in the bin or Phil's room. On the odd occasion Adam met her from work, the only properties that caught his eye were those ample for three. If she was busy, he might quiz Mark-James about the size of an ensuite or a second bedroom; questions her boss answered warily, for he and Adam moved in very different orbits. Mark-James rowed and lived behind gates in Putney, wore striped shirts with cufflinks, and referred to Adam behind his back as 'Emin-Ad' on account of his taste in music. It was a dig intended to wind up Mari – which failed, since the last thing she wanted in a boyfriend was approval from a man who hoisted his trousers up around his kidneys.

On the contrary, Mari loved Adam for the way he did his own thing. And never more than on the morning Mark-James had breezed into the office, braying tales of the weekend into his Blackberry:

'So we're two bottles down, yeah, and I'm with Velvet. Meanwhile Pigsy's getting it on *big stylee* with her mate, Electra, who's falling out of her blouse before she's even in the cab. We're halfway up Westbourne Grove when Pigsy says, "Where the eff's Rudders?" ... *Exactly!* ... Well, mine apparently, though why the eff I'm supposed to have the keys, blowed if I know ... *Quite!* Or would, if her mouth was empty for long enough – *fnaar*!'

His rowing team's drinking games and the incarceration of their ever-stoical cox were the staple subject of Mark-James's Monday phone calls.

'Nice weekend, Mari?' he asked, between munches of ginger biscuit. They were making coffee in the shop's cramped kitchen. Mari's weekends could never compete with his, happy as she was to spend Saturday nights in bed with a book and Adam, twitching away to his iPod. Or, if they were at his place, watching one of his precious wildlife DVDs, on a laptop balanced on a stack of vinyl.

'Fine, thanks,' said Mari. 'We stayed in Saturday night. Watched a documentary about penguins.'

Mark-James snorted, nudging her till she slopped her cup of instant.

'Aye aye! *Natural history videos*, eh? Slippery slope, Mari!'

She smiled tightly as he tossed the biscuit wrapper at the bin and missed.

It was the same week Mari signed them both up for the TEFL course, and Adam booked their flights to Lima.

III

That night, after they left the Windmill, Ian and Agnes made love four times. Twice lying down and twice standing up, all in the back of his van.

It was parked in the drive as they pulled up in the Peugeot. Her fingers were spreading scurrilously over his thigh, picking at the inseam of his Levi's.

'We are not coming inside,' she said firmly.

Dear God, thought Ian. Talk about calling the shots! But maybe that's what girls were like these days … Then he realised she was talking about the house.

The passenger door opened and Agnes was up against the side of his racing-green van in one silken manoeuvre.

'I would like we go *here …*'

He slipped furtively out of the driver's side, resisting the urge to bundle her indoors under a tarpaulin. Ian walked briskly to the gates and scanned the houses opposite. Only the Robinsons had a view through the ornamental pines, and there was no sign of their Saab. Besides, it was none of their damned business. And it wasn't like he was doing anything – *wrong.*

Agnes still had her back to the van, one heel up on the wheel arch like a lady of the night in a Fellini film. As he moved in closer she looked mad, bad and irresistibly sexy. He brushed a stray reddish curl from her eyelashes. Took one last glance to make sure they were hidden from the road. And then he kissed her.

Ian Newton didn't count nieces or goddaughters on their wedding day; or playing Spin the Bottle with Pete and Trisha Smedley that heinous night in Crete. So, when he pressed his lips closely followed by everything else, to

Agnes Skirowska in his own front garden, it was the first time he'd been unfaithful by his own, impeccable standards.

His mouth felt alive with the taste of someone new. His fingers found the warm, taut flesh of her stomach, tormented by the choice of going up or down. His chest tensed in a spasm of manly pride at the pressure of her breasts, soft yet curiously firm. Different breasts. *Naughty breasts.* Breasts that pressed into him a rib or two higher than he was used to … Agnes's fingers were inside his shirt, then touching his groin with an urgency akin to aggression …

And here he is: seventeen again, burdened with the pressure to perform! His entire body trembles at the proximity of Jessica Gidley's tantalising curves across the handbrake.

Is it possible? Can this really be happening?

With the Capri's custom sports seats reclined to near horizontal, Ian's legs and the steering wheel are magnetically drawn. Rose Royce cuts to the Commodores as he lunges for a breast. He catches his shin a glancing blow that sends him into spasm. Bites back a yelp as he slides a clammy hand up Jessica Gidley's thigh. But the die is cast; the wicked twins of Pent-Up Longing and Pants-Down Ridicule are upon him as he snags the winder of his Timex in the mitten-thick mesh of her tights.

It's enough to keep his virginity in stasis for a further two and a half years.

Ian returned to the moment. Where Agnes was young and lithe, fired up in a carnal frenzy; and he was willing but tired, and frankly out of practice.

What if he couldn't-?

'Big man,' she crooned with an approving squeeze.

Relief and terror mingled as he felt himself rise to the challenge – if anything, a little too eagerly. It took most of his strength and all his willpower to escape her sinuous grasp.

'I'll get the keys,' Ian whispered.

But Agnes wouldn't let go. From the way she nipped playfully at his lower lip, he had an inkling she was quite prepared to do the show right here. He pushed her back against the metal panel.

'Two seconds ...'

He strode away like he did this sort of thing all the time; composed himself as he rounded the bonnet of the Peugeot, though he deeply wanted to vault it like Starsky and Hutch. As the Yale turned in the front door, Ian ignored the shucking noise behind him that sounded suspiciously like sinking jeans.

Jasper was in his basket at the bottom of the stairs. He swapped the car keys for the van fob in the pot on the hall table. Left his wallet too, rather impressed that his head was clear enough to do the sensible thing, after a shameful second pint of Guinness and the same again of testosterone.

Condoms!

He should ...

He had to!

He wouldn't be surprised if Agnes had some anyway but it seemed unchivalrous to ask. He bounded up the stairs in threes. There were still some in the bedside drawer, from when Carla had come off the Pill.

He found them, checked the expiry and ran back down again. And as he did, Ian caught sight of himself in the hall mirror ... *Ruddy, if invitingly tousled. Not bad at all!* He allowed himself a little smile (Carla, girl – you had this coming!)

There was nothing to feel bad about. He was only doing what they'd agreed. And besides, he had stuck to their vows a darn sight longer than she had ...

Outside, Agnes was still there. Very still. And very, very there. Her jeans and T-shirt were folded on the wing of the

Peugeot and – *Dear God, she was naked!* Naked as a newborn by the side of his van, where the stencil read:

I. NEWTON Ltd
Big Ideas For Gardens

The logo was Carla's idea, with falling apples for dots on the Is. But as he skirted the back of the car, Ian realised Agnes wasn't naked at all. She was still in those skimpy white panties, and now he could see them in all their glory: simple and spotless, with a tiny motif. Another daisy, right where – *right where he was going to be!*

'You leave me any longer, I go home,' she said, doing her best to sound neglected. 'Dressed like this.'

The night was warm; there wasn't a goose bump in sight. She snatched at the keys. He held them away.

'I'll do it …'

Slowly, calmly, Ian took her by the hand and led her to the loading doors. With a practised flick of the key in a lock that could reduce a lesser man to tears, the doors sprang apart. Any trepidation Ian felt at that moment was not about what he was going to do. Rather, it was for the consequences of what he had already started with that first extramarital kiss.

Or second, to be strictly accurate.

The difference was that, this time, Ian knew he was genuinely running the risk of further temptation. Which, he could safely say, had never been the case with Pete Smedley.

Whatever Carla said.

In the week that followed, he allowed himself a little euphoria at pulling a cracker like Agnes.

Agnes! Who'd have thought it? The only other woman he'd ever met with that name was his grandmother's bridge partner when he was ten years old, who smelled of face powder and wore her hat indoors. But as this year's model soon explained, her real name was Agnieszka, anglicised for the sake of her clients.

In fairness, Ian reflected, her interest shouldn't come as a total surprise. He was in good shape, after all; eleven years of lugging wheelbarrows and felling leylandii had seen to that. And what his mates said was true: he did catch the occasional lady client looking him over. Gentlemen too, come to that, but that was London for you – gaylords everywhere! In his business a touch of the Lady Chatterleys went with the territory. Some of his clients liked their bit of rough, mooching around the garden in boots and shorts.

The following Wednesday, as he and Jasper let themselves in through the Wallaces' back gate, he hadn't the foggiest idea what to expect. The last he'd seen of Agnes was her perfectly proportioned rear swaying up his road at 3 a.m. She kissed him goodbye in the shadow of the ornamental pines and told him he needn't walk her home.

'I am not a baby... You know that, no?'

Today there was no sign of life at the house. Jasper made himself at home in his spot by the bamboo as Ian set to work, sweeping the path and deadheading petunias. When he clipped the hose to the outdoor tap, he allowed himself a peek in the lounge windows. And another in the kitchen as he plugged the hedge trimmers into the all-weather socket. It was while he was bent over Bernard Wallace's petrol-driven lawnmower that he heard a noise behind him.

'You should have cleaned that properly last time!'

He smiled as he fought the urge to doff an imaginary

cap to the son of the house. Sebastian Wallace's outfit of red wellingtons and blue football strip looked unconsciously patriotic, teamed with his pasty white face.

'Come to help me mow the lawn?' asked Ian through gritted teeth. Boots indicated Sebastian intended to assist.

The boy bent down over the engine casing. He stroked up a veneer of mulch with a snappably delicate finger and presented it to Ian at arm's length.

'*See?*'

Ian nodded and eyed the ignition thoughtfully, wondering if he was about to take issue with that twig, jammed under the cutlass-sharp rotor blades. The Wallaces' mower was an antique, and the bane of his Wednesday afternoons. He had suggested upgrading to a quieter, greener model but Wallace Senior was too stingy to oblige. Or, too in love with the attention the old mower's cacophony drew from his neighbours, who looked up only to be reminded that *Mr Wallace had a gardener.*

Ian resigned himself to letting Sebastian copilot the contraption as it etched its pattern of parallel stripes. Or until his own, lumbering feet clipped the boy's heels enough to kill his interest.

'Sebastian! Cartoons!'

The voice of salvation came from the back door. The boy scampered into the house, swerving past Agnes without a word.

Unscrewing the petrol cap, Ian held his breath. This was it – the encounter-after-the-fuck-before; he'd seen it in a hundred movies but never played it out himself. As he topped up the tank from a battered can, he wondered how on earth—

'Hello,' said Agnes. 'I got lemonade. You want I bring some?'

Jasper looked up from the shade.

She smiled. In fact, she bloomed. She very nearly sparkled, to the extent that Ian changed his mind all over again and wondered how on earth he had ever lit her fire.

'You look beautiful,' he said.

But her face betrayed nothing as she disappeared inside. To fix him a glass of lemonade, with ice and a slice and a mint leaf cut into a heart; watching him from the draining board with her eyes half closed and her lips half open. Until another of those smiles, like a sudden sunbeam, told him he'd be watching Sky Plus again tonight.

That she was ready for a rematch Ian took as a compliment on his sexual prowess. It was also a bit of worry.

Aside from their one torrid night, he hadn't had sex in six and a half weeks – and that had been the first time in ages. In the history of their relationship, the initial passion between Ian and his wife had been short-lived. A year or two in and sex tapered to once-weekly intercourse, then kept on tapering. Marriage, money and making house were happy diversions from the Holy Grail of spontaneous sex, and as an issue it was rarely broached. Until one night, in a tipsy heart-to-heart, when Ian told Carla he applied the same rule to their sex life as he did to repotting the yuccas: *Every other spring, whether they needed it or not.*

He was only half joking. On a scale of One-to-Sex-Beast, his own libido held steady at a three. Ian preferred cricket to sex and always had. Shopping and holidays did the same for his wife; or so he believed. Her affair in the thirteenth year of their marriage was a wake-up call to them both.

Carla's confession came three weeks after the fact. It was strictly a one-off, she insisted, with a Maltese car mechanic she'd met in a tapas bar while Ian was at Edgbaston for the Second Test. She had gone to meet a friend who was going through the wars with her latest, impractical lover. Carla was alone in Rincón España, halfway down a bottle of rioja, when the friend called to bail. Her liaison with the man on the next table was hatched in a red-wine blur, and culminated in an hour of garlicky grappling, in a bedsit ironically close to the Oval. Ian was torn between his wife's misdeed and his own inadequacy. He reacted with resentment rather than rage; and even that hadn't lasted.

He and Carla were sensible, rational people. They discussed therapy and researched counsellors on the internet. They lay in bed reading self-help books and answering questionnaires; a poor substitute for lovemaking, which if anything became even more perfunctory.

And then … it drifted. A problem swept away in the flow of life; of weekends into weeks, into work, into holidays. Before long they were back where they started: Ian-and-Carla again. Carla-and-Ian, rolling along, singing a song, banging a gong if not each other. And out of that, forged on the cinders of Ian's dwindling indignation, came an understanding:

One-offs were permissible, if immediately disclosed.

It boiled down, he said, to trust. A single straying needn't spell the end of their marriage, but duplicity might.

Whether he meant this rule as a way of sidestepping all but a modicum of marital duties, or as a get-out clause for the wife he loved but feared he would never satisfy, neither of them cared to ask. To Ian's knowledge, their rule remained untested until now. And there was the rub: in the circumstances, he could be excused for not coming clean about a harmless fling, because Carla was incommunicado.

The trouble was that sweet, beautiful Agnes desired further escapades – was ready, willing and thoroughly insistent – and Ian found he was powerless to refuse. Thus came their second encounter.

And their third, a few days later.

Before he knew it he was embroiled in a full-blown affair, far beyond the agreed parameters. More startling still, every time passions were rejoined Agnes demanded a new and unconventional locale; a development which delighted him in the saucy rush of the first instance, since it tapped into a fantasy of his own. Ian had always harboured a not-so-soft spot for the idea of making out in his van. He and Carla had tried it once, in the exploratory period after her affair; an attempt to "give full rein to one another's desires" as the books advised. Back then he drove a cantankerous old Vauxhall, a smaller model than now. They had talked of waiting for the perfect moment, of driving out somewhere windswept and deserted. But, since his jalopy was up on bricks awaiting a new axle, they seized the moment and did it in the drive.

It was not a success; though more so than Carla's idea with the blindfolds and candles, which proved very nearly lethal in the setting of her new, four-poster drapes. By contrast, van sex with Agnes was a delight. She didn't tut at the oil patches Ian tried to hide with Jasper's swimming towel. She laughed, when his elbow brought a sheaf of garden canes tumbling down around them like jack straws. And so, in the weeks that followed, he found himself going to ever-increasing lengths to please her.

They made love in the greenhouse when the Wallaces were away … Behind the raspberries in his own back garden, a whisker beyond the reach of his motion-sensitive arc lamps ... After an hour of foraging and two false starts, they found the only head-high thicket on Clapham Common not reserved by homosexuals. But. while her own loft room remained understandably out of bounds, Ian put down her spurning of his own bed to the willfulness of youth. It aroused him, up to a point. Though by their fifth liaison, he couldn't help thinking a nice, dry kingsize divan would be welcome.

Their assignations were arranged by text. Agnes liked him to message her with a time and place on a Sunday and Thursday, her guaranteed nights off from childcare. Precoital drinks proved unnecessary and his offers of dinner were rebuffed. Ian might have wondered if she liked him at all, were it not for her passion during the act itself. For, when they made love, Agnes was a creature of attentive and savage tenderness. She held his gaze fearlessly whenever she was facing in the right direction. Her mouth and hands implored and explored, as they made love in ways Ian had only read about, in positions he thought impossible. And she did things – *with things* – he would never have asked Carla to do, and all without being asked.

Anything, in fact, except make love in his bed.

But Agnes Skirowska was twenty-two, beautiful and uncomplicated. She wanted everything – and yet nothing. How could anyone wish for more?

He didn't have to explain about Carla, because she never asked. Didn't have to hide his wife's clothes or photographs, because she never set foot in the house. If the Wallaces knew where Carla was, Agnes might have picked up on it. But Ian wasn't in the habit of discussing his wife with clients, and he doubted they would make the connection unprompted.

So all in all it was rotten luck, the night she texted to say she'd be twenty minutes late, adding:

BLODDY CHILD. TONIGHT I NEED DRINK

The bar of the Windmill was hosting an event. Twenty sheepish boys sat opposite twenty girls, all of whom managed the trick of looking over- and under-dressed at once. A buzzer sounded at five-minute intervals, the signal for the boys to pick up their drinks and shift along in a sort of parlour game.

Speed-dating, according to the poster.

Ghastly, thought Ian. He was waiting for Agnes in the relative quiet of the annexe. If he was still single, he couldn't think of anything worse than—

She appeared, cheeks puffing as she collapsed into a chair.

'Sorry,' she said in exasperation. 'That boy. His name should be "Se-bas-*tard*-ian", no?'

He smiled as he slid her vodka across the table. 'What's he done now?'

Agnes swiped away the straw which was impeding a mighty swig.

'He refuse to go to bed for his *mozzer*. He say he *only* go to bed if I read him story. Me! Like I am his best friend in the world!'

'Well, that's very sweet. You're obviously a very good nanny.'

She shrugged. 'But the *bloddy* child is reading *Lord of the Rings*! Every page take ten minutes!' She slapped down her glass, making the ice chink. 'And when I get one of the stupid names wrong, he correct me and I have to say again!'

The fluster had given her a glow. Her tiny shell pendant bonded awkwardly to her cleavage and Ian fought the urge to unstick it. Whether it was anger or the stimulation of deciphering Tolkien, she was positively chatty, which made a change. She was usually so controlled. Till she got going.

She told him about her day, of waiting in specially for a parcel from Poland the postman had failed to deliver.

'… So then I have to go to post office to pick it. When I get there I queue, I don't know, maybe fifteen minutes. Then they tell me I need passport or my drive licence! So I go home *again* …'

It was ten past eight. Street lamps were coming on outside, but the night was young. Ian had left the car at home. His plan for tonight involved the groundsmen's lockup: a six-foot-high corral the size of a tennis court at the centre of the Common. He and Jasper had found it, on one of their walks which had become more frequent of late to his little dog's disquiet. It was padlocked at night and the fence topped with barbed wire, but a loose plank had allowed for a recce when no one was looking. Inside were a couple of beaten-up sheds, parking for the council grass cutters, and not much else.

From the bar the buzzer sounded again. Cue whoops and the sound of chairs scraping floorboards. Ian had his back to the flat-screen TV, which was playing identikit hip-hop videos – all gold-toothed girls and slouching homeboys. Every now and then the soundtrack was swamped by the clatter of the fruit machine.

Agnes was chasing a slice of lemon around her glass. She had forgotten to eat. 'Please – may I have a packet of crisps?'

Ian was delighted when she asked him for anything, and this didn't even risk putting his back out. He smiled at her furrowed brow; were crisps a big ask in Poland? He fished the wallet from his jacket and set off for the bar.

Three steps later he stopped.

Her eyes followed his to the TV. The barman had switched channels.

Two women and a man in wetsuits were chatting on the deck of a boat. One of them was crying, while the other two tried to look concerned without obscuring their best side. Only the blubbing woman was oblivious, her hair all over the place, and mascara spotting her cheeks with sooty freckles as the camera zoomed in for a close-up.

At the exact moment she opened her mouth, the fruit machine jangled. But Ian could lipread her words perfectly:

'I – want – to go – HO-O-OME!!!'

Ian knew their precise inflection. The very pitch of the accompanying yowl.

'My God,' said Agnes. 'Who is that woman?'

He slid the wallet into his trousers, all thought of crisps forgotten.

'She's my wife,' he said. 'Come on, let's do it.'

Dusk was slipping into darkness as they followed the path to the lockup. Ian was lost in his thoughts. He expected her to have a thousand questions yet they walked in silence.

They reached the gap in the fence, which he'd taken the precaution of marking with a Tango can. Agnes nudged him: a cyclist was heading towards them, headlamp blinking Morse code. They pretended to look for something on the ground until he whisked away.

Steadying each other, they slid down the bank into the unlit enclosure. Meaningless shapes resolved in the darkness: a mound of rubbish here, a bonfire of branches there. And all around the odour of earth, a curiously country smell that suggested they were further from the city than they were.

Agnes took his hand as she searched for a location that pleased her. Checked the lock on one shed then the other.

Ever hopeful, she tried the door of a Land Rover hitched to a glinting grass cutter, its engine still ticking from a hard day's decapitation.

Ian wondered if she understood about the woman on TV; if she was silently furious or in denial. But the thought retreated as he sank groin-deep into the familiar plunge pool of fear, guilt and the unabating horn.

Agnes found what she was looking for – a waist-high tower of fertiliser sacks, sheltered on two sides by a hedge and a piece of corrugated iron. She tested it for firmness as if buying a mattress in Selfridges.

'Put your jacket here, please.'

Ian did as he was told.

She hopped up on the sacks, watching him carefully as she made herself comfortable. Her skin was pale and her eyes reflected the moonlight.

'You know,' she said, 'we have *Big Brother* in Poland. Is *werry* popular programme. For people who want change their lives ...'

She reached down and unbuttoned his jeans.

Carla's show was not *Big Brother*, but the premise was the same. *To Hell in a Houseboat* was in its second series. It took eight disparate members of the public and moored them on a converted coal barge in the middle of Loch Ness. The barge was seventy feet long with hidden cameras, bunk beds, and ceilings so low no one above average height could stand upright. And, in case being marooned on a gale-blasted loch with unknown neurotics wasn't hellish enough, it had an extra twist. Every week the shipmates were set a series of challenges. Those who scored high won the right to stay aboard, edging closer to the much-trumpeted prize of a seven-star cruise for them and half a dozen friends. But whoever scored lowest was ejected from the boat in an original manner, based loosely on the principles of medieval torture. All in the name of minor-channel primetime TV.

Carla had applied for reality shows before, which Ian put down to her restless soul. When they'd first met, she hated her City job even more than he did, and when his severance package proved more than enough to pay off the mortgage, she gave up work at the first opportunity. Like him, she had no yen for children; Jasper was the only baby for her. Carla was happy at home, fringing pelmets and testing paint effects, turning shabby little properties into palaces to sell on for a tidy profit. Or so she said.

Ian knew she'd been looking for something since the day they met. Briefly he thought it was him. It explained the affair and her other forays into the unknown – retreats in Sri Lanka, camping on Kilimanjaro ... When you married a woman ten years your junior, there were bound to be differences. But Carla wanted her independence too, and he'd learned to let her have it.

'*Good old Carla!*' said their friends, when they heard she was going on the box. Everyone wished her luck before she flew up to Scotland, and Ian knew they were following the show. One or two rang for the inside track; any gossip that didn't make the edit. The challenge in Week Three – weaving a lobster creel – prompted a volley of calls when Carla and Dougie, the ginger-haired deputy head, clashed over the pincer-proof twine. But Ian had to disappoint them; he knew no more than they did.

For emergencies, he had the number of the production office, and they had his though as yet no calls had been made. So he was following her progress like everyone else, on TV three nights a week; or later on Sky Plus if he was going – out.

It was a strange feeling: making love to another woman, then coming home to watch your wife on TV. Sort of pornography in reverse.

To Hell in a Houseboat hadn't topped the ratings, but the producers still had hopes of scandal. The first series caused a tabloid buzz, when graphic designer Jake came out as bisexual and dumped his girlfriend live on air. Engineering a threesome with a singing air hostess and the location cameraman, he'd won the approval of the nation and ultimately the show. He and the cameraman had done the gay marriage thing, and now Jake had his own slot reviewing menswear on daytime TV.

'Is that what *you* want?' Ian asked as they ate dinner at their local bistro the night before Carla flew to Scotland. 'Break into telly, get your own show?'

His wife looked back at him across the carnations. She had been waiting for this.

'Ian, I don't know *what* I want.'

She took another mouthful of veal. 'But maybe this will help me decide. Don't worry, I'm not expecting to win. Though the cruise'd be nice, as long as we can take Jasper. And it would be fun watching our friends fight over the tickets ...'

The car picked her up at quarter to seven next morning. Ian had a fuzzy memory of kissing her goodbye. He ought to have gone down to see her off, but he wasn't at his best in the mornings – and that one in particular. The night before, Carla had all but worn him out.

And so, for the last eight weeks, her presence in his life had been strictly two-dimensional. He surprised himself by feeling quite detached. He'd expected to get swept up in the drama of life on the Houseboat, of competitive tapestry-making in the shadow of the ducking stool. But initially his wife's exploits left him unmoved; sometimes even embarrassed.

Since the weeknight shows weren't live, whatever he saw had already happened. Ian knew he would get a call if Carla was ejected, when he'd be required to catch the shuttle from Gatwick to Inverness. Partners were always there for the cameras on Saturday, as the latest victim was hauled ashore on live TV in whatever contraption had been dreamt up for their departure. A quick towel-down, then it was onto the tartan coffee-bar set for their exit interview with the show's breezily cynical host.

Carla's knack for handicrafts stood her in good stead for the challenges; though she had faltered in Week Four's task – making a NessiePeriscope™ – by failing to grasp the principles of mirror alignment. Luckily for her, Tremelle, the mouthy gender-belligerent go-go dancer, had made an even bigger hash, and it was he/she who floated ashore in the leaky iron maiden.

But now, and against his better judgement, Ian was aware of becoming inexorably sucked in. Last week he'd almost been tempted to put a bet on Carla to win. But the longest odds he could find were five to one, which considering there were four contestants left seemed less than generous. It was a decision he regretted as soon as she made it through to the last three.

So that night, as he returned from the Common, the latest tearful instalment was set to be the closest to high drama yet. There were four messages on the landline and another two on his mobile; doubtless voices of concern from friends who'd already seen the show because they had not been screwing the night away.

They could wait. Ian found the episode on the hard drive and whizzed through on fast-forward ... There was no sign of Carla for the first six minutes. Suki and Mitch-the-Geordie were making breakfast in the galley. The loch was choppy, and tensions ran high when an egg nearly rolled off the worktop. This was followed by a confessional piece from Mitch in the HeadSpace, the converted toilet cubicle where contestants went to unburden themselves into the mirror that concealed a live feed to the studio.

'We're all feelin' it nah, like' said Mitch, brushing a lank strand of badger hairdo from his eyes. 'Suki's worried aboot her kids. Carla's missin' her dog. An' it's killin' me not knowin' if the Toon are ga'an doon …'

There was a splutter of static. The presenter's voice oozed through from the NessCafé™.

'But Mitch, in just two weeks' time one of you will win the seven-star cruise of a lifetime. Doesn't that make it easier to hang in there?'

Mitch nodded. 'Oh aye, in a way ... Cos, er, it'd be truly marvellous to wake up in loadsa different countries … Experience different cultures, an' that …' He leaned forward, taking a peek up his reflected nostrils. 'An' you could always eat on the ship, like …'

Ian paused on this distasteful image and fetched a beer from the fridge. He forwarded through Suki pegging out pyjamas on deck beneath a steel-grey sky. And again, as she took her turn on watch, eyes peeled for plesiosaur activity at the rudder-mounted NessieCam™. Then Carla appeared, apparently hammering nails into a wall with the palm of her hand.

He stabbed the remote until the pace decelerated. She was doing tai chi.

'Carla has the bunk room to herself,' explained the voiceover. *'She's not spoken to the other shipmates all morning and is relaxing with a burst of yoga!'*

Ignorant shit, thought Ian.

Bollocks. Adverts.

He skipped the break, which was topped and tailed with messages from the programme's sponsor, a well-known instant coffee. At last he found what he was looking for: Carla, Suki and Mitch on deck in their one-piece wetsuits with integral lifejackets.

'It's twelve noon and the shipmates are preparing for today's challenge. Who can collect the most NessTicles and avoid an awkward swim home in the thumbscrews?'

The director cut to a two-shot of Suki folding her arm protectively around Carla's shoulders.

'It's all right, babes,' she cooed. 'You'll be brilliant. You was the only one who didn't capsize last time …'

Carla sniffed, trying to gather herself. 'I know, it's just ... It's not that.'

'What, then?' Suki pointed at Mitch. 'Is it 'im? I know it ain't fair. I told them in the 'eadSpace, he can get more balls down his wetsuit cos he ain't got no boobs!'

'*Oh, Suke!*' Carla smiled through her sniffles but didn't pursue it. Compared to the other woman she was positively flat-chested.

Mitch's matted highlights appeared in frame: 'Hang on, pet!' he protested. 'I've got big balls doon there 'a begin with, remember!'

Both women laughed weakly as the voiceover chimed in.

'But there's more to Carla's woes than the prospect of a dip in the deep …'

And right on cue, she started to sob.

'I WANT TO GO HOME! I want to see my husband! I want to fall asleep in front of the telly with my dog ...'

'Don't start, babes,' implored Suki. 'If you start, I'll start. It's the twins' birthday tomorrow and we always go down

Chessington World of Adventures!'

Ian was choked. He gripped the remote control like a stress toy.

Good God! Carla was missing him!

He felt suddenly possessive as two strangers had their arms around his wife. But a moment later, at the sound of a familiar claxon, the shipmates unhuddled and ran pell-mell for the side. They were overboard quicker than a well-drilled SWAT team, landing astride waiting inflatables in the shape of cartoon lake monsters. The challenge had begun!

The director cut between footage from an airborne camera and another on the loch. Carla, Suki and Mitch both grabbed the paddle strung round their creature's neck and manoeuvred furiously for NessTicles™. The green rubber balls were a staple of the challenges dreamed up by the show's less-than-imaginative production team. Dozens of them were bobbing in the black water round the barge, as far as the eye could see.

The voiceover leapt in:

'And it's Suki taking an early lead! She's got one down her wetsuit already … Looking good, girl! … Moving onto Mitch – remember how we got the Houseboat Doctor out to him last time for a touch of hypothermia? ... Going well! Good lean, Mitch! ... And what about Carla? We've seen the strain get to her this morning but she's a plucky one, we all know that … That's right, Carla! Under the rudder – well spotted! Yup, she's tucking that away nicely ... Oops, zipper up, love! We don't want everything bouncing out …'

Ian's jaw fell open. Carla was plucky all right. As the commentary delighted in regaling, the temperature in the loch was less than five degrees Centigrade; cold enough to turn a red mullet blue.

'A minute to go … And this is where those insulated waterproofs

get tested to the max! Suki's slowing down – she looks tired! Those NessTicles are getting few and far between … Oh, Carla's spotted one. Mitch has seen it too! Look at them go! I make that five apiece, so this is crucial—'

Ian sat forward in his seat.

'They're going for it! Who's gonna get there? Mitch has got the upper body strength but he's prone to cramping ... It could be Carla—'

Her closeup filled the screen, teeth gritted, forehead crinkled in exertion.

'They're paddling like porpoises! ... Neck and neck round the bow. It's Mitch—'

Ian's heart went out.

'It's Carla!'

Another closeup: his wife, shoulder to shoulder with the Geordie, bearing down on a solitary green ball.

'No, it's Mitch – he's got it!'

He grunted, sinking to his knees on the carpet.

'BUT HE'S CAUGHT A CRAB! Mitch has caught a crab!! He's wobbling. He's losing his grip on the inflatable … HE'S GONE!!!'

Ian let out a manly squeal of delight.

'Mitch has gone! Carla's got the NessTicle and she's tucking it where the sun don't shine! Or wouldn't, if there was any … Well done, Carla! Ten seconds to go, as the NessieRescueCrew zoom in to fish out poor old Mitch …'

The director cut to Suki, bedraggled and exhausted. She'd given up the chase and was clinging to her monster with one arm while the other clasped the lumpy front of her wetsuit. She looked as if she was smuggling turtle's eggs as she smiled for the camera.

Cut to the three contestants on board the Houseboat. Mitch was shivering in a foil blanket as they took turns to unzip and count their balls.

Suki: 'Six … seven … eight!'

Carla: 'Six!'

Mitch: 'Er … t-t-two.'

Sympathetic groans and hugs for Mitch from the women. But the voiceover was less benign:

'Oh, and that's a disastrous haul for Mitch!'

Sniffing, he swallowed audibly as he explained himself to the girls:

'Aye, well – *hhonn-kkk!* – three of the f-f-fookers fell out, like …'

And at that, a familiar tune struck up. The *To Hell in a Houseboat* closing shanty, played over a montage of highlights: Carla and Suki, hugging mutual congratulations for getting through to the final week; lime-green NessTicles™ rolling over the worktop like an animated Bridget Riley; and sad, shivering Mitch, slouched in the galley with his hands round a mug of something steamy, dreaming of lands he'd never see or St James's Park.

Credits rolled over these faces of mixed fortune as the voiceover gushed:

'Poor old Mitch! We'll see more of him in our live Saturday show as he shapes up for the next chilling departure – Breaststroke in Thumbscr—'

Ian froze the picture.

Good old Carla! She was going all the way!

He rewound so he could watch again ... How did she feel at this moment, he wondered, tucked up in her bunk on that godforsaken loch? Best check the odds again before he turned in – now more than ever, he had a suspicion she might win the bloody thing! And if they did go off round the world he'd need to think about his business – maybe even subcontract ...

He paused the flailing footage as Carla counted her balls

again. She had dried her hair since the previous shot; it was sticking up in that way she hated and he found rather endearing. She was hugging the awful Suki.

(God – would there be reunions?)

Ian was almost ready for bed. His hand dangled over the chair arm as he paused the programme for a final time: his wife, looking proud and resilient before the watching world. Smiling, sort of – but not with a smile he recognised.

Christ!

He flinched at the sudden wetness on his fingers.

It was Jasper, out of his basket at this time of night. He ambled to the rug in front of the TV and folded down with a thump. For a moment his chin touched his paws. Until the sight of Carla's giant, flickering face brought it up again.

'You see it too, don't you, fella?' whispered Ian.

Something wasn't right.

IV

Mrs Molyneux had called an impromptu meeting in the staffroom. The care home inspectors, she said, would take a week to issue their report.

'But all the indications are that we've given a *very good* account of ourselves. So well done. We all deserve a pat on the back. Now, onwards and upwards!'

And with that they returned to their posts. Glory caught the eye of the caretaker's boy, hunched in a chair by the noticeboard. A gold crucifix was snagged over the top of his vest and his boots were filthy.

'Don't let Mrs Molyneux see those,' she said, nodding to his mud-encrusted feet. 'We did all the floors today, you know.'

The boy smiled, head bobbing to a silent beat. 'You callin' me a dirty man, Glory?'

She turned away before he could see her smile. 'I'm not calling you any sorta man. You want to show some respect, boy. I'm old enough to be your ma!'

She doubted this was strictly true. He had to be seventeen at least, which would make her the youngest mother in her family for a generation. Not counting that cousin in Mandeville, and no one did any more.

The boy bent down and unlaced his boots, arrogant eyes upon her like one of those saucy Chippendales.

'So, Glory, when we going for that drink?'

'We're not,' said Glory. 'I'm not available. And by the way, you'll undo that knot a whole lot quicker by watchin' what you're doing.'

'You sayin' you got a boyfriend, then?'

'I'm saying I'm not available.'

'You a lesbian?'

Glory fixed him with a stare.

'No. I'm not.'

She picked up the pile of laundry she'd been folding. He followed her up the corridor, one boot on and the other in his hands.

'You finish half four, same as me. Come for a walk on the Common!'

Glory smiled over the snowdrift of clean nighties. He was persistent, she'd give him that.

'No means *no*. But thank you for askin'.'

The caretaker's boy said something under his breath as he pushed past and skulked off down the passage, leaving a single trail of muddy treads on the polished floor.

'Look at the mess you makin'!' called Glory. 'That's the last pat on the back you'll get from Mrs Molyneux!'

But the boy kept walking, his swagger more pronounced for wearing one boot.

'An' she a cow too,' he said. 'She can keep her pats to herself.'

That night the bus was packed and Glory had to stand all the way.

Two of the tills were down at the Brixton Lidl. She queued for what seemed like an age, and by the time she got back to the flats, three bags of shopping and six flights of steps had all but done her in.

Mercy wasn't home. She could tell from the squall that greeted her as she dropped the bags in the hall. What sounded like a prison riot in the front room was Sam, Sherelle and twenty lengths of car-racing track.

'What's all this foolishness!' shouted Glory.

A pair of tiny racers flew across the room, narrowly missing Sam and a leaning tower of CDs on the window sill.

'Sherelle's messin' with me cars!' said her nephew. 'Every time I send one down she kicks it away!'

His sister's tiny hands flew to her face to fend off the accusation, a picture of stung innocence.

'I didn't do *nuffin'*!'

'Liar!' howled Sam, hurling a length of plastic track at her like a javelin.

'*Enough!*' Glory's bark froze them to the spot. 'There's groceries need puttin' away and chores to do before you get your tea. Sam, you can start by clearin' up this mess. *Now, boy!*'

He dropped to his knees without a word and began pulling apart the track.

'Sherelle – kitchen!'

Her niece scurried past her, head tucked low to avoid a cuffing.

As they stacked tins in the cupboard, Glory sighed. Sam was six; Sherelle four. Mercy had no right leaving them alone.

'How long's your ma been out?' she asked as the little girl handed up a can of kidney beans.

Sherelle thought for a moment. Held her hands together, then opened her fingers as if releasing an invisible dove.

'Ten minutes,' read Glory. It was still too long.

The front door slammed as she stowed the sweet potatoes. Sherelle followed the noise of wooden sandals clacking into the front room. Glory took a breath and closed the cupboard. She could smell her sister before she saw her.

Mercy was sprawling on the couch, one leg over the arm with Sherelle in her lap, peering up like a baby bird.

'Where you been?' said Glory. Her hands were on her hips.

Mercy didn't look at her as she flicked on the TV and riffled the channels in a herbal daze.

'Auntie Glory says: where you been?' repeated Sherelle helpfully.

Mercy tutted at them both. She cocked her chin at the wall but said nothing.

'She says she's been to see the painter man,' interpreted Sam. His arms were round a sheaf of track as tall as he was.

'*Your auntie knows what I sayin'!*' snapped Mercy. 'Now put your toys away and help her with the tea.' She settled on a soap opera and dropped the remote. 'What we havin', anyway?' She looked at Glory for the first time, her eyes a challenge that had nothing to do with the evening meal.

'If you got your fat backside to the shops instead of smokin' weed all day,' said Glory, 'you would know.'

She went back to the kitchen.

Mercy cleaned and Glory cooked; that was the deal. One Glory had considered fair at first, until she realised that while her sister expected to eat every day, often many times, she had no intention of cleaning with such regularity.

Mercy, as always, had an answer:

'*If I clean as much as you cook, I'll waste away. Then I'll have to eat even more!*'

She had enough to do, she said, running round after her kids. Though for the life of her Glory couldn't remember the last time she'd seen her sister run after anything under six feet tall.

When Glory finished school, a year after Mercy, she saw it as her duty to get a job to help Ma. Their mother had brought them up alone since she fell pregnant the third time; worked six days a week until the day she died – on the buses, the cabs, or cleaning for folks up the hill.

Folks not worthy of wringin' out Ma's mop, in Glory's opinion.

So the day after her last exam, Glory was down at the job centre. She had started at Cedars Hall the following week. Just cleaning like Ma, but it was a start. Sometimes she wondered if Ma would still be alive if Mercy had done the same. Their little brother would have helped too; if he'd lived. Between them they could have stopped her working herself into an early grave.

Fifty-six. It was no age at all.

But Mercy had no sense of duty and never had. Her attempts at holding down a job began and ended washing heads at Mizz Frizzie's salon on Coldharbour Lane. To this day, women on the estate whistled to each other from the balconies when she went by with her squeaky pushchair:

'There she goes – the one that scalded the Wilcox girl's face half off on her wedding day.' They would nod until the swaying hips were out of sight. 'Aye. Groom had to kiss her through the veil for fear of frightenin' her kids ...'

Some days Glory felt bitter, coming home to her sister in her hollow on the batik-print couch; leaving those children to run amok, bawling echoes into the stairwell like a piss-stained pirates' cave. But, as Mercy never tired of reminding her, they had her to thank for the roof over their heads. (Didn't the Housing Association give priority to single mothers? And wasn't it only out of kindness that Mercy shared her room with the kids – gentleman callers permitting – so their Auntie Glory could be there to see them grow?)

What Mercy didn't know was that Glory's name was on the list with a different housing association. One of these days she'd have a place of her own, one she could buy a part of if she liked. She longed for the day she could tell Mercy she had a home, and a mortgage. That would wipe the smile off her lazy face. And so would cooking her children's tea.

Mercy was happy to admit she was no career girl. Her talents, she said, lay in another direction; currently, through the front-room wall. Alfonse Bidman was the latest man to fall for her charms. One in a line that would reach from here to the town hall, assuming they could summon the energy to stand. For if Mercy lived up to her reputation, she did not live up to her name. In Glory's opinion, it was a miracle her sister had only two children; though if Mercy had a way to make her sister carry her babies the way she carried everything else, there would surely be more.

Later that evening, when the children were asleep and the flat was quiet, she slipped out again.

'Laters,' mumbled Mercy, slamming the front door.

Glory was drying the dishes. She listened for her footsteps on the walkway.

Six, seven, eight, nine …

She was outside the adjacent flat. Then: nothing. No knock. Until the *clunk* of Alfonse Bidman's front door closing.

Mercy had got herself a key!

As she stacked the children's bowls, Glory couldn't resist a wry smile. That caretaker's boy touched a nerve when he asked if she was a lesbian. She and Mercy had been mistaken for a couple before. *Co-parents* it was called nowadays. The idea repulsed her, for more reasons than one, but she was a better mother to those children than Mercy had ever been.

That said, it would do them good to have a man around – especially Sam. One man, mind. Not five.

When Alfonse Bidman moved in next door, Glory had

taken a shine to him herself. He was tall and thin, the way she preferred, with almond-shaped eyes and hands that had an artist's sensitivity. She thought he noticed her, too; enough to get her hair extensions done by the lady downstairs. Then her sister stepped in and ruined everything. Before she knew it, Mercy was knocking on his door with slices of neighbourly spice cake she claimed to have baked herself.

Alfonse painted abstracts. Glory had seen them drying outside; garish things in a dozen colours that left you dizzy if you stared too long. Not that it stopped Mercy offering herself as a model. Whether she'd ever made it onto canvas, Glory didn't know – though, judging by the smears of paint that appeared on her sister's neck, knees and heaven knew where else, she could do with standing further from his palate.

When she was ready for bed, Glory turned the second lock on the door but left the bolt unfastened. You never knew with Mercy. She turned off the TV and peeked in at the children. Fast asleep in their little camp beds and all the more perfect for it. Sherelle's hands were clasped outside her sleeping bag, the very image of her grandma on the day they laid her out. Sam was restless, still for hardly a minute, blowing spittle bubbles. His skin glistened like melted chocolate in the moonlight.

As she got into her own bed, Glory noticed the empty hanger on the back of the door.

Where had her best blouse gone now?

As if she couldn't guess.

Two minutes later, a squawk like a molested chicken broke the silence. Her sister's laugh, seeping through the wall only inches from Glory's ear.

She sighed and pulled the covers over her head. The

next time she saw that blouse, it would stink of weed. At the very least.

When Glory went to answer the front bell at the Hall the following Wednesday, Archie was between her and the door. Residents were not encouraged to let in callers, though in his case it wasn't likely.

The gentleman on the doorstep recognised Glory as she stood aside.

'Morning, er …'

He might have been avoiding the old joke, but he had probably just forgotten her name. Gerald Stanley was sixty and balding. His hat was in his hands, as always. Glory was suspicious of men who wore hats; white men in particular could rarely carry them off. Apart from that Boy George, who was still a man of sorts.

'Mornin', Mr Stanley. Lovely day … Don't mind Archie, now.'

He wiped his feet daintily for a big man, edging past Archie, who stood against the wall like a sentry. Mr Stanley nodded, but Archie did not respond. Just drummed his fingers softly on the anaglypta.

He pointed vaguely up the hall. 'Is my mother, er … ?'

'I expect she's in her room,' said Glory. 'Do you remember the way?'

It wasn't meant to sound cutting. How often relatives visited was no business of hers. She led the way up the hall to spare him the reply.

'Is – is that chap all right?'

'Oh yes,' said Glory. 'Archie's fine. That's his place by the front door, till a quarter to twelve. On a Wednesday. Then he'll be on the landing till teatime … Mornin', Daisy!' She waved to an old woman sitting in an armchair on a kink in the hallway. 'Does it all without a watch.'

'Ah,' said Mr Stanley. 'Important to have a routine.'

Glory shucked her chin. 'We had these walls decorated a month ago. Caretakers had to paint round him in the end.' She stopped at the door of Pearl's room. 'Here's your ma – do you want I should take your hat?'

'I'll keep it, thank you.' He knocked and went in.

Aye; all the better for a quick getaway.

Glory was in the middle of compiling a list for the chiropodist, but she stopped to see to Daisy. The poor little thing was craning over the side of her chair, like a child in a sailboat watching for fishes. She bolstered her with a cushion and turned the page of her magazine.

'There, Daisy. We don't want you tipping out now. It's nearly coffee time!'

Daisy seemed surprised by her *Woman's Own*.

'Thank you,' she said, in a voice as small and dry as pebbles. 'I've been looking for that everywhere ...'

Further down the hall, Archie was still drumming. Some of the residents spent the day in their room, while others liked to mix. And some liked the television – though not Archie, who never set foot in the lounge when it was on. *Prefers the pictures in his own head,* thought Glory. He was content enough at his sentry points, depending on the time of day. And sometimes, if it was sunny, he took a turn in the back garden, watched by old-lady eyes from the wheelchairs in the shade. But mostly he just liked to stand.

The able-bodied residents had rooms upstairs. Archie's was next door to poor old Dennis, which meant hour upon hour of that moaning with its foghorn regularity.

'Enough to drive anyone mad!' had been Mrs Molyneux's opinion when Dennis arrived from St George's. She had given him the room next to Archie, reasoning he was too far gone to notice.

Wednesday was hairdressing morning. The rota had Glory overseeing the flow of ladies down to the makeshift salon in the basement. That meant lifting some of them from their armchairs, then wheeling them into the creaky old lift with its gates and smell of engine oil. It was one chore Glory savoured, if only for the look on the ladies' faces as they came back up and caught their own reflections in the mirrored walls. Seeing their hair set, all prim and proper, always perked them up. Except for the ones who flinched and looked away politely before the other lady caught them staring.

According to regulations, manual lifting was a two-person job, and the first thing you learned as a care assistant at Cedars Hall. Lesley-Anne, the podgy trainee, was helping Glory today and her technique left much to be desired. Glory had seen her more than once, hefting a delicate body like a sack of potatoes.

'One arm under the knees – like this …' she explained, as they hoisted another lady from her spot in front of a chat show. 'Don't worry, darlin', he'll be here again tomorrow. Think how pretty you'll look for him with your new perm …'

'Look like there's nothing of 'em, don't they?' puffed Lesley-Anne as they lowered her into the wheelchair. 'I swear they've got sandbags up their jumpers, half of 'em.'

Two ladies later, Glory was coming back up in the lift when the outer doors opened. Mrs Molyneux was framed through the metal gates, crisscross shadows falling across her face in a fishnet mask.

'Glory, can you come to my office, please? When you've seen to Mabel.'

Mrs Molyneux was the sort of woman who thought too much praise was harmful. She could be as curt with you whether she was pleased or vexed.

Glory let herself into the senior manager's office. A drab little room, with a desk and filing cabinets and the same air of old-school headmistress as Mrs Molyneux herself. On the wall hung a single watercolour, a railway station in the rain. It belonged to the previous senior manager, who allegedly forgot to take it with her. Underneath, the guest chair was occupied by Gerald Stanley.

'Mr Stanley,' began Mrs Molyneux, 'I have asked Glory to join us in her role as your mother's designated care assistant. As you'll remember from Pearl's induction, every resident has a qualified member of staff who takes a one-to-one interest in their lifestyle enhancement ...'

This was straight out of the Cedars Hall Handbook, as written by Mrs Molyneux herself. Mr Stanley nodded, turning over the hat on his knees. There was nowhere to sit, so Glory stood, still unclear if she had done something wrong. There was a lull, until Mrs Molyneux caught the gentleman's eye.

'Yes. I was just saying, I'm rather concerned about my mother's, er, condition.' His tone was apologetic, like a rumbled schoolboy. 'She's not been herself for years, we all know that. Been seeing things, ever since my father died. It's why we had to – why we thought she'd be better off here in the first place.'

Mrs Molyneux wanted to breeze things along. 'As we know, Glory, hallucinations are a sad but inevitable side effect of Pearl's Parkinson's medication ... I've *explained* this to Mr Stanley.' This she underlined with a winch of her eyebrows. Glory realised she was here in support, not defence.

'I'm quite aware of that, Mrs Molyneux!' The gentleman's tone put her shoulder blades in contact with the hard-backed chair. 'But I'd be failing in my duty as my mother's son if I didn't express my—'

He broke off at a knock on the door. It was Jan with the tea things and a plate of custard creams. Mrs Molyneux made a space by shifting a stack of *Gerontology Now*.

'I only brought two cups, shall I—'

'Thank you, Janet!' snapped Mrs Molyneux. 'That's fine.'

Jan put down the tray. She picked up the teapot and gave it a swish.

'Leave it. I'll be mother.'

Glory's friend tiptoed past her, eyes bulging in silent camaraderie.

Mr Stanley reconnected with his argument. 'Look, I'm used to Mother's funny ideas. Whenever I come and see her, it's always *"When are we going?"* or *"Has the manager got our bill ready?"* All piffle, of course – thank you, yes, one sugar.' He took the proffered cup. 'But today was different. Mother's talking about someone coming into her room at night. Someone trying to harm her!'

'Yes,' said Mrs Molyneux. 'Last week it was the Vietcong.'

'*No!*' Mr Stanley rapped a biscuit on his hat and made crumbs. 'I think this is real.'

Now Glory was concerned. 'Who did Pearl see?'

'That's just it. She says she couldn't, in the dark. But they were going through her chest of drawers, and when she called out she felt a hand on the side of her face. When she pulled the alarm cord, they ran off.' He looked at them both. 'I only bring this up because for once it sounds plausible. When Mother sees paratroopers in the snapdragons or a tiger on the commode, you know it's nonsense. But this …'

Mrs Molyneux lowered her cup to the saucer.

'Mr Stanley, it is not Cedars Hall policy to lock residents in their rooms at night, unless it's for their own safety. Now, if you and your mother decide that she would prefer to be secured in this way we'll consider it, but it contravenes fire regulations for the swift evacuation of the Hall in an emergency. You remember the Gateshead nursing home fire last year?'

The prospect of making a decision seemed to make Mr Stanley uncomfortable. 'I'm not telling you how to do your job, Mrs Molyneux. Merely bringing this to your attention. All I want—'

'And so you have, Mr Stanley, you have.' She stood. 'But I don't think you have any reason to worry. Pearl's safety and comfort are our prime concerns.' This was the senior manager on automatic; the tone she reserved for anyone making a suggestion she had no intention of heeding. 'Rest assured, Glory and I will be keeping a close eye on the situation. Won't we, Glory?'

The younger woman nodded. 'I'll go an' have a chat to Pearl now.'

Mrs Molyneux smiled from the lipstick down. 'Good. Once you've finished with the hairdressing.'

'I have finished with the hairdressin'.'

The Senior Manager checked the rota on her pinboard, between a clipping about herself from the local paper and a single raffle ticket.

'Probably better after lunch. Pearl's always chattier when she's eaten.'

Glory returned her glare. What she meant was: Pearl was dopier and easier to manipulate when she'd eaten.

Mr Stanley stepped in. 'Mother's having a nap anyway, but thank you.'

He smiled at Glory, who smiled back, and thought how easily men gave up on their loved ones when money was changing hands.

Mrs Molyneux leaned across the desk on bony knuckles. Shoulders hunched and gimlet-eyed, like a navy-blue vulture.

'See Mr Stanley out, please, Glory.'

Glory paused, helping herself to a custard cream from the plate. The door had almost closed behind her as Mrs Molyneux said:

'And Glory?'

She opened it a crack.

'You can come back for the cups.'

It was not part of the Hall's hallowed policy to let residents nap in their rooms during mealtimes, but for once Glory let Pearl doze on. If she'd really had a disturbed night, she would need the sleep – and better that she was rested when they had their chat.

Pearl came round as Glory was clipping the tray to her wheelchair.

'I'm not asleep,' she yawned, answering a question only she heard. 'Just resting my eyes.'

Glory turned the handle of her mug to face her and lifted the plastic cover from the bowl. It contained a lake of mashed potato and two brown shapes, half submerged like hippos.

'Here now, Pearl. Sausage and mash. Your favourite.'

Pearl considered the scene with a philosophical '*Hmmph*'.

Glory cut up the sausages and pushed the knife and fork gently into the old lady's paper-skinned fingers. Ordinarily Pearl ate like a horse, but when she was distracted her food went cold and forgotten. Glory was about to ask what she'd said to her son when Pearl piped up:

'I'm sure Gerald thinks I'm talking nonsense. But you believe me, don't you?'

Glory folded her hands in her lap. She looked the old lady squarely in the eye.

''Course I do, Pearl. Tell me again what happened.'

An attentive audience delighted her. 'Well, there was someone here in the night, you see. Could have been more than one – it was too dark to tell.'

'What were they doin'?'

'Banging about, going through my drawers! I thought they were after our biscuits! Then I heard a creak, like someone opening the wardrobe. Unless it was the door – does my door creak?'

Glory smiled and helped her load the fork. 'All the doors creak in this place. What happened next?'

Pearl paused while she chewed her lunch politely.

'Well, I called out – of course I did! I'm surprised I didn't wake you ... I asked what they wanted and told them I was calling the police. Could you pass my sherry?' Glory handed her the mug of ginger beer. Pearl glugged a mouthful and lowered it shakily to the tray. 'Then they were standing over our bed, right where you are now. I thought they were going to kill us!'

'Did they touch you?'

Pearl looked out of the window, past the empty bird table at something far away. 'I think so. I'm not sure ... When you go over things again and again, it's hard to know what happened and what you only thought. Don't you find?'

Glory loaded another forkful. The problem with Pearl was, you were never sure what she was sure of herself.

'Was that when you pulled the alarm?'

She nodded. 'Mmm ... Fat lot of good that thing is!

When's the last time you saw a policeman round here?'

Glory sighed. 'Well, it must have been very frightenin' for you. But I'm going to keep an eye out from now on, make sure it doesn't happen again.'

Pearl finished chewing. She shook her head stoically.

'Oh, I wouldn't worry unduly. I've always got Ernest, at a pinch.' She leaned towards Glory unsteadily, with a look that said *I'm telling you this because you're a woman.* 'Needless to say, he slept through the entire thing ...'

The cuff of her cardigan had come to rest in the mashed potato. Glory took a paper towel from the dispenser by the basin and wiped it clean.

Telling white lies was easy with folk like Pearl, though that didn't make it right. But sometimes they were a comfort; and anyway, five minutes later they were forgotten.

Glory was scheduled to be off for the next two days, so it wasn't strictly true to say she'd be watching Pearl herself. But she made a note in the diary for staff to check her regularly. While she was at it, she looked at the previous night's entries. And sure enough, Pearl was right: her alarm was logged at 04:18. Underneath, the investigating care assistant had written: *04:21. Pearl fast asleep.*

In her heart of hearts, Glory thought it was another of her dreams. Pearl's dwindling hold on reality made for extraordinary tales, recounted to Glory with conviction as she washed and dressed her each morning. Sometimes Glory wondered where they came from; Pearl read nothing more scandalous than the parish magazine, and by all accounts had led a quiet suburban life. Probably never worked at all, and certainly not for the Secret Service. They had persuaded the GP to alter the drugs that kept her Parkinson's tremors at bay, for a better balance of side effects. But Pearl continued to see people and things that weren't there; things she nonetheless took in her stride, existing as she did in a sort of bubble, with only the vaguest concern for what went on outside it.

It was Glory's intention to spend the first of her two days off catching up with cousins over Harlesden way. But as she knew from experience, an idle sister and two small children were a burden that expanded to fill the space available – and before long, her plans had been washed away in a tide of chores and dramas.

On top of that, the community crèche Sherelle attended three mornings a week was taking one of its many holidays. Which made it all the more surprising, on the second morning, when Glory awoke to a perfect hush. Her last recollection was the sound of the front door opening in the small hours: Mercy, back from her nightly jaunt, albeit with a muffled squeak of hinges rather than a careless thud.

It was twenty past eight as Glory shuffled into the kitchen. She picked up the cereal packet to pour the children's Krispies – but their bowls had gone from the shelf.

'All done,' said Mercy, behind her. 'I was jus' about to bring you a cuppa tea and toast.'

For a moment, Glory wondered if Pearl's condition was catching. Mercy hadn't made breakfast for anyone since three men came to fix the boiler, and this time she was even dressed. She suspected a practical joke.

'What you up to?'

'I ain't up to nothin'!' said Mercy, wounded. 'Just givin' you a lie-in on your day off. Go on, back to your bed!'

Through the door of her sister's room the children were sitting on the end of their beds, angelic-eyed and spooning Krispies into their mouths. They were dressed too.

As Glory got back under the covers she noticed her blouse. It had reappeared on the door in the night; more miraculously still, in a wrapper from the dry cleaners.

'I thought I had to be at death's door before I got a cuppa tea out of you,' she said as Mercy brought in her mug. The teabag was left in to steep the way she liked it, paper tag dangling over the side like a stranded kite.

'Less of your cheek!' scoffed Mercy. 'We're droppin' Sam off at school, then I'm taking Sherelle to see her Auntie Beula. So you got the place to yourself today. Won't that be nice?'

Beula Pomfret was a hussy from their youth-club days, and about as much the children's auntie as that Lady Gaga. Glory had no time for her, but Mercy and Beula were two of a kind: work-shy layabouts and magnets for the worst kind of babyfather. The latest word on Beula was that she'd fallen on her feet (which made a change) with some small-time property developer in Crystal Palace.

When Mercy marched the children in to say goodbye, it was barely quarter to nine.

'Back in time for tea,' she said. 'And don't worry yourself about that. We'll pick up something nice on the way.'

The children chorused '*Bye-bye, Auntie Glory!*' and Sherelle leapt up on the bed to give her a kiss.

'Aye,' said Glory. 'An' be sure to check your ma's bag when you leave. I wouldn't trust Auntie Beulah not to slip in a kid of her own ...'

Time alone in the flat was such a luxury Glory hardly knew what to do with it. It seemed a waste to sit and do nothing, but a shame to go out and miss it completely. So she compromised.

She began with a deep bath, with bubbles and the luxury of the door open so she could shout out the answers to her favourite quiz on TV. She dried herself, then creamed her skin from top to toe with her favourite moisturiser. Not that lightening stuff that Mercy used; just good, honest skin cream, fresh with the scent of oranges like the jar that stood on Ma's dressing table all through their childhood.

Then Glory started to clean.

She changed into fresh clothes – sweatpants and a T-shirt. Wasteful in a way, considering she was about to spend the morning on her hands and knees, but she wasn't about to put on dirty clothes after a nice long bath. And anyway, like that skinny woman used to say on the TV advertisements, *she was worth it*. Her own career might have taken a turn for the better, but Glory had no time for people who looked down on cleaners. There were precious few jobs that were more worthwhile or rewarded you with such satisfying results. And it beat staring at a computer any day.

Outside, the sun was shining. The tower blocks cast their giant shadows across the lawn, turning the grass from green to black. Glory locked the security grille, so she could leave the front door open and enjoy the fresh air as she worked. She began in the bathroom, attacking the lino with a mop and a pleasingly scalding solution of bleach, the likes of which Mercy never bothered with. She blessed the lack of distractions; she would be done in no time.

An old shopping list skated off the kitchen worktop on the freedom of the breeze. It landed in the hall, but Glory let it lie. Consequently, as she crouched by the bath reaching her mop into the corners underneath, she paid no attention to another fluttering noise behind her.

'*Lost your cat, Glory?*' said a man's voice.

She straightened up, almost snapping her mop in two.

'Good Lord! You scared the life outta me!'

From the walkway Alfonse Bidman smiled apologetically. He tapped his thin fingers lightly on the metal bars a second time. 'Jus' trying to get your attention …'

Glory stood the mop in its bucket and caught her reflection in the mirror. Her face was shiny and there was already dirt on her clean top. She leaned on the door frame and folded her arms over the smudge.

'Mercy isn't in. She gone to see a friend.'

Alfonse nodded thoughtfully. 'An' I bet Mercy got a lotta friends … But isn't it too lovely a day to be cleanin', Glory? How about I come and keep you company awhile?'

Glory peeled off her rubber gloves in a way he would not mistake for seductive. *What was this about now?*

'I'm too busy moppin' up after your girlfriend and her children to chat with you, Alfonse Bidman!'

The young painter, who was nearly as tall as the door, cocked his head on one side as he peered through the grille. A charred stump of reefer lay behind one ear, but he was dressed more smartly than usual, in proper trousers and a shirt. And his old Doc Marten shoes with straggling yellow laces, which Glory had never seen him without.

'Everyone deserves a rest,' said Alfonse, ''cept the wicked, of course.' He winked. 'You're not wicked, are you, Glory?'

She sighed and stared impassively, chewing the inside of her cheek. *Why was it men only ever thought o' one thing?*

'You can have one cuppa tea. Then you're out an' let me get on with me housework.'

She crossed the hall and unlocked the grille, drawing herself against the wall as he sauntered in.

'My,' said Alfonse, 'don't you smell grand? Oranges, is it?'

Glory ignored him. She left him in the kitchen to watch the kettle while she changed into another fresh shirt. One with sleeves.

'So,' she said, firmly shutting the bedroom door, 'not doing your paintin' today?'

Alfonse's clothes were clean, but the coloured splashes on his hands were there as ever, like battle scars.

'I been to a meetin',' he said, leaning against the draining board. 'At the council offices. Seeing a man about a grant.'

The kettle puttered. Glory lifted it off the gas. 'You studyin', then?'

'No. A grant for me paintin'. So I can put on *a' exhibition*.'

Glory filled the mugs with boiling water and said nothing. From what she'd seen of his paintings, he needed lessons not an exhibition. She squeezed the teabag on the back of the spoon and handed him the mug.

In the front room, she waited for him to sit. When he chose the couch, Glory took the other chair and wondered what to say next. Alfonse had been part of their lives for a good six months, but since he and Mercy did all their courting next door, this was the first time they had been alone together.

He filled the awkward pause.

'Well, it's nice to finally spend some time with you, Glory. And if you're anything like your sister, I bet you're a whole lotta fun ...'

'My sister's fun enough for both of us,' said Glory, tucking up her heels under her backside. Something about Alfonse Bidman made her want to make herself very small; his louche way of sitting, with those great long legs so wide his kneecaps almost touched the ends of the couch.

'Aye,' he nodded, 'she knows how to enjoy herself. An' thank God she does, with those two scamps around her all day long, wearin' her to a frazzle.' He shook his head at the thought of poor Mercy, flogging herself to exhaustion in the name of motherhood. 'Some nights, she come round my place an' she can barely keep her eyes open! I fetch her a' elderflower tea but she asleep before she finish it …'

Glory looked sideways. She had never known her sister touch elderflower tea, but it was more believable than the rest of his portrait. Alfonse put the mug to his lips. He watched her through the rising vapour.

'An' that's why I been thinkin' – wouldn't it be nice if Mercy had a break?'

He swallowed, though he hadn't sipped, Adam's apple falling in his throat like an elbow passing through the sleeve of a jacket.

'What sorta break would that be?' asked Glory warily.

Alfonse sat upright and pulled a wad of paper from his trouser pocket.

'Well, I was thinkin' about taking her to see Trinidad. Where me folks are from. It's *beautiful* this time of year ...'

The papers were pages from a holiday brochure. He spread them out on the rug, pointing at pictures and losing himself in reverie.

'… I wan' to show her the beach where me Great Granny had a cottage. Where she used to watch the flocks of scarlet ibis when she was a girl. They're still there – thousands of 'em, beautiful ... When they comes home to roost, it's like a bloodstain on the sunset, an' when I tell Mercy about them, she got a tear in her eye …'

Lord, thought Glory, what sort of spell had her sister cast this time? The only birds she had any time for were coated in breadcrumbs.

'A trip like that costs a fortune!' said Glory. 'You know she got no money.'

'Ah,' said Alfonse, digging something from his other pocket. 'But I got me grant today.' The letter was headed *Lambeth Council Funding for the Arts*. 'Goes in the bank tomorrow!'

Glory eyed him disapprovingly. 'That money's for your paintin'.'

He nodded, hard enough to loosen his head: 'An' it is! Believe me, there ain't nothing more inspirin' to a' artist than the colours of Trinidad!'

'Oh? And how much you gonna have left when you bought tickets for Mercy and the kids? Did you work that out?'

Suddenly Alfonse was absorbed in the small print. 'Ah – well, I was meanin' to talk to you about that …'

And that was when Glory understood.

Mercy! That girl had had the luck of the devil since the day she was born! And here it was, happening again – with Glory running along behind, holding her sister's forked tail out of the dirt, same as always!

Alfonse spluttered. 'I was thinkin' it'd do her good to get away *without the children*.'

'Oh no—'

'I gotta half-sister in Camberwell – you wouldn't be on your own!'

'*Oh no!*'

'She could pick them up from school when you're workin' …'

Glory's ears were on fire.

'… maybe have one o' them at the weekends?'

'*How many weekends?!*'

Alfonse was trying to shrink into the couch. His skin showed rosy through his wispy beard. He looked like the world's tallest ten-year-old.

'One!' His voice clawed back the risen octave. 'Maximum two.'

Glory rocked back in her chair. Now it all fell into place! Mercy, playing the good sister, bringing her breakfast in bed then hauling the kids off to see Beula Pomfret. All so her Casanova could work his silver tongue on good old Glory! The cheek of her! The cheek of them both!

Before she knew it she was standing over him.

'Alfonse Bidman, if Mercy thinks she can dump her kids on me and go swannin' off with a man who can't even clean his fingernails, then she's stupid as you are!'

'Mercy say—'

'Mercy say a whole lotta rubbish – an' by the sound of it, you swallowed the lot! The only children she ever exhausted herself over are great big babies like you! Now get your carcass outta my house before I kicks you out!'

He was up in a swirl of brochure pages, gone without a word. Through the grille so fast he might have slid through the bars.

Glory heard his Doc Martens squeaking down the walkway, followed by the slam of his own front door. She slumped on the couch. Then she reached down and picked up the one page he'd missed: *Coconut Bay Beach Club. Snorkelling, swimming and sunbathing beneath an azure sky.* The photograph showed a smartly jacketed waiter shouldering drinks down a jetty, to where a white couple dangled their toes in the milky blue water.

Just the sorta sea for sharks, thought Glory.

She screwed the page into a ball. Tossed it into the bin, along with the stump of reefer that had fallen from Alfonse's ear.

With Mercy around, those sharks didn't stand a chance.

V

When Tony got back to the flat, Geoff was twiddling with the microwave.

'Hi darling! How was your Back, Sack 'n' Crack?'

'Actually, you call it a Back Facial over here,' said Tony. 'The intimate waxing option *was* on the table, so to speak. But I'm a bit fussy who I let down there.'

His mate made a face. 'Really? Since when?'

'Behave!' Tony took a ready meal from the magnet-encrusted fridge. 'Can I have one of these? I'll hit the supermarket tomorrow, promise.'

Geoff nodded. 'Well, I hope it's helped your jet lag.'

'Me too. Plus, twenty-four hours in a tin can always brings me out in zits.'

Geoff scratched around in the cutlery drawer. 'That'll be the delightful combination of nylon seats and recycled flatulence. I go club; calfskin and a better class of fart!'

Tony laughed. He'd met Geoff on his first trip to London in '97, when he was freelancing at an advertising agency in Knightsbridge. Tony was an account handler, as buttoned-up as his Auckland city tailoring; Geoff was in the creative department, the only other gay guy in the place. Their paths hadn't crossed much, but they whipped up a lively enough email banter when they were back on their respective sides of the planet. When Geoff took him up on his invitation and said he was coming to Auckland the summer before the millennium, Tony could hardly remember what he looked like – but his office was firmly imprinted on his memory. The décor combined a row of advertising award catalogues with two shelves of fairground kitsch: My Little Ponies, snow domes from selected destinations around the world, and flamenco dolls guaranteed to have their skirts up round their ears on a Friday afternoon. Geoff was camper than a Winnebago convention – out, proud and very loud. The night he turned up at Tony's apartment needing dollars for the cab from the airport, he wondered what he'd let himself in for. Turned out they got on fine, to the point where Tony took two weeks off to drive them both round South Island in a hire car. In some ways, Geoff was the kind of guy he'd give a wide berth, but as a travel buddy he was a delight. With no hint of mutual attraction to make it complicated they had a ball; bunking down in youth hostels and cheap hotels in Christchurch, Queenstown, Dunedin – even Invercargill. By the end, and despite some less than seasonal weather, Geoff said he'd had the holiday of his life. Now here he was, all these years later, returning the hospitality.

Or that was the idea. He was also up to his Gaultier eyewear in a pitch for a deodorant brand, and since Tony arrived they'd hardly had a chance to catch up.

'Geoff, you know yesterday – did you mean it when you said I'd put on weight?'

Geoff took a heatproof plastic cauldron from the microwave. He peeled back the film lid and stirred something that was caramelising nicely.

'Let's see … Stand up straight … Turn round.' He looked Tony over with an art director's eye. 'Yep, you've definitely slapped it on a bit.' He slid the bowl back in the oven. 'Don't you weigh yourself?'

'Used to,' said Tony. 'At the gym. Till I stopped going.'

'Well, there you are. I always know from my belt hole if I'm putting it on.'

'Ah, but elastic waists are back in again at home.'

Geoff snorted. 'Like they ever went out! New Zealand's not Milan, is it? Talking of which, I see you've still got that manky old bag …'

Tony's hand baggage was on the kitchen table where he'd left it.

'Hey, keep my trusty rucky out of this! We've been all over the world together.'

Geoff picked at the collage of souvenir patches that all but swallowed up the original fabric. 'Don't tell me – Chernobyl, Baghdad, Detroit … I'll say one thing though, your needlework's improving.'

'Anyway,' said Tony, 'You can't have a go at my bag while you're still hoarding those bloody fridge magnets!'

It was a fair point. The cavalcade of tack in the corner was an echo of Geoff's office, the one concession to bad taste in his tastefully understated apartment. He picked up magnets wherever he went in the world and encouraged friends to do the same.

'It's art! I'm creating an installation. Look, I've got a new one …'

He unclamped one plastic horror: a white-faced figure in flowing robes, with what appeared to be spaghetti drying between its fingers. Beneath it read:

FUKKIENESE PUPPET THEATRE SINGAPORE

'Fuckin' easy string puppets!' he crowed. 'I love it.'

As he fitted it back into the mosaic, Geoff caught Tony's expression.

'Come on, don't beat yourself up. So what if you've put a bit of weight on, it's not a crime.' He ran a hand down his well-toned side '*Exactly.*'

Tony laughed. Then he noticed the cardboard sleeve

from Geoff's dinner on top of the rubbish tin, from a range called TastyTrimmers. He looked back at his own Beef and Ale Pie with All-Butter Mash.

The microwave pinged like a gameshow clock.

'And you're tall,' said Geoff. 'You wouldn't suit skinny.' He held open the oven door. 'Your turn.'

But Tony's meal was already back in the fridge.

'Can I have one of those oranges?'

Geoff's spare room trebled as his dressing room and study, though the lack of a spare bed made Tony wonder if he really liked having guests. The inflatable mattress, mustard with a velveteen finish, was at odds with the colour scheme. And with the reclaimed-timber wardrobe, desk and chair there wasn't much room for Tony's stuff. Most of it was still in the suitcase.

Geoff had said he could use the computer, which made for a welcome diversion that night as Tony found himself awake long hours before dawn.

He logged onto his email, and was delighted to see one from Greta.

g.daniels@shermansumnerinc.com ***01:05***

Hey gorgeous.

Hope you arrived safe and that London's welcoming you with open arms. Geoff still his bubbly old self? Don't tell me, girly as ever!!

All fine here in NYC, though more fun if you were here. Could have done with you last night actually. Got cornered by the client at after-work drink (Note singular! Jeez do they NOT know how to party!!) Mr Sherman Senior is a total sleaze ball – 70 if he's a day, on his fourth divorce. And reading between the lines of his $2,000 pinstripes, I think he was proposing I play cowpoke at his ranch in Connecticut, EWWW!!

So of course I made my excuses and left. Then got stuck in the lift. THEN got cab going the wrong way down 5th. Took me an hour to get home, but worth it to escape old Anchovy Breath! Got to get out of this job!!

Anyway drop me a line ASAP. Big kiss to Geoff, bigger one to you and remember me to Leicester Square!

Luvya

Gret xxx

PS How are the fridge magnets?!

Tony smiled. He hadn't seen Greta since her transfer to New York. They had vague plans to catch up while he was on his travels and he couldn't wait; that girl never failed to cheer him up. He slid the roller blind halfway up, letting in the street lamp's yellowish glow. Then he clicked reply.

TTorrence1010@hotmail.com 04.56

Hi there sweetheart,

Flight ghastly as expected, thanks! You were right, it wasn't worth saving $100 to transit in Abu Dhabi. Just meant I got cooped up in a fish tank with 200 people and a drinks machine that didn't take dollars, pounds or a bloody good kicking. Bloke from Rotorua nearly clapped in irons for vandalism. We all kept quiet after that, watching Al Jazeera with sound off.

And no, Geoff hasn't changed, except for hairdo (one of many?!) He's got a cool apartment five mins from the subway, though we haven't discussed how long I'm staying yet. He's swamped at work, so looks like I'm flying solo for now. Suits me. Came here to think, didn't I?

Took your tip and went straight to the beauty parlour. Staff a bit ornery, but they all look the same when you've got your head in the glory hole, eh?! :-O

Oh, one thing. Geoff says I've put on weight, cheeky bastard. Could be right though. Reckon I better restart the old health and fitness while I'm here too. Gym nearby and there's a big park at the end of the road. Time to cleanse body AND soul, no? Hints, tips, websites of cute Cockney personal trainers all gratefully received!

Big squeeze to my fruity babe in the Big Apple.

T x

He closed the blind and got back into bed, which was like negotiating a giant blancmange. Tony kept one eye on the screen in case she replied. Until his mailbox morphed into Geoff's screensaver: a line of glitter-pouched go-go boys shimmying into infinity.

No one real had abs like that.

Retouched. *Definitely.*

And then he fell asleep.

Tony took it easy over the next few days to let his jet lag subside. He soon regained his London bearings, with a little help from the Underground map and the 137 bus that went all the way to Oxford Circus.

He rediscovered Covent Garden with its acrobats and mime artists, including a guy in Tin Man face paint he was sure had been there last time. High Street Kensington and the King's Road were irresistible too, particularly at the current exchange rate on his Kiwi dollars. Barkers department store had gone; but World's End brought back happy memories of his first trip overseas. A time when life was less stressful.

He walked to Kensington Gardens, to the gates where an ocean of flowers had bloomed on the death of Diana. That was right after he got back to NZ: he remembered watching the funeral at Ma's house with the rest of the family, already nostalgic for the brash, familiar streets that looked so dispirited. The almost-pagan outpouring of grief reached around the world to their lounge in Blockhouse Bay; Ma, a fervent royalist and never averse to a wallow, sitting with her treasured copy of the *Auckland Herald* from the day she queued for a glimpse of Charles, Diana and baby Wills at Government House.

Last time round, Tony's experience of south-of-the-river amounted to a single night and hungover morning in Tooting with a curate he met in a sauna. Not much to show for eight months in London, but, as he soon learned, not unusual. Most the natives were trapped in their own little rat runs, as likely to pop to Paris for the weekend as set foot in Peckham or Penge.

But this time, with Clapham as his base, South London was his stamping ground. So on days when hitting the city centre was too much effort, he amused himself closer to home. With Geoff at work, he had the run of the apartment and free rein on the laptop. It took him no time at all to find tempting deals to Rome, Prague and a dozen other cities he longed to see.

Financially, he had his three-month sabbatical covered – or less if Geoff got antsy about him bunking down in the spare room. The bigger issue was whether Tony was going back to his job at all. He was forty years and seven weeks old; and since the day he blew out the candles, those midlife clichés had come tumbling in on him. He needed time to regroup, to ponder his next move; though admittedly coming twelve thousand miles to do it was a trifle indulgent.

His dilemma was this: in the last year he'd been marking time at work, doing a good job without doing a great one.

The trend-bucking revenue stream swilling through his department had buoyed him to a career high of group account director on New Zealand's biggest telecoms account. A reading of the runes – *aka* a memo spotted on the fifth-floor printer – suggested he was up for a seat on the board. It was everything Tony had been waiting for, and longer than most. If he was going up the corporate ladder, now was the time.

That was the good news. The bad news was that advertising didn't excite him anymore. It was a truth he did his best to ignore, as it skulked at the back of his mind, waiting for attention like a dogged hypochondriac. And again next morning, as he lazed fitfully on his lilo, watching a silent stream of jets make their descent into Heathrow; later, on the subway, strap-hanging back from a West End matinee; and again that night, when Geoff was still at work and Tony found himself alone in the apartment, shuffling between the DVD player and his host's poorly hidden stash of gay porn.

Since his reliable old Virgo buddy kept his smut alphabetised, he could view without fear of discovery. It was an easy if mischievous way to while away an hour when he still felt woozy from the flight – watching a bunch of hot Dan Carter-lookalikes rolling around and scoring aplenty without so much as a rugby ball in sight. Particularly, when accompanied by a glass of the rather fine Marlborough pinot Tony had found for a crazy price at the local Sainsbury's. Daytime drinking wasn't his style, but hey – what were holidays for?

Pleasurable distractions aside, he followed Greta's advice. (*How about power walking, like we did in The Domain?*) Back in the day, his best friend had embraced the latest exercise fad along with the fashion for hip-skimming jeans.

Examining her muffin-top belly at his kitchen counter, she explained how power walking would strip the fat from her waist, hips and thighs, tone her arms and give her pikestaff posture. All in three, forty-minute sessions a week.

Tony had joined in to keep her company, though hipsters did him no favours either. It was also an excuse to splash out on new exercise gear, and when they met for their first after-work session they fell about at the sight of each other, Lycra'd up like a couple of gone-to-seed superheroes. Their new regime lasted precisely two arm-swinging, bottom-tucking weeks, till work in her case and a certain bespectacled solicitor in his chipped away their resolve.

If you listened to Greta, Tony had men falling at his feet (*Remember the time I nipped into the Winter Gardens for a pee? Came back and found you chatting up a hot horticulturist, bursting to show you his orchids?!*) To him, it never felt like that. Tony wasn't much of a one for putting himself out there; liaisons only came his way when the other guy did the work. Not because he thought he was something special; more because he didn't. And yet, by Greta's straight single-girl standards, he had it easy. Tummy roll aside, she was in great shape: attractive, easy-going, career on the up and boobs to match. But for reasons he had never fathomed, she'd been on her own for ten years – and the closer she got to forty, the more it needled her.

So when Tony met Jarvis, he felt like apologising.

It was a business meeting. Tony's ad agency was suing a client for unpaid bills, and Jarvis was the solicitor on the case. For Tony, it was instant attraction; like walking into a clothing store and seeing a jacket you couldn't leave without. And from the way the little guy in the shade-too-big suit was blushing to the top of his shaven scalp, the feeling was mutual. For once, Tony took the initiative. Email did the rest.

Two nights later, they were sharing a bottle of wine on Auckland Harbour, listening to the mast cables rattle on the breeze. Within a week, they were seeing each other – officially, except where work was concerned, since Jarvis wasn't out to his colleagues. In fact, he wasn't out to anyone but a small group of friends – which amused Tony at first, along with all the clandestine texts and the emails peppered with few enough double entendres to get past Jarvis's secretary. A bit old-school, but then he didn't rally to the rainbow flag much himself anymore.

Even so, there were disadvantages to dating a guy so far in the closet he smelt of mothballs. Jarvis approached their relationship like an undercover operation. Monday and Wednesday lunchtimes, they would meet at the beach equidistant from their offices. There, in the evergreen shade of a pōhutukawa tree, they laid down their suit jackets and ate sandwiches a respectable hip-width apart. Usually in silence, with Jarvis looking out to sea. And every lunchtime ended the same, as he checked his watch and said, '*I better skedaddle* …' He would stand and dislodge the sand from his blazer by shaking it three times and wiping it twice; then they walked to the bus stop where Jarvis said, '*Text you later,*' before crossing the street without looking back.

In the end, Tony couldn't remember why he'd been so smitten. It wasn't the sex, since Jarvis's idea of passion followed a similarly rigid agenda. Tony had a thing for guys even hairier than he was, and the solicitor's well-thatched chest was more of a turn-on than what passed for technique. But Jarvis was good company, when he relaxed enough to let his well-read wit out to play. They spent long evenings sifting through each other's past. Tony told him things he never usually spoke of. And Jarvis reciprocated: about the pressure of staying on the right side of the grandmother, who controlled the family fortune; and his uneasy relationship with his parents, whom Tony soon realised he would never meet. When the revelations dried up, Jarvis was content with a kind of lazy symbiosis; having made his niche in Tony's life, he was going to lie in it. And once there, he reverted to Mr-White-and-Uptight, albeit now with a presentable boyfriend he could call on when required.

So after three and a half months, their relationship stalled, at wordless lunches and two nights a week of *Groundhog Day* passion. When Tony had told Jarvis he was taking a sabbatical to go abroad, neither of them admitted it was the end. In that final, stilted lunch hour on the beach the day before Tony flew to London, the silence was loud enough to drown out the surf. So the next morning, when the cab arrived to take him to the airport, Tony locked up his apartment with Jarvis's austere little folding toothbrush still in the mug on the bathroom shelf. Stiff and upright, giving nothing away.

A few days later, Tony was striding round Clapham Common, keeping tight to the railing that separated him from the grumpy perimeter traffic. The Common was dull, even in the sunshine. Nothing but a few trees and a cluster of flaking swings disrupted the green concrete of its lawns.

He chose mid-morning, when there were fewer people around, though after his first couple of power walks he hardly felt self-conscious at all. The clockwork-soldier arm carriage had become second nature and even felt exhilarating. Today, he was following the example of a particularly svelte jogger by shouldering his rucksack, in which three bottles of pinot wrapped in a sweater acted as ballast. His route took him past the bleak little pond, where geese dabbled or took to the path to menace the pigeons. Two boys sat over their fishing rods with a stack of tinnies; as he passed, one of them said something Tony didn't catch. The other boy laughed but kept his eyes on the water.

In forty-four minutes his circuit was complete, at the bandstand in the centre of the Common where the thrum of traffic was hardly audible. Panting, Tony chose one of a circle of benches by the tawdry little café. He unhooked the bag from his damp shoulders, toying with the idea of buying a Coke until he realised he'd forgotten his wallet. He sat back in the sunshine instead.

Toddlers on tricycles clattered gleefully over the bitumen. Well-dressed mums and indifferent nannies hovered, rushing to the rescue of riders unseated by the tree roots that broke the surface like Triffids. A red-faced man whistled to a dog chasing a crisp packet; as the spiral-tailed mutt paused at Tony's feet to sniff his sneakers, the man watched without making eye contact. Tony remembered that from last time – the way Londoners kept themselves to themselves. His spatial awareness was back too; it was always worth knowing who was around you in the big city.

The young woman who had walked up behind him was blond with a ponytail, maybe a few years younger than him. Pretty, with no makeup except a shade too much mascara. She was wearing trackie bottoms with a sweatshirt round her waist; at the end of a run, judging by the way her chest was heaving. Her vest said *SMART BLONDE – Deal With It.* She lifted one foot onto the bench-back in a graceful arc, leaning into a hamstring stretch. Her "Must be mad!" smile as she caught Tony's eye told him she wasn't British. The woman repeated the move with the other leg, then walked away, hands linked overhead in a shoulder stretch.

From the other side of the bandstand, the red-faced man was also watching. The dog he was trying to persuade back onto its lead was more interested in a squirrel, capering round a tree trunk with roller-coaster grace. The dog looked at its master with one ear cocked – then it was off, tail jiggling like a rattlesnake.

Just like Chippy! thought Tony. The Labrador/Collie cross from his childhood was the soul of obedience, till he wanted his own way.

'*Cute, eh?*'

He was startled to see the young woman at the other end of his bench (so much for his personal radar!) She tucked her hands under her thighs as she spoke again:

'Don't mind me asking, but – are you a Kiwi?'

The voice was no surprise; every other white face round these parts seemed to hail from Down Under.

'Yeah!' said Tony, lifting his sunnies to look her over and hoping she wouldn't misconstrue it. 'Auckland. You?'

'Wellington.'

She turned away, rubbing the side of her face. Something was bothering her.

'Funny, I actually thought you were going to say Wellington too.'

'Oh, why?'

'Because – look, I know this sounds bizarre, but I think I recognise you!'

They laughed at the absurdity of it – but not too hard. Back home, travellers' tales were legion of heading into the wild blue yonder only to bump into the girl or bloke from next door.

'I don't get down to Wellington much,' said Tony. 'And when I do it's on business. You know, plane-taxi-meeting-taxi-plane.'

The woman shook her head. 'That's just it. I don't think it's home I know you from.'

The man with the lead had given up. He sat down, leaving his dog to its quest. Tony and the woman frowned at each other from either end of the bench like the poster for a feisty romcom.

'I'm Tony, by the way.'

'Shelley – sorry, I sound like a total loon!'

'No worries. Maybe you saw me here. I'm on the Common most days.'

'Nope,' she insisted. 'God, this is crazy, I know your face so well! You're not on telly are you?'

He laughed and shook his head. 'Maybe we've got a mutual Facebook friend. Oh, hang on – I was on the local news a couple of months back. They stopped me in the mall, asked if I thought we should become a republic when Camilla becomes Queen …'

'Wait a minute!' She lifted a hand to her eyes. 'Did you – did you go to the University of Otago?'

Tony's mouth fell open. Then closed. Then opened again.

'Yeah, but that was—'

'Don't tell me. Late eighties, right?'

'Yeah, more or less. Were you there too?'

'No, no. It's way weirder than that.' Shelley laughed disbelievingly as the dog appeared beside her, squirrel forgotten. 'Do you remember a bloke called Vince Hardy?'

'Vince …'

'Tall, dark hair, played rugby. Big shoulders and hands like bunches of bananas.'

He sounded like the kind of guy Tony would remember.

But then hundreds of students passed through in his years at Otago.

'Vince and I had been together since we were kids. When he went off to uni, I came to stay a few times.'

'What was he studying?'

'Sports medicine. Ended up physio-ing for the Kiwi women's rugby team. Enough said about *that* ...' Shelley reached down to pet the dog as it truffled for smells. 'You were in his photo!'

Tony had lost the thread. 'His what?'

'It was by my bed all the time he was away, and in my purse for years after that. *Vince, raising a tinnie at the uni bar*. You were standing right behind him.'

'Well, well ... Small world.'

Shelley sighed. 'Men, eh? Can't live with 'em, can't shoot 'em.'

Tony wasn't sure how to take that. Had he come all this way to get cornered by a nutter from home? He felt for the comforting rub of his rucksack – it was time he got these bottles back in the wine rack.

'How about you? Did you have a guy at uni?'

Now, that unnerved him. Strangers rarely latched on to which way his bread was buttered; so he liked to think.

She wasn't deterred. 'I mean it can't have been easy, back then. Not like today – and not like here! Some friends of mine took me to this great little gay bar in Soho last week. Terrace had the cutest parakeets hopping around. It sounded just like home!' Her nose twitched. 'I'm not so sure about English blokes, though. Bit standoffish, don't you find?'

A genuine pause.

'Dunno,' said Tony. Barring a weakness for a few of the cuter rugby players, he hadn't given the native totty much thought. 'To be honest, I'm still mulling over a guy I left back home.'

'Ah, gotcha!' said Shelley. 'Then that's something else we've got in common!'

She nodded to the empty tables outside the café.

'Fancy a coffee?'

Running into Kiwis was one of London's drawbacks. Since Tony had come to get a fresh perspective, the bouncy twang of voices from back home usually made him shrivel. But this one, he was warming to. She was also more likely to be familiar from the telly than he was; Shelley was an actress – not to mention a pop star.

'Hardly!' she said. 'Just backing vocals for a few bands that nearly made it. Oh, and I did an INXS video once – there, that dates me! Played one of a dozen chicks flirting with Michael Hutchence before he runs off with the girl in footie shorts.' She picked at the cardboard cuff of her cappuccino. 'Talk about life imitating art …'

Tony didn't delve. 'Are you singing over here?'

'No. I'm taking a break from all that. I've got another project on the go, sort of. Excuse the cliché, but I suppose I've come to find myself.'

'Haven't we all.'

A girl came out of the café and started clearing tables. Shelley turned the conversation back to him.

'Must be a pretty pressurising business, advertising. When I've done shoots, the agency guys are always the ones looking harassed. Muttering on their mobiles, like they're talking someone down from a window ledge.'

Tony laughed. 'You're playing with other people's money at the end of the day. Lots of it, usually.' He flicked crumbs onto the tarmac as a pigeon appeared from nowhere. 'So who are you escaping from?'

Shelley rested her cup on the edge of the table.

'My ex. *Husband*. Though technically I've already escaped. We divorced two months ago.'

Now that did sound familiar. She was, what – thirty-five, thirty-six? Tony knew of at least three marriages that were grinding to a halt round about now.

'There's a lot of it about. How do you feel?'

She took the sweatshirt off the back of the chair and draped it over her shoulders.

'Sad. Empowered. Terrified. Take your pick! We'd been married nine years.'

'It wasn't, er – Vern?'

'Vince? No. Actually, my husband was the one who saved me from Vince. Picked me up and dusted me down when he went off with Fly-Half Phoebe. I was on the rebound, should never have done it but … Life runs away with you sometimes.'

Tony didn't know what to say. He settled for what he was thinking:

'Nine years sounds pretty good to me. I still measure my relationships in dog years. Nine months is practically silver anniversary!'

Shelley smiled. 'Yeah, tell me about it. Some of the guys I was chatting to in that bar changed partners every week! Nice work if you can get it.' She drained the last of her coffee. 'Gay guys have it sussed.'

'Hmm,' said Tony. 'Grass is always greener. Talking of which, it's time I headed home. Which way you going?'

The sun had gone in and there was already a chill in the air. He was tempted to get the sweater out of his bag as they walked back to the road.

'I never asked,' said Shelley. 'Who's the bastard you're escaping from?'

'Oh, he's not that bad. Actually, he's only part of the reason I'm here. I just needed to take a step back. From everything.'

The red-faced man overtook them at the duck pond with his dog on an extendable lead.

'What's your project, anyway?' asked Tony. 'Find-a-New-Husband?'

'Not exactly, but close. I'm looking for a sperm donor.'

That made him catch a breath.

'Blimey! You've come far enough for it. Couldn't your husband, er … ?'

'Oh, he could all right. But he never wanted to. Said we were better off just the two of us. Till the day he came home and told me he was in love with a woman at work – who also happened to be eight weeks' pregnant.'

Tony whistled. 'Nasty. That's a bastard, all right. But why the distance?'

Shelley watched the dog as it paused to sniff a tussock of dandelions.

'So then, I decided to do it on my own. Oh, I know I could go to a clinic, but that's all so – *clinical*. I guess I'm an old-fashioned girl.' She paused, thinking it through. 'I could have a one-night stand – leave the guy none the wiser. But that'd be mean, to him and the kid. I just want to be straight about it, without involving someone who wants to pop round and check on his handiwork every weekend. Does that sound crazy?'

Tony shook his head. 'Not at all. My dad wasn't around when I grew up and it didn't do me any harm. Apart from turning me into a *great big poofter*.'

Shelley looked startled. 'Do you really think—?'

He nudged her shoulder. 'Joke!'

They reached the railings at a bend in the road. The traffic was bumper to bumper, like a fairground ride.

'I'm staying with a mate down that-a-way,' said Tony.

'I'm the other way. Nice meeting you. Maybe see you again?'

'Maybe. I'm working off all those business lunches while I'm here, so ...'

He wasn't sure how to say goodbye, so he settled for a pat on the arm. Her triceps were enviably firm. Tony watched her skip smoothly over the railing with that scissor kick he had never quite mastered.

'You look fine as you are,' said Shelley. 'See ya!'

She waited for a break in the traffic that never came, until a grubby white van drew to a respectful halt. As she crossed the road, three heads turned in unison behind the windscreen. The driver whistled approvingly and Tony found himself included in a conspiratorial nod from the dark, stubbly bloke at the passenger window.

Who was actually quite tasty himself ... But then Tony always was a sucker for a guy with painty elbows.

One way or another, he couldn't see Shelley being short of volunteers.

VI

Quito was a culture shock, after a month in the rainforest and the Toblerone ruins of Machu Picchu. Mari had had her doubts from the start. Every urban stop they'd made on this trip brought a sense of disquiet she never felt when they were off the beaten track. But if they were going to extend their adventure, they needed to earn money – and Adam said the Ecuadorian capital was the place to do it.

They fell into jobs at the first college they tried. Took to teaching readily enough – particularly Mari, who spoke the better Spanish. But with each other to go home with at night, there was little incentive to mix with the natives, or their fellow teachers. Before long, the city's beggar families and the interminable honking traffic had taken their toll on Mari's pioneering spirit. Her long fair hair singled her out; with its endless queues and guinea pigs on the menu, Quito made the gritty parts of London feel as edgy as her hometown of sleepy Hove in Sussex.

Mari reminded herself that they had come to see a different way of life; it was that all right. She knew she had to stick it for a while, because Adam was having a whale of a time – until his second iPod disappeared in the college café, and the life of indoor camping started to pall even for him. So, barring a dusty bus ride to the Indian market, the day when their plane lifted out of the Quito smog was the first time they'd left the city in nine weeks. Two hours later, they were in the Galápagos.

By the standards of the archipelago, the island of Baltra had little to show for itself but an airstrip left by the US Marines. Soon Mari and Adam were mustering on the quay, with the three other couples who were to make up their cruise boat's payload. They were the youngest by a generation.

Their guide, Paloma, was finishing her introduction in perfect American English.

'And here she is now!' she announced, as the *Beluga* glided in through the harbour entrance. The vessel, a 'prestige-class motor yacht', was as white and glossy as its photograph. The brochure promised air-conditioned cabins, and the kind of cuisine their well-heeled travelling companions probably took for granted. The trip was well outside their budget; or would have been, but for a late cancellation at the travel agents on Avenida Amazonas. Mari and Adam's luck was in, as they scored eight nights on the *Beluga* for the price of five on a glorified fishing boat.

Their regal craft came to rest fifty metres offshore; her anchor chain slipped into the water as she idled, sleek as a supermodel. Mari scratched mud from her backpack as the first of two inflatable launches pulled up at the quay. A pair of thickset sailors clambered over the wall and nodded to Paloma.

'These guys will take your luggage,' she explained. 'We're boarding on the other panga.'

The sailors hoisted Mari's and Adam's shabby bags onto their shoulders, freeing up a hand to pull Louis Vuittons across the concrete on squealing wheels. One sailor dropped into the inflatable boat, while the other passed the luggage down piece by piece. Mari was watching the first inflatable speed back towards the *Beluga* when lifejackets appeared, popping up on the quay like surfacing penguins.

'Life vests are compulsory whenever we cross to or from an island,' explained Paloma, passing them round.

The men of their party grumbled. But once everyone was

suitably trussed, Paloma and the other sailor demonstrated the surefooted way to climb aboard a panga. They made everyone practise, to more tutting from the ranks. But as Mari took her place on the launch, Adam's face lit up like a kid on Christmas morning.

'Hold on tight, babe. Here we go!'

She braced herself as the engine roared.

Two seconds later they were scudding across the water to where the other panga was already disgorging their luggage onto the boat. Mari touched the band on her wrist, which the chemist had assured her would ward off seasickness. Felt in one pocket, for the tablets she'd also bought while she was there; and in the other, for the candied-ginger remedy that usually lived at the bottom of her wash-bag.

For a girl who had jacked in a perfectly good job to travel halfway round the world, Mari wasn't one for taking chances.

Next morning, to her surprise, she felt quite acclimatised.

They had sailed through the night and the sea was calm – as expected, according to Adam's guidebook. He was engrossed from the moment they retired to their cabin, reading out passages from the top bunk. But not even the copper-coloured iguanas of Española could keep Mari's attention for long. According to Paloma's after-dinner briefing, the following day began at 6 a.m.; a time Mari had no intention of seeing for any iguana – copper, tin or paisley. She was still pondering the best way to fake *mal de mer,* when the chin-to-ankles rocking of the ocean sent her to sleep.

Adam's alarm went off impossibly soon after that. He bounced her out of the lower bunk, into the least effective shower she had encountered outside a caravan. There was no escape.

Mari passed on breakfast since it was too early to eat. A decision she immediately regretted as they teetered onto one of the two inflatables, bobbing off the stern like giant flip-flops.

'Remember – Galápagos Handshake,' reminded Paloma, clasping the fleshiest part of Mari's forearm as she guided her aboard.

The rest of their party were already seated, bright in anticipation and yellow lifejackets. A sailor sparked up the engine, and they pulled away in the direction of a stony beach just visible through the morning mist. The sea air was whistling by at a rate of knots when Adam's belch hit Mari square in the face. Nausea rose behind her nostrils, mingling with the aroma of his black coffee, bacon and morning fag.

'Can you *not* do that?' she snapped.

'Can't hear you, babe,' he mouthed, leaning over to kiss her on the cheek. Nothing on the equator of the earth was going to spoil his day.

The inflatable's motor slowed near the shore. Something in the water caught Mari's eye. She shuddered at the smooth dark shape half a dozen metres away, that looked a lot like a—

'Galápagos sea lion,' smiled Paloma, as the rubber-bottomed boat skidded on the shingle. 'Nothing to worry about!'

Their guide hopped into the surf to secure the bow, helped by Jorge Luis, the dark-eyed pilot.

As the aliens prepared to land, Mari realised she was the only one without waterproof sandals. Taking off her trainers and knotting the laces, she hung them round her neck in a Nike bolas. She waited her turn, then jumped for the sand.

She was still drying her toes on the hem of her T-shirt when Adam said, 'Come on, we're off!'

The rest of the troop were halfway up the trail. Mari sighed, managing to squeeze her gritty feet into the trainers before he dragged her after them.

Terra firma had settled her stomach and she was starting to feel hungry. But according to Paloma, taking food onto the islands was prohibited, along with everything else except water, sunblock and a camera. She would just have to rumble.

Fifty metres up the carefully marked path, there didn't seem to be much to see on Española. They meandered on, through the rocks and round a bend until-

'*See! Down there!*'

Ah yes, thought Mari: another sea lion.

But soon fingers were pointing again. Motors whirred and shutters clicked as creatures emerged from crevice and camouflage. Birds hopped onto the trail, fearless of the goggling spectators, and something skittered from a cascade of foliage, coming to rest at Mari's feet. It was a tiny grey lizard with a ridge of spines along its back.

'Baby iguana, no?' asked Heike, the German lady. She stooped for a closer look through her ever-present camcorder. The tiny reptile stared back, arrogant as a Chihuahua on a cushion.

'Actually, it's a lava lizard,' Paloma corrected kindly.

Adam sniggered.

It was only 8 a.m., but the sun was already intense. Three months on and Mari was still heeding the warnings, applying high-factor cream to her exposed bits and making Adam do the same. She hung back, dawdling in the warmth, and reflected that a week of this might not be so bad after all.

Adam read her mind. 'Good here, innit?'

She nodded. It wasn't quite the teeming cradle of creation she had fallen asleep to on his *Wild Galápagos* DVD

– but then this island was only the first of many. And she didn't have to go ashore every day if she didn't want to. The boat had a decent-sized sundeck, with padded recliners, and a shady little nook in front of the wheelhouse. The lounge was cosy too, even if the furniture was bolted to the floor. All places where a girl could curl up with a book, if all this nature became too much for her.

The party snaked off down the trail, with Paloma at the head in her bush hat and voluminous shorts. Every few metres a bird or reptile strayed onto the path; but as the signs pointed out in four different languages, trespass was strictly a one-way affair. Española was an odd combination of wilderness and perfect order, like the Garden of Eden run by the National Trust.

Rounding another bend, they were greeted by squawking pandemonium. Tangled branches rising cliff-high were intermingled with the nests of birds. On some, oversized parents teetered like saucepan lids on teacups. Others were filled with raucous juveniles, brazenly careless of passing eyes. They were different species, all roosting together: gulls, albatross and something else – a black-feathered giant with a hooked beak and scarlet patch at its throat.

Paloma halted in front of a particularly fine specimen.

'And here we have one of the most amazing birds of the islands – the Magnificent Frigatebird. Keep your eye on him and he may show you how he got his name ...'

In less than a minute, the bird rose to the challenge. Drawing back its head it raised its wings; then, with a noise like a drum roll, puffed out its throat pouch alarmingly to form a balloon it proceeded to waggle from side to side. Further down the trail others followed suit, until the branches were dotted with scarlet baubles.

'Like switching on Blackpool Illuminations!' murmured Adam, snapping away.

They walked on for another half-hour, more at an amble than a yomp. Pausing at a rocky promontory for the oldies to take a breather, Mari looked out to sea.

'So, where's all these iguanas, then?'

'Around,' said Adam. 'Gone fishing, maybe.'

The breeze carried their words to Paloma.

'You want iguanas? Then you came to the right place ...'

Ten minutes later, they were down on the shore where the breakers crashed like white thunder. Sea lions coughed and blue-footed boobies flapped off in search of breakfast. But the human specimens, lined up on the shingle, were motionless; all they could do was watch.

The pumice-grey rocks were alive, with beasts from a Boschian nightmare: marine iguanas strewn three-deep like a mass burial, the nearest an arm's length away. Most of them lay motionless, soaking up the sun in their morning ritual of reanimation. But every now and then one uncoupled itself, shifting around in its veiny, barnacled skin. Such a tableau of primeval nature silenced everyone – even Mari. The closest she had come to an iguana was a gargoyle on Quito Cathedral. The real things weren't as big, or their claws as scything. But they were every bit as macabre.

'Bollocks,' breathed Adam in her ear. 'Memory's full.'

He fiddled with his camera, scrolling for any shots he could bear to delete. Abruptly, a big male iguana detached itself from the rookery, lurching onto the path. Sun rays caught the coppery sheen of its crusted verdigris hide as it staggered towards them. But the beast turned sideways and stopped, one black eye trained in their direction. They were close enough to make out the motion of its breathing, the salty pellets it expelled from its nostrils like a Sunday-morning footballer.

'Is he a beauty or what?' whispered Adam.

Mari remembered a sticky, airless night in Quito when they stopped for a beer on the way home from the *colegio* that turned into three. How Adam had pointed to the portico as they swayed past the cathedral, trying to convince her that the gargoyle had just moved.

Another time, she would take a closer look.

Life on the boat had a rhythm of its own, as reliable as the throb of the engine that carried them between islands overnight. Over the next couple of days, Mari found herself slipping into a routine of jovial mornings and panga rides, gentle treks and communal meals, saline showers and siestas.

She surprised herself by going ashore on every trip. She was never going to match Adam's passion for wildlife, but watching it up-close had a certain addictive thrill. She was entranced by the dabbling flamingos of Floreana; the fur seal pups of Isabela that padded after her like friendly strays. Less so, the turtle as big as a smart car that appeared for an instant in a cresting wave, like a monster caught on celluloid. But where excursions were concerned, Mari was game for anything. Except snorkelling.

Adam was keen, and keener still to scuba. But she had a thing about open water and the cosmic emptiness beneath. Not to mention sharks, though Paloma insisted the species found around here were harmless. And so, on days when the others went off to splash around unmissable wrecks and reefs, Mari stayed on the boat. Until the fourth morning, when she awoke to a circle of ethereal crags framed in the cabin porthole: a sunken crater, according to Adam – the Devil's Crown. This time, Mari decided to take her book and tag along, if only for a closer look at its eerie beauty.

Once everyone else had plopped into the water, she lay across the seat at the back of the panga. Now and again she looked up; glanced at the rocks and tried to spot Adam splashing about among the penguins and flightless cormorants. But mostly she just lazed in the unbroken sunshine, rereading the same paragraph of her novel until the words became a meaningless mantra.

'You don't like *es-swim*?' asked Jorge Luis.

She had almost forgotten he was there. It was the first time she had heard any of the sailors speak English.

'Sometimes,' she replied. 'On the beach or in a pool. But I don't like deep water. Scary!'

The little pilot smiled. It made his flattened profile look distinctly handsome.

'You shouldn't be afraid,' he said. 'Beneath the ocean is very beautiful.'

To her irritation, Mari blushed, and hoped it didn't show through her tan. He made her think of Javier and the tension he brought to her English class. The way her heart sank on the days when he deigned to turn up – and the disconcertingly similar feeling when he didn't.

Jorge Luis bent down to tie his tennis shoe; a manoeuvre that brought his V-shaped torso into relief through his faded T-shirt. No socks, she noted. Unlike Adam, who believed that shoes-minus-socks-equalled blisters, if you were walking further than the fridge. He would live and die in his socks, that boy, English to the last.

At that moment, a bizarre creature torpedoed out of the water in a silvery torrent, its forelimbs slapping over the edge of the panga …

It was Heike. Her auburn hair was plastered to her scalp, and an expression of sheer terror lay behind her snorkel mask. Mari sprang up to help her from the water, making the craft list giddily. But before she could reach her, the other woman slipped onto the deck with a thud.

Mari was shaking. 'Are – are you all right?'

Heike unhooked her flippers, looking at her suspiciously. 'Of course! The water is perfect. You should swim!'

As she peeled off her mask, Mari noticed the crayon-stroke lines behind what remained of Heike's viciously plucked eyebrows. They were the work of a tattooist's needle; with the sparse hairs slicked away, she looked like nothing so much as a startled drag queen.

Mari went back to her book and tried not to laugh.

Two minutes later, Jorge Luis was standing at the stern. He gave the signal for the others to come aboard, and smiled at Mari as the whistle dropped from his lips.

'Time for tea, no?' he said.

He was still flirting as they climbed aboard the *Beluga*. Mari made sure it was Paloma's arm she took to steady herself.

Up to now, Jorge Luis had barely registered. After Mark-James, she was dubious about any men with double-barrelled forenames, which she viewed as the height of pretension, if possibly different for Hispanics. Presumably he'd been there that first night on the boat when Paloma introduced the crew after dinner; half a dozen of them, all lined up in their dress whites to toast this week's complement of passengers. Now she thought of it, hadn't there been one who had cut a better figure in tennis shorts and polo shirt than the rest?

That was the night Adam asked about sharks.

Hammerheads were his favourite animal (fish; whatever) and always had been. Mari still remembered his adept if slightly sinister doodles on her notebooks at university. Swimming with hammerheads was one of his dreams, along with a box at Old Trafford and buying Dogg

Street Bruvvaz acetates on eBay. Paloma replied that their chances of seeing them were slim on this route through the islands, though she knew one place he might get lucky. And it was not a million nautical miles from the Devil's Crown.

So that afternoon, while the *Beluga* and Mari idled at anchor, Adam, Paloma and one of the sailors sped off in search of nature's answer to a plastic-surgery disaster. As she made her way to the foredeck with her book and a generously stiff drink, Mari stumbled upon the giggly English couple at the bow. They were staging the figurehead scene from *Titanic* for digital posterity, until her presence sent them slinking off in naughty-child embarrassment. The rest of the oldies had retired to their cabins, as they did after lunch, for unthinkable sex or mahjong. Agreeably alone at last, she lounged on the bench in front of the wheelhouse. As she began to read, the English couple's sniggering drifted back on the breeze, and once again concentration eluded her.

Adam would be back before long – flushed with the sun and full of stories. Mari still found it sort of sexy, the way he got so enthusiastic about things. Just not with the same intensity as in the early days, when their eyes met across a canteen tray-tidy. Their days and nights of fevered pawing were long gone; of urges answered up alleyways, in sand hills, and once, memorably, on the roof of the vice-principal's study. Nowadays, sex was for Sundays, when Adam came back from his run; pre-lunch and preferably post-mouthwash.

She wasn't complaining. Mari knew all about boyfriends; she'd had one ever since she was eight. Adam was good stock, and you knew where you were with a Cosgrove; solid, dependable people, if never likely to set the world on fire.

Except of course for Cousin Harry.

Cousin Harry the wide boy, who was always at Cosgrove weddings. Who slipped Mari her first and only tab of ecstasy by the loudspeakers, when Adam was out having a fag. Cousin Harry, with his soft olive skin, who whispered something so utterly, crassly obscene in her ear that Mari bawled with laughter, then felt bereft when she couldn't remember what it was. Cousin Harry, who made her feel like a very pretty, very naughty schoolgirl; as if her lungs were floating free inside her, ready to emit a squeaky balloon-toy shriek the moment she opened her mouth ...

She often thought of Cousin Harry. Usually when she shouldn't.

The afternoon was perfect. The sun struck a silver path across the water all the way to the horizon. She shuffled round until her skin met the rays at an even more pleasing angle.

Little old Mari! Drifting through the Galápagos with a rum and coke in one hand, racy novel in the other. *Who'd have thought it?*

A solitary cry marred the hollow lap of ocean on hull. A frigatebird soaring; an italic eyebrow on the face of the sky, delicate in a way Heike's beautician could only dream of.

When Adam came back, he'd be full of more than shark tales. Exercise never failed to make him horny, and Mari doubted she would have the heart to reject him. All the more reason why she should make the most of—

She flinched at the sudden incursion of Rod Stewart, as the opening lines of 'Sailing' rasped out of the wheelhouse.

Jorge Luis was smiling down at her through the glass, holding an ancient CD case featuring Rod in leopard-print ski pants.

'You like?' he mouthed.

Mari nodded, not wishing to hurt his feelings. She went back to her book. By the bottom of the page, he was still there, judging by his rousing singalong.

'We are sailing … We are es-sailing … Home again, cross da sea …'

She chanced another look … Still smiling; but now he was looking past her, as if for something to steer around. Pointlessly, since the boat wasn't moving.

'Sailing' faded into 'Maggie May', the words of which he also knew after a fashion. Mari wondered if song lyrics might have been a way to engage the Quito kids in her language syllabus. She could just see Nine Inch Nails sparking a bit of interest on the back row …

Her ears pricked up again. Was she imagining it or did he just sing:

'*Oh* Mari *I wish I'd never – es-seen your face …*'?

He was looking down again. Cheek of the devil!

During the middle eight, Jorge Luis sauntered out of the wheelhouse. He picked up a nylon rope and coiled it round a tawny, brawny forearm. With a flick of the wrist that deceived the eye, he tossed the free end over one shoulder and caught it deftly behind him.

Good catch, thought Mari. (Wasn't he just?)

She took another sip of her drink as the sailor repeated his party piece with the other end, snagging the loops into an authentic-looking knot. He bent down to sling the rope into the starboard locker, causing her to peer over her sunglasses.

You had to laugh! Here they were, in the middle of the Pacific Ocean; and there, peeping over the top of his shorts, was that same designer-underwear waistband she saw at every bar and bus stop back home! Everywhere, in fact, except on Adam, who was a boxers man through and through, refusing to switch to anything sleeker on the improbable grounds he needed the room to manoeuvre …

As Jorge Luis straightened up, Mari couldn't help notice the way his buttocks retained their chunky roundness. (Make that cheeks of an angel!)

She was still smiling as he turned round.

'You wan' come inside?' he asked. 'I show you very nice.'

She paused. Flushed, for the second time that day, and scrabbling for her bookmark as it fell to the deck.

'I don't, er ... What do you mean?'

Jorge Luis looked puzzled. 'On the bridge. I show you how to steer the boat.'

Mari stifled a nervous laugh; now who was being cheeky? Regaining her composure, she slipped in the bookmark at random.

'Why not,' she said. She smoothed her bikini straps as he held open the door.

Inside the wheelhouse, Rod was giving full throat to 'Baby Jane'. A whiff of diesel took Mari back to her childhood – the tractor shed on her uncle's farm. On one side of the tiny cabin was the ship's wheel, and a low platform for the pilot. A clipboard swung from a hook, and a box lit up the dashboard with a red digital display.

'Es-satellite tracking,' explained Jorge Luis, motioning her onto the platform. 'Came here ... Hold the wheel.'

She did as he said, inadvertently flattening her hair against the ceiling.

'Too tall, no?' he smiled. 'Did you see the captain? He a very little man.'

He wasn't the only one; now they were side by side, the top of Jorge Luis's head was level with Mari's eyes. He leaned in, brushing her shoulder as he demonstrated where to put her hands on the wheel. It moved freely in her fingers with no effect on the boat.

'So,' he said. 'Now you are the captain.'

The tinny music faded out. She was about to reply when the CD player expelled the disc with a thrust, like a silver tongue. Jorge Luis pushed it back in and skipped to a favourite track. Then he began to tidy, picking coffee cups and sweet wrappers from the footwell. Rod was singing about a downtown train, as he produced polish and a rag and set to work on the brass without a word.

Mari spun the wheel in silence, contented as a toddler on a supermarket ride. She revelled in the tranquillity of being adrift in paradise; family, friends and career all blissfully out of reach – and not so much as a mobile signal to break the spell.

Adam could keep his hammerheads, and his lesser-spotted land iguanas! The real magic of the islands was out there – on that endless, empty seam of ocean and sky. If only she-

'*Mira!*'

The word brought her back with a jolt.

'It's "Mari", actually ...'

Jorge Luis shook his head. '*Mira!* Look!'

He was pointing at two black shapes. No – black and white shapes, breaking the surface on the port side.

'*Orca!*'

At a distance, the giant fins resembled conning towers, their glossy sides the battle-scarred hull of a submarine. But even Mari knew killer whales when she saw them, and she shuddered. Wherever Adam was, she hoped he was out of the water. Wait till he heard he'd missed this!

The fins disappeared, surfacing again a few metres away. Jorge Luis's voice rose as he pointed at something else.

'Y niño también!'

Mari followed his finger but couldn't see anything. And in a moment he was behind her, steering her gaze with a hand on her arm. His palm was as warm and dry as the breath on her shoulder; he smelt of brass polish and whatever he washed his T-shirt in.

'See! Baby, no?'

She stared, but still she couldn't make it out.

An adult emerged one last time, massive and magnificent, unleashing a plume of spray that hung in the air for an instant, like a light sabre.

Then they were gone – one, two, possibly three of the fabled beasts, diving down into infinite darkness. Leaving Mari and the sailor tucked one behind the other at the wheel; alone before a thousand miles of glittering sea. His breath moved subtly from her shoulder to the back of her neck. Mari had a sudden urge to lean into him – to feel his torso against hers.

'All my dreams,' sang Rod, *'All my dreams fall like rain ...'*

'Nice one, mate,' said Adam's voice from the door. 'You should hear the grief I get when I ask her to drive.'

FOUR

I

Wednesdays meant Camberwell. The Parkers in the morning, for whom Ian was building a rockery, and Mrs Higgins in the afternoon. Mostly trimming and tidying and any other jobs the old dear could find for him.

Feels like Carla's been gone forever, he thought, as he cut back the chives.

His wife's wanderlust meant time apart was nothing new. When she'd gone off meditating in Nepal, he got a call from the airport when she arrived, and another seventeen days later when she was on the way home. They'd never been the sort of couple to phone each other three times a day. Even so, this was different.

The old lady's bird box had blown down at the weekend. Ian fetched the stepladder from her lean-to and a hammer from the van. Jasper was still inside, perched on the spare tyre. He shook his grubby white muzzle but didn't get up. Too hot for him today.

When Carla went on one of her treks, Ian slid into his own routine and didn't worry about her after a day or two. But this time there was the show, a one-way peephole from his life into hers; and this time there was Agnes. In the best case scenario, she'd be back victorious in a fortnight, with a fistful of golden tickets and the requisite surrounding publicity.

Dear God. Publicity!

As the blushing spouse, waiting at home for Plucky Carla, Ian had half-expected enquiries from the press. But calls there had been none, at least after the first few days. Week One of *Houseboat* caused a minor media splash when a leggy dental nurse was ejected for hoarding NessTicles™

in her makeup bag. A man from the tabloids left a message, seeking Ian's incensed reaction, and never called back. Since then, nothing. The show had hardly set the red tops alight – no doubt to the disappointment of the production company.

He rested the steps against Mrs Higgins' beech and hopped up with the bird box. But if Carla won … That would be a different kettle of fish.

Last year's winner, Jake, had been on and off chat-show sofas for weeks, thanks largely to his deviant behaviour on board. Dental nurse aside, this year's crew were relatively player-free; there'd been no sex and hardly any nervous breakdowns, which explained the less than spectacular viewing figures.

Nails.

Nails would be good. He jumped down and went back to the van.

Hopefully it would only amount to a couple of interviews. Ian couldn't see Carla opening garden fêtes or going into panto, let alone courting the networks for her own show. And there was no way they were agreeing to photographers on the cruise – he'd put his foot down there, whatever they were paying! He pocketed an assortment of nails and climbed out of the van.

How much *did* they pay, exactly?

If Carla made it through the next challenge then he would have one last week to decide what to do about Agnes. Talking of whom, she didn't seem a bit bothered about being the Other Woman. He was pretty sure she'd known he was married all along, and he was secretly rather pleased with himself for the way he'd handled it. With a little more skilled manoeuvring, it needn't be an issue for Carla, either; because, in a sense, he had no reason to tell her.

The way Ian saw it, he was simply exploring new …

terrain. Like Carla and her Himalayas. It wasn't like he expected her to come back and give him a blow-by-blow account; fill him in on every yak and temple.

He paused at the top of the steps. Then he sighed.

She was missing him! Carla – his Carla, who got on with life in her own sweet way and rarely asked for anything more than his sturdy presence in the background – was missing him! It had to be true; she'd told the nation.

He was hammering in the final nail when a chirping erupted from the back of his shorts. Text message … He dropped the hammer to the lawn and stabbed at his mobile with grimy fingers.

Uh-oh: Agnes.

CAN YOU MEET TONIGHT. ONLY FOR TALK. I CAN BE AT 8.

Shit. Still, probably for the best. They needed to talk all right. He tapped out a reply.

OK. See you Windmill 8pm

When he put away the ladder, it was nearly quarter past six. Just time to water Mrs Higgins' pots, then he could nip home for a shower.

The traffic was heavy. A bus had broken down halfway up Brixton Hill. Two seat cushions stood on the tarmac at the rear in an inverted V, like hands begging forgiveness of the fuming motorists.

It was gone seven by the time he got home. Ian dashed up the steps with Jasper under one arm, fumbling for his door key.

He showered and found a clean shirt that was tolerably uncreased. Ran a comb through his hair (*Memo to self: go to barber before Carla gets home*). Wolfed down a ham and cheese toastie, followed by rice pud straight from the tin. If he left in ten minutes, he could still walk to the pub … No, hang on, he would drive. He wasn't going to drink anyway, and they were only talking, so it wasn't as if there was anything to get fired up for …

What were they going to talk about?

Ian felt that creeping awkwardness of adolescence all over again. Perhaps he would need a drink after all.

One last look in the mirror ... *Not bad at-*

Whoops! Jasper.

They were down to the last tin of Turkey & Mackerel (*Sainsbury's tomorrow!*) He found the can opener and gave the feeding bowl a rinse; forked the meat into smaller pieces, remembering to toss in a few biscuits.

Bowl down on coconut mat? Check.

Water in water bowl? Check.

All done. Now he could relax. It was just …

No Jasper.

As a rule, there was no keeping the old fella from his tea. His hearing may have lost its sharpness, but that dog could still detect slicing metal at fifty paces.

Ian ran into the hall and yelled his name.

Nothing. Just the tiniest thud of wood on wood.

Balls! He'd left the door open.

He bounded down the steps, scanning the drive for signs of fluffy white life.

'Jasper! *JAAA-sper!'*

Not a twitch.

Checked under the car. Then under the van.

Checked *inside* the van, in case he'd hallucinated

bringing him in altogether.

Looked up and down the road.

Under the nearest parked cars …

Nothing!

The side gate to the back garden was locked – but there was that gap in the mesh the little chap had been known to shuck through. Ian used to tie it down, but he'd given up when Jasper lost his roaming instinct.

He unclipped the gate and went through to the back, calling again … Checked the arbour and behind the compost, not forgetting the little hollow under the hawthorn, Jasper's favourite hidey-hole when it rained.

Not a sausage.

He checked his watch. Twenty to eight! He'd have to take the car now.

He couldn't go anywhere till he'd found that bloody dog. What if something had happened to him? What if he'd been run over?

Carla would kill him. He could see it now:

'Congratulations, darling! Welcome home! … Sorry? Welcoming party of one? Yes, actually, I've got a bit of bad news …'

Christ. He'd rather confess to screwing a Polish au pair!

Ian returned to the front. It wasn't like Jasper to go gallivanting. These days he was too timid to go past the garden gates, which was why they hardly ever—

Then he remembered. Last winter, when they'd lost him for the best part of an afternoon. He wasn't in the house and he wasn't outside, but the gates were shut, so he had to be here somewhere. It was Carla who found him in the end. Tracked down his faint, cheeky whimpering to the van's back axle. And there was Jasper under the wheel arch, tail wagging and black with dust, exercising his dog-given right to selective deafness.

Little sod! He's done it again … Ian had a good mind to start the engine.

He checked the left-side tyres instead … *One, two – no.* Ran behind to the loading doors. The van was parked so close to the wall, he had to breathe in as he slid his torso into the gap, chafing his clean shirt on the brickwork. The far wheel wasn't visible from this angle, but if he just – *squeezed* – in a bit further, he could see right under the—

Feet!

Two feet.

Smooth and pink and attractively shod, as opposed to white and furry! Standing in the drive on the other side of his van, like they owned the place.

Agnes! What the hell was she doing here? He'd told her to meet him in the pub. God – women!

'Hang on!' snapped Ian, hauling himself out of the gap. 'You didn't have to call round, I'm just running a bit—'

It was Carla.

Wearing a tracksuit top and a kilt, *it was Carla!*

And now he looked, those weren't her sort of shoes at all.

'You're back!'

'What are you doing there?' she asked, as if his presence was the more incongruous.

'I can't find the bloody d—'

Yapping cut his confession short, as Jasper bowled out from beneath the dwarf conifer like grubby tumbleweed.

'Baby!' cried Carla. The old Westie leapt unwisely; she caught him halfway. 'Baby … yes, it's wonderful to see you, too!' She tickled him under the chin, looking askance at Ian. 'Well, I'm glad one of you is pleased to see me.'

'I am – I'm just … What happened? You weren't ejected!'

'I know. I jumped ship.'

'You – what?'

'I missed you, Ian!'

'You … ?'

'I missed you!'

The way she was looking him squarely in the eye said she wasn't in the mood to explain. Carla dropped Jasper lightly to the gravel.

'Let's go upstairs!'

Ian stared oafishly at the stone steps to the front door.

'Up … ?'

'BEDROOM!' she boomed.

She took his hand and they followed Jasper indoors.

Ian lay on their bed and kicked off his brogues. Her kilt was on the floor beside those flat pumps. His day had taken a surreal turn. While his wife was in the shower, he texted Agnes.

Sorry. Aphid crisis. Can't meet tonight. Text tomorrow promise

He switched off his mobile and hoped to God she didn't turn up on the doorstep. There was only so much French farce a man could take.

The door to the ensuite was open. Carla's voice rang out as the cascading water ceased.

'I can't believe Production didn't phone you! I never thought I'd make it off the boat, let alone all the way home! Must be my lucky day … I mean, what were the chances of hitching a lift with a lorry driver who'd never seen the show?'

Pretty good, thought Ian. But it would keep.

She sauntered out of the bathroom wrapped in a towel. Paused at the window as she peeped over the sheer voile nets.

'But you were so close to winning,' said Ian, trying to sound concerned, not resentful. 'Just that Suki woman between you and the cruise. Was it so bad?'

Carla flopped across the duvet at his feet and peeled his socks off, one at a time.

'Bad? No it wasn't bad. It was just so – brainless … I doubt they showed it, but there were times we just sat there for hours, with no one saying a thing.' She ran her fingers over the soles of his feet without tickling. 'Some days I'd just lie on the bunk, looking for faces in Dougie's sleeping bag…' She pushed up one leg of his best khaki chinos, planting a kiss on his shin. '*Mwaah.* It was like one of those old Magic Eye pictures. If you – *mwaah* – half-shut your eyes, you could—'

'Carla!'

Her fingers were running up the inside of his thigh. Ian felt unaccountably coy.

'*Carla* – you can't just walk out on a national TV show! Didn't you sign something? We've got to call them!'

'Oh, stuff their bloody contract! And their bloody cruise!' She shuffled up the bed, dislodging the towel from her breasts. 'I said all along this was going to help me clear my head, didn't I? Well, it has.' She rucked up his shirt, nuzzling his belly. She stopped and sniffed. 'You've had a shower, were you going out?'

'No, I just … Clear your head about what?'

'*Me!* My life! I tell you, nothing gives you a fresh perspective like six weeks dodging the midges with a bunch of screwballs.' She returned to Ian's belly, unbuttoning his shirt from the bottom up.

He was staring at the ceiling, sweating. Not in a good way.

'And?'

'Well, the more I thought about it, the more I thought we've got it right.'

Right? Got what right? Was she talking about their little understanding – the monogamy get-out clause? If she was, he was home and dry! Maybe she'd had an adventure of her own the cameras didn't catch. Is that what she was trying to tell him?

'I want *you*, Ian!'

Carla reached the top button and kissed his clavicle.

'I want *us*! Oh, I know we've had our wobbles … Okay, don't look at me like that – *I've* had my wobbles. But I've really learned in the last six weeks, from seeing the stuff people go through. And meditating, of course. Did they show me meditating?'

Ian tried to cast his mind back as his wife's lips hovered round his nipples.

'Once or twice, in your … *wetsuit*. Intercut with sunsets and … *ripples* on the loch …'

She paused. 'God, very lyrical!'

For a moment, she laid her cheek on his chest.

'I'll never watch it all. You did Sky Plus it, didn't you?'

'Oh yeah ...'

Her crown rose from under his chin. She was smiling as she swept her damp hair to one side, rearing over him like a mermaid emerging from the deep. Then she sank down again, engulfing him in *Eau de Carla,* the signature scent of their sixteen years; their home, their car, their duvet. A smell that was with him every day of his life, even when she was not.

He thanked his lucky stars he'd never got Agnes into bed.

And then they were kissing. Carla was kissing him, and Ian found himself responding in kind. As if they'd tripped a switch and fallen into a long-forgotten groove, a tune they hadn't played in years. He rolled on top of her so that her hands were wedged between them both. She was fumbling with the zip of his trousers, her fingers persistent, if not as brassily assured as-

Waves of love and guilt clashed inside him as Ian tried, in every sense, not to think of Agnes. *For this was their moment* – him and Carla, adrift ... Their bed was a raft on the swell of the ocean, far from land and sight of man, woman or camera. No green rubber balls, no temptation, and as close to the first time as it had been in years.

The tangle of her towel was all that divided them. He pulled it away. And with it went his own delusion.

She was right. As usual, damn her, she was right!

The towel slid to the floor, the warmth between them intensifying to heat, familiar, soft and burning. There would be a reason for all this, Ian knew. Perhaps Agnes had put them on an even footing – made it easier to draw a line under the past ... Now they were Ian and Carla again. Carla and Ian, the way they were always meant to be. They'd been right all those years ago and they were right now! The two of them were a unit – the perfect team, strong as ever. And who could ask for more?

'I want a baby,' said Carla.

Next morning the farce continued.

The phone started ringing at ten to eight as their friends opened the morning papers. Ian made the round trip to the newsagents in six minutes flat. For the first time in years, he bypassed the cricket reports and read from the front.

Daily Express, page three: 'HOUSEBOAT HEROINE JUMPS SHIP'.

Daily Mail, page seven: 'WHERE'S OUR PLUCKY CARLA?'

The Sun, page five (*Exclusive!*): 'TV BABE IN MONSTER MYSTERY – Did She Fall or Was She Pushed?'

At half past nine, he put the phone down for the seventh time and realised he'd been holding the same piece of toast for an hour. He shambled into the kitchen, where Carla was still in her robe. She looked up hollow-eyed from the breakfast bar, which was smothered in tabloids.

'Christ,' she said. 'They're dredging the loch.'

This was not Ian's first brush with celebrity. One of his clients, a Premier League football manager, lived in Notting Hill with his shipping-heiress girlfriend. Their Georgian pile was regularly under siege from the press when he arrived to see to the hydrangeas. Ian had learned to field their fetid queries with a shake of the head and an enigmatic smile. But not even the hover mower stemmed the propositions, tossed over the wall like chicken bones; lures for the inside track on affairs, transfer fees and Arianna's ever-expanding bust.

As if he knew! Or cared.

But now, without warning, the eyes of the press were on him.

He was at Carla's shoulder as she called the production office. She was passed on to three excitable people before she got the right person. Ian moved closer to listen in, grimacing as the producer barked down the phone like an angry father. There would have to be a meeting … Someone would be round by midday … She was not to speak to anyone or leave the house till then … *Legal reasons.*

Carla blubbed as she put down the phone. It rang immediately and Ian answered.

It was a woman from the *Mirror*.

Then the showbiz editor of the *Star*.

Publicists and journalists, phone-ins and talk shows, all

wanting 'a little chat'. But Carla did as she was told, and Ian, rather getting into the part, confirmed she would be releasing a statement later.

Not even their friends could get through on the landline. Jasper, who disliked the ringer at the best of times, retreated to the second spare bedroom. By ten-thirty, they had unplugged the phone altogether. Fruitlessly, since the press had got hold of their mobile numbers.

It was the scale and speed of it that staggered Ian. He tuned into the daytime TV sofa slot at eleven-fifteen, to find his wife's disappearance being debated by scrubbed homosexuals and a woman with nylon hair. He turned it off as the doorbell rang.

'I'm not here!' whispered Carla, ducking under the frosted panes and running for the stairs.

He put his eye to the peephole. A pale woman in violent-red lipstick was on the top step. There was the sound of heavy feet on gravel, then an older man in a blue checked shirt appeared behind her. He was carrying a camera bag and smoking a roll-up. The bell rang again as the woman leaned into the lens, which distorted her into an angry insect.

'*You in there, Carla?* It's Maisie from News Direct! We won't keep you – just want a little chat!' She turned and said something to the cameraman, before pealing out again in her Irish brogue: '*Ian, are you there?*'

He backed away from the door as it was pounded by a fist.

'Only take five minutes, love. Best you get it over with now ...'

He went to find Carla. She was squatting at the bedroom nets, shoulders aquiver with disbelieving laughter.

'What have I *done?*' she implored. 'There's more of them now, look!'

A van and another car had parked in the road. Two women and half a dozen men were loitering on the pavement, fiddling with tripods and talking into phones. One of them was assembling a microphone like a stick of grey candy floss, and three more haggled over change for the meter. The media circus hadn't just come to town, it had pitched camp on their doorstep.

'You'd better get dressed,' he said. 'That production bod will be here soon.'

The knot of reporters stood their ground, milling at the boundary of the drive like idle teens. They all seemed to know each other, and every few minutes one of them broke ranks to ring the bell or shout through the letterbox. Ian switched on the bedside radio, keeping a lookout through the curtains. Carla was on the carpet by the long mirror, doing her hair. She was still chortling at the madness of it all when the news came on at eleven-thirty.

"… And missing Houseboat contestant Carla Newton is safe and sound, back at home in leafy Clapham with her husband, Ivan …"

'Let that be an end to it,' she said.

Fat chance of that, thought Ian. A black cab was drawing up outside.

'Tell them to fuck off. I do!'

Raj Sinatra's skinny frame sank into the sofa as Ian closed the sitting-room door on another volley from the doorstep. His chrome-effect business card lay in Carla's lap. With his jeans, rubber-pimpled trainers and thumb rings, Raj didn't look old enough to be on work experience, let alone

Production Liaison Director at FloatYaBoat TV.

Best to treat him carefully, thought Ian.

'I'm making coffee. Would you, er ... ?'

'I will, fanks Ian. Proper if you've got it. Two sugars, no froff.'

Carla looked up. She was grinding her teeth perceptibly. 'Just water for me.'

Ian went through to the kitchen, leaving the connecting door ajar. The boy was irritatingly laid-back, as if a horde of slavering journos was something he dealt with every day.

Carla was trying to explain herself, becoming more flustered by the minute.

'Raj – first, let me apologise. I never should have run out on the show like that. I left you in the lurch and if I'd known, I —'

Raj interrupted: 'Whoa, Carla, whoa!'

Ian could see him holding up those manicured hands, clear as if the wall was glass.

'That's legals, and legals is later, yeah? Right now we need to talk about how we can – *progress this.*'

'Progress, in terms of ... ?'

'The best way forward! For you *and* FloatYaBoat.'

His voice was all assurance. As Ian filled the cafetière, he heard the sofa creak; Raj sitting back, probably with a wink and a toss of that hair, jet black, bobbed and brilliantined.

'The way we see it, Carla, we can play this two ways. We get contractual about it – lawyers, small print, all that shit – or we pull together. Salvage the situation in a way that benefits *everyone* ...'

Ian waited. The kitchen clock ticked, echoing Carla's brain.

'Could you be more specific, Raj?'

'*The big P!* Publicity! Look, Carla, you weren't to know, but Houseboat Two has seriously stiffed in the ratings.

So bad the first week, the producer was all for airlifting in an iceberg and ploughing you into it. No offence, but you weren't the liveliest bunch. We had hopes for Mitch and Miriam getting it on, but then the silly cow hid a stash in her toiletries ... What wiv her gone, it was hard to see where the scandal was coming from. Then *you* got lovesick.'

Ian tried to take down the good crockery without a sound.

'Carla, what I'm saying is, it wasn't a *total* coincidence there was an inflatable Nessie outside your porthole on Tuesday night. Or that you got off the boat wivout being seen by the cameras.'

A cup hit a saucer with an audible chink. In the sitting room, Carla's jaw fell in synchrony.

'You mean – you knew I was making a run for it?'

Raj laughed. 'FloatYaBoat knows *everyfink*, Carla! Why else do you fink there was a nice dry kilt and pair of shoes on the pebbles where you came ashore?'

'I – well, I thought they'd been left by someone having a ... tryst.'

'Yeah? Size six? *Wide fitting?*'

'Hang on!' blustered Carla, 'That was the day before yesterday! You didn't call my husband – there was nothing on the news till this morning. What were you going to do, leave me to perish in the Highlands and make a documentary? If I hadn't hitched a lift with that long distance lorry driver—'

'Jed.'

'*Eddie,*' corrected Carla.

'His name's Jed.'

'His name was Eddie!'

'His name,' said Raj, 'is Jed. He does me photocopying.'

Ian took a bottle of water from the fridge. The sly bastards!

'Now, while you were trundling home from Inverness, I was a busy boy … I've got a mid-market daily twitching for a nice, straight "Who Says Marriage is Dead?" story. You know: *Plucky reality girl jumps ship from Hell in a Houseboat ... Hitches home to London in a Primark kilt to the husband she loves* … It's got it all!'

'Primark!' yelped Carla.

Christ! thought Ian. That greaseball was selling them to the tabloids! He sank the plunger into the coffee and poured. Black for Raj, like his heart.

As he came through the door, Carla was saying: 'Oh, I don't think we want anything to do with the papers, Raj. They'll get bored if we sit it out, won't they? Storm in a teacup. What do you think, Ian?'

He put down the tray.

'Carla's right, Raj. Not really our scene, showbiz and all.' He was trying to sound decisive, but the dice were against him. 'Personally, I think the show's been jolly, er, gripping. Everyone I know's excited about Mitch's ejection this week!'

Raj took his coffee without a word. He sniffed it and stirred in another sugar.

'Ian – Mitch is a total mong. He finks fumbscrews are what you give girls behind the bike sheds. The only viewers who identify wiv him are glue-sniffing ferals with the disposable income of woodlice, and that ain't the audience our sponsors are after. Now, if you fink I'm gonna—'

He was cut short by a bleat of synthesised bhangra. Raj whipped out his iPhone and read an email.

'Shit! Okay, guys, that's the office. Time is tight. I don't know if you've noticed, but there's a Rottweiler on your doorstep by the name of Maisie O'Grady. Tits like torpedoes and lippy like she's been in a fight, which half the time she has … She strings for the red tops and she's onto us. She knows Carla didn't spring herself unassisted, and we don't want that in the papers. It ain't good for the integrity of the show.'

Carla was still holding her mineral water; she hadn't taken a sip.

'Dear God,' she quavered. 'I never meant for all this!'

Her hand reached for Ian's as he sat down on the chair arm. He squeezed it.

'Cool it, Carla,' said Raj. 'I got a plan, yeah? Now, if we sign you up to an exclusive with the daily I'm talking to, you could be on a nice little earner. Way I'm hearing it from the features ed, if we get in now, we catch the zeitgeist.'

Ian froze. He made it sound like a superbug.

But Raj was on a roll. 'Apparently, monogamy's the next big fing. Again … Marriage, romance and all that. They're planning a sixteen-page pullout on how to shag the same bird for the rest of your life wivout closing your eyes and finking of girl scouts. They always need somefink topical to hang this sort of shit on, and you're it! You know – jumping overboard at midnight, swimming naked across Loch Ness—'

'I was *not* naked!' said Carla.

'—flagging down a hunky heavy-goods driver. And how, after six weeks of total surveillance, you wrestled wiv committing adultery in the back of his lorry.'

'I did not!'

'No, I know.' Raj sighed. 'I said it was a waste of time installing the camera.'

'You what?' Carla was incensed. 'For Christ's sake! What sort of person has sex with a total stranger in the back of a lorry?'

Ian's frown didn't waver.

Raj was up, pacing the rug like a beleaguered general.

'This is *news,* yeah? It doesn't have to be true! They're

gonna position you as a heroine. Standing by your man an' that. A beacon of heterosexual womanhood like – Joan of Arc!'

Ian closed his eyes.

Raj was warming to his story, unrepentant as the Maid of Orleans: 'Fink about it, Carla. This is your springboard! You could end up an icon like – *Lorraine Kelly!* TV show, your own column. How about novels – can you write?'

She almost spilled her water. 'Actually, Ian, do you remember I did that course? I've still got that manuscript in the loft!'

Jesus! She was falling for it!

'Get it out, babe!' cajoled Raj. 'I know publishers. Well, I know their PAs. Look, I tell you what—' He picked his shiny camouflage blouson off the sofa and produced a piece of paper. 'Now, this is only preliminary – it ain't binding, entirely. But sign this, and I guarantee we can be talking about looking at negotiating a five-figure contract before tomorrow night's *Houseboat* goes on air!'

Carla increased her grip on Ian's hand. Excitement was chasing confusion across her face. Soon it was winning.

'Hang on,' said Ian. 'You can't do this just like that! We need to talk. Think of the impact this could have on – everything.'

Carla spluttered, 'Yes, I know, but – on what?'

(Christ! How could she forget about wanting a baby?)

'What we talked about last night! Trying for a – *you know*?'

The front doorbell trilled again as a flash, like sun on a knife blade, caught his eye. It was coming from the bottom of the garden.

'Arseholes!' he yelled. 'They're round the back now! I'll take a shovel to any bastard who damages my fence.' He ran to the French windows and closed the curtains. Carla couldn't remember the last time she'd seen him this fired up.

'Guys!' snapped Raj. 'There's still *the other* contract, remember? The one Carla broke when she buggered off the boat early? Now, if you wanna take your chances with our legal department, fine – but I'm telling you, they don't mess about.' He glanced around their immaculate sitting room. 'And I'm not being funny, but you don't look like you qualify for Legal Aid.' He checked his watch. 'Right. I've got to be at Battersea Heliport in twenty minutes. There's an understudy taking your place, and if I don't brief her on the chopper up to Inverness, we won't have a show at all.'

Carla looked at Ian. He was peeping through the damask drapes. He felt her eyes upon him and turned.

'It's your decision,' he said. 'Do what you want.'

His hand was through the curtains. He unlocked the French windows.

'What are you doing?'

'Going to light a bonfire. The smoke might drive them off – and if any of those shits come over my fence, they're going straight on it ...'

He slammed the glass door behind him.

Raj produced a pen, laying it on the coffee table beside the contract. It was printed on FloatYaBoat letterhead in sea-green ink.

'He's dead right, Carla. It's your decision.' His forehead had developed a sheen. 'But I'm telling you: lose your grip now and we'll have Maisie O'Grady up all our arses like Dale Winton on Viagra!'

Carla's eyes rested on the dotted line at the tip of his finger. She wondered if his mother knew what he did for a living. She scanned the page and scribbled her signature.

'Nice one!' said Raj Sinatra. 'You won't regret it!' He peeled off the top copy, pushing it across the table as she stood from the chair.

'See yourself out,' said Carla. 'There's something I've

got to do ...'

She opened the sitting-room door and ran upstairs.

If Ian was burning anything, he could start with that kilt.

By four o'clock that afternoon, the last hyena had left, with photos of nothing more saleable than Plucky Carla's husband lighting a bonfire.

It was after eight before Ian turned on his mobile. Six messages, none of them from Agnes; that was something. His world was collapsing. Twenty-four hours ago, he had barely a care. His marriage and this ridiculous affair were four hundred miles apart, till Carla brought them snapping together like a telescope. Add sudden celebrity, life-altering sums of money, and a wife who changed her mind about motherhood after sixteen years, and the effects were dizzying.

He needed time to think and he didn't have it. Carla had set sail on something a lot more unstable than a converted coal barge, and he was along for the ride. Everything hinged on the two of them, packaged and sold: *Houseboat* Heroine Carla and Loyal Husband Ian (*Sexy! Silent! Soily nails!*) A shining paragon of marriage, all set to light up the summer-weight duvets of Middle England from the Sunday supplements. It went against his nature to believe it could end in anything but disaster.

Christ. How had he got himself into this?

Carla was on the phone to Trisha Smedley and had been for an hour. Ian gave Jasper his tea. He should make something for them too; they'd missed lunch completely. He checked the drawer of the fridge and decided to surprise her with cauliflower cheese.

He was slicing away the stalky outer leaves at the breakfast bar when the truth of his situation struck him: in any normal circumstances, he would have told Carla about Agnes without hesitation. Oh, it would be a blow but she'd bounce back, same as he had. Polish nanny, Maltese car mechanic – what was the difference?

But now was not the time; his wife had enough to contend with so Ian had to deal with this himself. He whisked off a text as he listened at the kitchen door. She was still talking on the bottom stair. Carla loved the phone; had taken calls on that exact spot for as long as they'd lived here, even now they were cordless and there was no flex to thread through the bars.

A minute later, his mobile chirped. It was the answer he'd hoped for.

He took a bottle of silver-top milk from the fridge and poured it down the plughole. Wiped the vegetable knife and slotted it into the rack, leaving the cauliflower head half-severed on the chopping board, like Mary, Queen of Scots.

Carla hardly looked up as he took the car keys from the pot. Waved the milky bottle in front of her face and mouthed, *'Just popping to the shop.'* She nodded without breaking her conversation.

Ian let himself out.

Part of him thought it was madness to meet at the Windmill. But it was the only place he could think of, and anyway he had to be quick. He would tell Carla the Indian grocer was out of milk and he'd driven to the high street. Drama at the checkout, tills down, blah-de-blah ... Chances were she'd still be on the phone anyway.

Agnes was already there, in the same old place. She had bought him a Guinness, which Ian told himself he wouldn't be drinking. He thought she looked a little forlorn as he slid in next to her on the torn banquette.

'Look, really sorry about last night! Nightmare in Notting Hill. Prize-winning hydrangea with galloping greenfly and—'

'Your wife is come home, no?'

Ah.

'I hear on the radio.'

Perhaps he would have a sip of that Guinness after all.

'Right. Well, we may need to have a chat about that.'

'She come back because she love you. She swim across the lake where the monster lives.'

Agnes was smiling, but her eyes were sad. Her thigh, which usually rested an inch from his in public, butted up unexpectedly. Ian pulled away, which made him feel like a shit. He let his leg fall back.

'Agnes – it's been wonderful. Meeting you and – everything.' How the hell did he say this without sounding like a cheating sleazebag? 'But we always knew, didn't we – that it was going nowhere? Us, I mean.'

Her hand on his arm startled him. He looked up in case someone had walked in.

'Me, I got something to tell *you,*' said Agnes. 'Is why I call you yesterday …'

Inexorably as marbles on a sloping floor, Ian's eyes rolled down to her belly … *Please God, anything but that!*

'I have to go back to Poland.'

Oh, you beauty!

'My sister is helping my mum to look after my – *babcia,* how do you say? My *grandmozzer*. But my sister is get married in one month, so now is my turn to help. You follow?'

Ian followed. He tried to look disappointed.

'Well, that's a shame. But you're a very good girl, going home to help your mum. A very good daughter!' He took another swig of stout. 'When are you, er … ?'

'One week. I have hand in my notice three weeks ago, so I leave one week on Sunday.'

Oh, right; bit strange that she hadn't mentioned it. For a second, Ian felt slighted, almost expendable. He dismissed the thought and thanked his lucky stars – this could *not* be going better! He moved his arm for a surreptitious look at his watch. If he just said the right thing now …

'Well, you must have lots to do before you go. Not to mention the little Wallace bastard.' He checked the time again. 'God, I must run! Got to get to the shops, so I'll love you and, er …' He pushed away his pint. 'I'm driving, so … Thanks, though!'

Agnes drained her glass and stood up too. Her mood had visibly lifted. She hardly even seemed put out as they walked back through the pub. As they did, a poster at the end of the bar caught Ian's eye:

Karaoke @ The Windmill
Every Thursday 8.30pm

No shame that they'd never caught that. He couldn't see Agnes taking to being serenaded. Young people these days! It was all *find 'em, fuck 'em, forget 'em!*

Lucky he'd mentioned the shopping; it meant he didn't have to offer her a lift. He couldn't believe his luck; this was all going infinitely better than he'd dared hope! Saying that, he did think she might have hankered for one last little session. They were good together, after all …

'Okay,' he said, holding the outer door for her.

Agnes stepped onto the path. Gave him a little wave.

'Maybe I see you next week,' she said. 'In the garden. But is Sebastian's school sports day, so I don' know.'

'Right. Right, then.'

God, this was all a bit sudden! The gentleman in him

wanted to end it decently, with dinner or something. He should give her a watch, or a necklace to replace that little shell thing she was always wearing ... Something to remember him by. Ian looked round. There was no one in the car park. He had half a mind to take her behind those wheelie bins right now. (*Ha! Not such a gentleman after all!*)

He stepped forward to kiss her.

Agnes giggled, pushing him away. Then she changed her mind.

Strange! To think he would never hear that laugh again!

Their lips met; she didn't resist. Ian felt her hands on the back of his neck, combing his hair with her nails.

'I better go,' she said, half like she meant it.

But she giggled again as his hands moved lower, from the small of her back to the mounds of her buttocks. All so maddeningly tempting ... They could just get in the car and —

The flare caught them both by surprise.

A silent, brilliant instant, minus the sulphurous hiss of the cameras in old movies.

It was over before they knew it. A flurry, three cars away, and a blur of blue. A figure running low, as if dodging snipers—

Blue checked shirt! The man on his doorstep this morning!

Ian sprang away from Agnes as a car door thudded shut and the Renault sped off in a spray of chippings.

Christ alive! He'd been papped!

II

By Saturday, Glory was glad to be back at work.

Even Dennis's moans were better than the stony hush that had fallen over the flat since Thursday. She and Jan were on nights for the next three days, and as they changed into their uniforms Glory was bringing her up to date.

'... an' the worst of it was, he'd already bought the tickets!'

'No!' said Jan, struggling to marry together enough Velcro to close the tabard round her hips. 'What's he gonna do?'

'Get a refund, that's what I said. Or get two more tickets for the kids.'

Jan sighed. 'Tell 'im three. I'll go along and babysit. I could do with a break from my lot. Callum brought home a plasma telly last night ...'

Upstairs in the office, the day duty manager was eating his dinner by the stool chart; a salt-beef sandwich and a protein shake. On the edge of the desk was a steam iron and a very small T-shirt, baby blue and wrinkle-free. He was finishing up his sandwich as he handed over to Glory and Jan.

'Nothing much going down,' he said, 'except the tummy bug on Second Floor West. Been through eight of the poor sods in two days.'

Glory had no time for this young man. He was frequently late on Monday mornings, and made no secret of the fact that Cedars Hall was just a stepping stone in his high-flying career.

He dabbed crumbs from his mouth with a sterile wipe.

'You've missed the worst of it, lucky you. Stank like a fucking horse box.' He drained the last of his shake and picked up the T-shirt.

Two minutes later he was off in search of his Saturday night. Glory sat at the desk and flicked through the diary.

'Hang on, what's this?' She beckoned to Jan. '*Friday 11.30 a.m. Pearl Stanley, East 9. Bruising to left forearm* ... What's old Pearl been up to now?'

Glory found her in the dining room. It was first sitting, and Pearl was in her usual place from where she could see the garden. Also round the table were Daisy, Fred and Frances, the Hall's oldest resident at ninety-eight. They sat together every mealtime, but paid each other little attention.

Pearl looked blank as Glory hunkered down by her wheelchair. After a moment, she recognised the smile.

'I'm very well, thanking you,' said Pearl politely. 'What can I do for you?'

'I just came to see how you are, that's all.'

Glory wiped the old woman's eye with the corner of a serviette. She picked up the forgotten fork and helped her to a scoop of cottage pie. As Pearl chewed, Glory looked her over. Sure enough, there were bruises above her left wrist, like magnifying-glass burns on ancient parchment. Four of them, a hand-width apart, index to little finger. There would be another under her wrist, where the thumb had been.

She ran her finger gently over Pearl's crepey skin.

'What did you do to your arm, Pearl?'

The old lady looked askance at Daisy, who was drinking from a child's safety mug. The look went through her to an empty table.

'I don't know. I think it must have been those people ...'

'Was someone in your room again?'

Pearl didn't reply. Just took a breath as deep as she could muster and let her head nod onto her chest.

'Did you see who it was this time?'

But Pearl wasn't listening, preoccupied by the pattern on her tartan slippers. Frances, a little thing with white hair and china-blue eyes, cawed something softly across the table. Her face was a mask of frozen wonder.

Pearl smiled at her. 'In a minute, dear ...'

Glory wasn't deterred. 'Pearl, when they came in your room, could you see what they—'

'No!' The old lady snapped into focus, fixing her with an imperious gaze. 'And if I could, I wouldn't tell you. They'd be after you then!'

Glory sighed and helped her to more cottage pie.

It wasn't like Mrs Molyneux to be around after 6 p.m., especially at weekends. Glory was taking a bale of towels to the linen store when she noticed her door was ajar. She steadied the stack under her chin and knocked.

'Yes?'

The door swung open sharply. Mrs Molyneux had been right behind it, hanging up her coat on tiptoe.

'Oh, good evening, Glory. Settling in for the nightshift, are we?'

Her body language was even less welcoming than usual. Her garish outdoor scarf disappeared from her neck with a flick, like sucked-up spaghetti. It landed in a rainbow across her sensible mac, the only sunny touch in the room.

'Mrs Jessop's called in sick. There's no one to cover so you've got me in charge tonight.' Her heels tottered to the other side of the desk. She settled down and switched on the computer. 'I'm sure you and Janet can keep things ticking over, but I'll be on the bleep if you need me.'

Glory considered this change of arrangements. Ordinarily the care assistants on nightshift reported to the night duty manager, who was responsible for the Hall until eight-thirty the following morning. Mrs Molyneux only involved herself as a last resort, preferring to hire a locum before she gave up her own precious time.

She finished logging on. 'Was there something else?'

Glory steadied the tower of towels with one knee. 'It's Pearl again, Mrs Molyneux. She's got bruises on her arm. In the shape of a—'

'A handprint, yes, I know. It was brought to my attention yesterday. I've examined her myself.' She rolled back her chair and rested her hands in her lap. 'Glory, Pearl is a very sick woman. Very – deluded.'

'She says someone's been in her room again. She says—'

The senior manager shook her head. 'Glory, you know as well as I do that Pearl comes out with enough twists to fill a bestseller. With her form of dementia, it's not uncommon for the subconscious to construct events. It's the brain's way of staying alert as the body deteriorates. And, sometimes, the body plays its part ...' Mrs Molyneux took hold of her own forearm with the other hand. 'Right hand on left arm. Like this.'

She released the grip and went back to her computer; subject closed.

The mime left Glory speechless. She glowered over the towels as Mrs Molyneux carried on typing.

'Any disasters, you know where I am.'

Glory told Jan the latest when she got back to the office. But the senior manager's theory seemed to bother Jan less than her actual presence.

'Gawd, that's all we need! I fancied a nice quiet one in front of the telly, sorting the clean clothes.' She was flicking through a fitness magazine on the desk. 'I've had three lots of relatives complain about stuff going missing. Insist it was all name-tagged …'

She was missing the point. 'But Mrs Molyneux says Pearl's harmin' herself, Jan. When she's hardly got the strength to lift a spoon!'

Jan sniffed but didn't look up. 'Well, could be true. They bruise soon as look at them at that age, don't they?' She skipped a feature on stomach crunches. 'Like old apples ...'

She went back to a recipe for virtually fat-free barbecue dip.

The evening passed quietly. Just two alarm bells before the eleven-thirty drugs round, both on Second Floor West. One an accident; the other a request for an extra pillow.

Only a handful of the Hall's residents needed night-time medication, and most of them took it without fully waking. It was procedure that only medically-trained personnel administered drugs; the night duty manager, or in this case Mrs Molyneux. So when she didn't appear at the allotted time, Glory rang through to her office.

She answered on the eighth ring, sounding sleepy.

While they waited, Jan helped Glory lay out the prescription bottles and tiny paper cups. It took the little woman another fifteen minutes to appear and thirty seconds to count out the dosages against the chart.

'Now, I'm halfway through the district auditor's preliminary report,' said Mrs Molyneux as she finished. 'So I'm sure I can trust you to give out this little lot.'

And with that she was gone, clacking down the corridor back to her lair.

So much for her precious Hall procedure now, thought Glory.

'She'll be kipping in that empty room behind her office,' said Jan as they carried the tray along the hall. 'Keeps a bed made up in there, according to the caretaker's lad.'

'Oh?' said Glory. 'And how would he know?'

'Says he's seen it through the window when he was ripping down the creeper. Shouldn't wonder he's got designs on it himself – thinks he's a right little Casanova, that one.'

Jan was blushing. Her entire face glowed, joining up the spaces between her freckles.

Glory smiled. 'That boy been chattin' you up?'

Jan made a thing of checking the next room on the list.

'I pay no attention. Too much cheek for his own good, that one. Probably does it to everyone.'

Glory found the door. She pushed it open and said nothing.

The duty-office clock chimed two. It had been hanging there as long as anyone could remember, its face appropriately worn and mottled. Irritating though it was, it helped the night staff stay awake.

Glory rarely had any trouble in that department. Unlike some, she never complained when nights came round on her rota. They were a reminder that she'd come up in the world, since she started here as a cleaner. It was worth all those hours of studying for her NVQs to reach a position of responsibility. She also liked nights because they kept Mercy and the kids on their toes; Sam and Sherelle knew they had to be quiet as mice when Auntie Glory stumbled into her bed as they were leaving theirs. And Mercy had to act the responsible mother until she surfaced again. Or that was the idea.

The chimes of the clock had no effect on Jan. She was fast asleep in an armchair, with the TV remote sliding slowly down the groove of her thighs like a glacier. Beside her was the heap of old-lady-and-gentleman knitwear she was sorting before she nodded off. The television played on mute, a repeat of *EastEnders*, with a man signing furiously in a corner of the screen. Glory turned it off and wondered why the television people thought the deaf were awake in the middle of the night. Surely the quiet was of no consequence to them, and the dark more frightening?

She didn't like to wake Jan, but rules were rules; if Mrs Molyneux checked on them, there'd be hell to pay. She shook her by the elbow.

'Jan, I'm takin' a turn about. Keep your eyes open till I get back.'

Her friend shrugged and snorted. She looked round for the remote, which had slipped to the floor.

'Where's me programme? I was watching that ...'

Glory's feet ached. She wondered how many miles a week she walked around this place. She trudged up to the top landing, preferring to start there and work her way down. The only sounds on Second Floor East and West were snores and the occasional groggy cry. Same on the First Floor. Even poor old Dennis was quiet. Whatever played in his head on an endless loop by day left him alone at night; and whatever he dreamt, he dreamt in silence.

The night was warm. At either end of First Floor East the sash windows were open a crack. Glory checked the safety locks; all present and correct. Any intruder threading himself through there would have to be an even skinnier bag of bones than poor old Daisy. Back on the ground floor, she stopped outside East 9. It would do no harm to check on Pearl.

The room was black. The door gave a coffin-creak as it closed behind her. Glory stood for a moment to catch the rhythm of Pearl's breathing ... The outline of her single bed and her bits of furniture emerged in the weak glow of the street lamp chinking through the curtains.

What Pearl needed was a little night light, thought Glory. It was the kind of thing family were meant to provide, though if it was left to that dithering son of hers, she'd be waiting till Judgement Day. Glory was sure she'd seen one in the basement.

Content that Pearl was sleeping soundly, she tiptoed from the room. She reached the kink in the hallway with its ancient armchair – and stopped. The chair was a monstrosity of wipe-clean vinyl, with a button back and an extra pad of foam to bolster the seat. As it wasn't visible from the door, it occurred to her it was also just the place to keep an eye on any comings and goings from Pearl's room. A long shot; if someone was really up to mischief, there was no guarantee they'd be back tonight. But then if Glory didn't take the old girl seriously, who would? She sat down and looked at her watch.

02:28.

If she turned the other way and craned her neck, she could just see into the lounge. The volume was up on the TV, a murmur that swept into waves of applause. Jan's feet were framed in the doorway, crossed at the ankle. Glory couldn't tell if she was awake, but at least she was there if the alarm went off.

It went against Glory's principles, sitting down on the job. But even in a home the size of Cedars Hall, there was precious little to do in the small hours. And besides, she was still angry at Mrs Molyneux for being so dismissive. People in her position thought they had an unrestricted view of the truth. They pretended to welcome opinions, when in fact theirs was the only right one. What they forgot was, all that separated them from a fate like Pearl's was a few years and a bit of luck. Something Glory was quick to remind herself, if ever a day of lifting rag-doll bodies off toilets got her down.

The minutes slipped by. There was no movement from either end of the hallway as the duty-office clock chimed quarter to the hour.

And three o'clock.

Then the quarter hour again.

She thought of fetching that magazine Jan had been reading. But if Mrs Molyneux reappeared she didn't want to give her the satisfaction of finding her idle. If she asked what Glory was doing sitting here, she would tell her straight and make no bones about it!

This armchair was surprisingly supportive. Glory reflected how she must have passed it twenty times a day for all these years and never sat in it once. She leaned her head on the wing, settling back in its padded embrace. Loosened the fastening of her black sandal and let it dangle from her toes, so the air could reach her aching heel. As it was, she didn't care for those sort of glossy magazines, full of men like cartoon characters, with bulging muscles and veins popping out of unseemly places. It belonged to the day duty manager. You only had to look at him to know he liked that sort of thing. To hear him talk, he was pumping iron every spare minute of the day, which explained why he was so tired whenever he was needed to do anything useful.

Glory was dubious about people who were so absorbed in themselves. Mercy was another, though in her case it was all hair relaxers and skin lighteners, and those intricate fingernail designs, some of which she had to admit were more artistic than anything she'd seen come out of next door. It was all vanity at the end of the day. Mercy's interest in her health and wellbeing was similar to her interest in men: skin deep. She never troubled herself with exercise –

at least in the respectable sense. Glory hadn't the time or money for gyms either, though heaven knows she got enough exercise with all her lifting and carrying.

And with that in mind, she became distantly aware of a strange turn of events …

Her sister, Mercy, approaches the pole vault with a giant paintbrush.

Her Lycra outfit is typically immodest, and her dagger-length nails a safety hazard. Glory watches from the stand with serene indifference as Mercy prepares for her third attempt at the bar … And as Alfonse Bidman, who is sitting beside her, slides an arm around her shoulders with a snakelike grace …

Mercy runs.

Mercy soars …

Mercy fails!

With an almighty thud and some very coarse language, she lands headfirst in her very own dent in the batik-print couch-

'Glory! Glory!'

—A couch that has no right being outdoors at all, unless it's being treated for fleas.

'GLORY! Wake up, for Gawd's sake!'

It was Jan. She was beetroot-red and gasping for breath. *Has she been pole-vaulting too?*

'Someone's had another go at Pearl!'

'YOU ARE TO WAIT OUTSIDE!'

Mrs Molyneux's words almost blew the door back in their faces.

Glory caught a glimpse of her navy-blue suit bearing down over Pearl's bed. She was still befuddled.

Jan was hopping from foot to foot.

'Why did you fall asleep?' she gibbered. 'You knew I was dozing. At least you'd have 'eard the alarm! Sod's law, the Angel of Death comes looking for milk, just when we're both spark out!'

Glory was too ashamed to defend herself. She put an ear to the door.

'*... could have been the same person. It was very hard to tell.*'

Pearl's voice.

'*... had my way we'd keep the light on, and none of this would have happened!*'

Mrs Molyneux said something Glory didn't catch.

A pause. Then: '*... not my colour. And it certainly isn't Ernest's!*'

Glory and Jan almost fell through the door as Mrs Molyneux yanked it open. By the time they had trooped inside she was back at the bedside, hands behind her back. Glory had no idea of the time, but an early light was seeping under the curtains.

'Are you all right, Pearl?' she asked.

The old lady peeped over her bedspread of knitted squares. Her hair was flat against the pillow as it was every morning, as if she'd spent the night walking into a gale. She peeked out at them all, eyes as bright as beads.

'Very well, thanking you.' She looked from Jan to Glory and back to Mrs Molyneux. 'Goodness, quite a party ...'

Mrs Molyneux looked at her watch. 'At five-twenty-five this morning, I was alerted to Pearl's distress by the alarm in the duty office.' Her voice had the tone of a policeman giving evidence.

'I'm sorry, Mrs Molyneux, I must have—'

'*Let me finish, Glory!*' She straightened up to her full, low height. 'I had to answer Pearl myself ... Who informs me that she pulled the alarm cord when she woke to find someone standing over her bed. She recollects this is the third such incident in a week.'

'We've checked her every hour, on the hour!' blurted Jan. 'Haven't we, Glory? Taking turns ...'

Glory stared without a word.

Jan was panicking. 'You can't sack us, Mrs Molyneux! Not like this. There's procedures!'

Mrs Molyneux closed her eyes at squawking from the ranks. 'When I arrived, the intruder had fled. Leaving this – on the rug.'

Her hands appeared from behind her back. And there, balanced across the palms like a freshly caught fish, was a black T-bar sandal.

Jan snatched a breath.

Glory stared. She tried to swallow but couldn't. An uncomfortable pressure was coming the other way.

Mrs Molyneux's eyes narrowed suspiciously. A different emotion played at the corners of her mouth. Everyone looked down at Glory's feet, including Glory herself.

She was aghast to see she was only wearing one shoe.

Eyes lifted, as if at the end of prayer.

'Bloody 'ell,' said Jan. 'Who's been playing Cinderella?'

Mrs Molyneux cleared her throat. 'Glory, you'd better come to my office. Pearl, Janet will help you get settled again. Breakfast isn't for hours.'

But Pearl was thoroughly entertained. A smile lit her face beneath the bush-baby eyes.

'Oh, don't worry about me,' she said heroically to the retreating blazer. The smile dimmed suddenly, like a waterlogged ember. 'Ernest is the one who's in trouble! If I find it belongs to that flighty piece from the laundry ...'

She went straight to the filing cabinet. Glory watched her skip through the tabbed dividers and take out the folder with her name on it. The drawer rolled shut with a thud as Mrs Molyneux sat.

The careful handwriting had begun to fade. The picture, clipped to the inside cover, showed a girl who looked appreciably younger than Glory, or at any rate thinner of face. She was crestfallen; could think of nothing to say. Just stood there in front of the senior manager's desk, where her sandal lay between them in the manner of a novelty paperweight.

Mrs Molyneux finished reading and closed the cover.

'Well, well, Glory. It's happening again, isn't it?'

She prodded the shoe with a corner of the file.

'You'd better go and get your bus.'

III

When Geoff got in from work on Friday, Tony was sprawled in front of the early-evening news.

'Present for you, darling,' he said, dropping a parcel on the couch. 'I've been on a shoot, and guess what fell in my bag when the props lady wasn't looking?'

Inside was a set of stylish bathroom scales. The top was designed to look like sandy soil, with the paw prints of a bear or some other fearsome beast where you put your feet.

'Erm, thanks, mate,' said Tony, examining the clawed indentations. 'You know, if I had an image problem, I'd say this was another of your subtle digs about getting a back wax ...'

Geoff flopped down beside him. 'Please! If your body hair offended me, you'd know about it.' He flicked through the TV channels. 'Besides, when you walk down the hall it saves me dusting the dado.' He opted for teen delinquents going through their paces on a parade ground. 'I thought we could see how much weight you've lost. Plus they'll look so cool on my antiqued limestone tiles.'

'You're all heart,' said Tony, getting up. 'I'm making a mackerel salad. Want some?'

'No thanks, I need egg and chips. I might do something vigorous later – like open a magazine ...'

Tony stopped off at the bathroom. He put down the scales and kicked off his sneakers. Hopping onto the paw prints, he waited for the needle to settle.

Ninety-six and a half kilos!

It sounded a lot, and even more in pounds. Still, it had to be an improvement: he'd been power walking every day for a fortnight. Maybe he should be running instead ...

Geoff rapped on the door. *'Is that the sound of screaming metal?'*

'Piss off, eh!' laughed Tony, clambering back into his shoes. 'I'm right on target, thanks very much!'

Later that evening, after he'd loaded the dishwasher, Tony found Geoff with an A4 pad across his knees. He was sketching with a stubby felt tip.

'Don't tell me: you're doing my portrait before I shrink to a shadow of my former self.'

Geoff looked impishly over his designer specs. 'I would, but I'm right out of A3 ... Actually, I just had an idea for this deodorant pitch.'

He held up the pad. It was a stickman sketch of Jensen Button wearing nothing but a towel and crash helmet. The tagline read: *Pit Stop. For Men in the Fast Lane.*

'Nice one,' said Tony. 'How's it going? Is that what the shoot was for?'

Geoff shook his head. 'That was our home-insurance client. I only went to keep an eye on one of the junior art directors. Nice kid, but you wouldn't trust him to shoot a bowl of fruit, let alone a thousand litres of water coming through a bathroom ceiling.'

Tony smiled. 'So when's the pitch?'

'Tuesday morning. Back on the red-eye Wednesday.'

'Back?'

Geoff looked up again.

'Bollocks, didn't I tell you?' He turned the felt tip on himself like a gun and drew a question mark on his forehead. 'Duuh! The pitch is at their global HQ. In New York.'

'Oh. Cool.'

'Tony, I'm really sorry I've not been around this week! I need to nip into the office tomorrow, but I *promise* we'll do whatever you want next weekend. Paris, Prague – the choice is yours.'

'No worries,' said Tony. 'I can amuse myself. Your apartment's in safe hands.'

'Yes. Actually, that reminds me …' The change in tone made him wary. '*Back Alley Cruising Two* goes before *Back Alley Cruising One*. Because *Two* is the director's cut and *One* is the budget release, so …'

'Ah,' said Tony. His cheeks had turned tawsed-buttock red.

'Get it right!'

'Sorry.' There were one or two things you didn't want even your best British mate knowing. 'I was just looking for – er …'

'Forget it,' said Geoff. 'Movies are for watching.' He looked round for the cap of his felt pen. 'But lose my download of that *Blue Peter* presenter in the shower and you'll never press freeze-frame in this town again.'

Tony grinned. 'Fingers crossed for your pitch.'

He pointed to Geoff's forehead. 'By the way, that question mark's the wrong way round.'

His mate slid the pad off his knees and looked in the mantelpiece mirror.

'*No, it isn't!*'

By Monday, the house laptop was in New York.

The combination of big fingers and a fiddly new mobile meant Tony had never got round to setting up email on his phone. So he stopped off at The Glow Room on his way down Haverill Road.

He'd been avoiding the funky little internet café, with its excellent cakes and lattes, since he started his fitness regime. But according to the menu it also served low-calorie blackcurrant tea, so he ordered one and logged on to a PC.

He gave Facebook a cursory sweep, but the musings of folks he half-knew back home were less gripping than ever. He checked his emails – and as usual there was one from Greta.

g.daniels@shermansumnerinc.com **02:35**

Hey gorgeous.

Well summer's here right enough. Air con packed up yesterday, so old man Sherman sent out for ice cream sodas. Which was fine, till I glooped strawberry down myself and had to do a meeting in my squash T-shirt. Raised a few eyebrows, plus the inevitable comments about banging balls at walls (Hey guys, don't tempt me!!)

Hope you gave Geoff my number. I could do with some of his wit and repartee. He's probably too busy schmoozing, but tell him I know the best place in the Park for a squizz at the blader boys if he can get away.

Hey, get this: latest rumour from upstairs is that they're NOT renewing my contract! Obviously I'm devastated – cried all the way to Saks' bikini counter!! Dunno where next, but first I want beach, booze and boy-babes (I sound like Geoff already!) Did you think any more about coming over? London to NYC is only eight hours. Hardly worth the sit-down! Or we could catch up somewhere sun-kissed in about a month?

Whoops, better dash. If I don't finish up this project I'll never get out of here. BTW any more on Wellington's answer to Christina Aguilera? I reckon she's got designs on you, Tony my boy. Just you remember, I'm the one with first dibs on your wrigglers if Mr Right Salary, Right Shoe Size doesn't turn up soon!

Luvya
Gret xxx

Tony sifted through the rest of his emails. Mostly spam; still no word from Jarvis. He looked up as the Aussie bloke with the industrial-strength dimple and fun-fur forearms brought over his blackcurrant tea.

He took a sip and tried not to scope out the chocolate cherry brownies. Cute Café Guy was staring out at the traffic passing the overpriced dress shops across the road. He had a beard and funky hair; long at the back, like a grow-your-own Davy Crockett hat. The way his hips were wiggling to the ambient background music, Tony wondered if he'd read him wrong … Till a skinny babe in a micro T-shirt sashayed out of the back with a large carton. As she bent down to restock the Thai snacks, the guy peered over to enjoy the view, scratching his balls dramatically.

Tony sighed. Two mails left in his inbox: a gossipy diatribe from work and – amazing! – one from his mother. It began *'Hello Son it's your Ma here'*, and covered everything happening in the road, from next door's overhanging cabbage tree to the saga of Frank McLagan's water butt. Tony could almost hear the creak of her laminate apron as she steeled herself to send her first-ever email from his brother's computer. He thought she'd done it unassisted until the closing paragraph:

Anyway, I will say cheerio now. Brad is taking Jenna to the pictures and he does not trust me to switch this thing off without fusing the street. Write soon. Love Your Ma.

Blimey, Ma: welcome to the twenty-first century!

Tony was touched; for a moment, he even thought he missed her. Him and Ma got on better apart. He often wondered why living at home didn't drive his brother crazy. But then Brad always had the knack of sailing through situations that left Tony foundering; and now that his little bro was getting married and grandkids were in the offing, Ma was a new woman. Nothing thawed her iciness like the prospect of new lives to fret over. Just as long as they were born on the right side of the blanket.

He tapped out replies as he finished his tea. Still five minutes' web time left, so he surfed for cheap deals to Prague. Found two offering flights and three nights for a crazy rate, even in English pounds. He scribbled the links on a flier for a nightclub and tucked it in his pocket.

Miss Skinny was on the till. As she took Tony's money, the Aussie guy winked at him, in that gallingly innocent way straight guys did sometimes. He so wished they wouldn't.

Outside the sun was still shining. He was considering whether to nip into town for the Pollock retrospective at the Tate, when he spotted a familiar figure.

Two figures, to be exact.

Shelley was at the counter in Plush, paying the super-sized receptionist. He waited on the pavement and caught her eye as she came out.

'Hey!' she said brightly. 'Fancy meeting you here! What do you think of these?' She held out her hands with their new aubergine tips.

'Very nice. Special occasion?'

She shook her head, looking quite glam without the ponytail.

'More an expediency measure ...' She pushed her arm through his as they walked. 'The guys I'm staying with have got a dog. I took her out this morning and let her off the leash, like a fool. Soon as she spots this other mutt, she's off! I chase after her, just manage to grab her before she reaches the road – and leave a ten-dollar nail wrap under her collar!'

Tony laughed. 'The perils of being a girl.'

'As it is, I needed to hit the beauty parlour anyway. I've got a date tonight!'

'Oh? Potential donor by any chance?'

'Yup.'

'Where did you find him?'

'Aha!' said Shelley. 'Put a discreet little ad on the *Guardian* website. Nineteen replies in five days! Seems English guys are just bursting to come forth and multiply!'

'Wow,' said Tony. 'I took out a lonely hearts ad once. All I got was married men and a park ranger from Whanganui who wanted to see me in lingerie.'

She laughed. 'I won't be surprised if half of mine are spoken for. But that's between them and their consciences, far as I'm concerned.'

They stopped at the entrance to Geoff's block.

'This is me,' said Tony. 'Hey, I hope it goes well tonight.'

She took a breath. 'Actually, can I ask a favour? It's a bit awkward …'

'Oh? Well, do you fancy lunch? I'm having a sandwich and a cup of low-cal, low-taste soup.'

Shelley peeled back her cuff with a new nail to check her watch. 'I should be getting back to Ethel, but – okay, thanks!'

She looked around while Tony fixed the lunch. Chicken salad on rye for the two of them, and a mug of rehydrated moon dust for him. His blow-up mattress was peeping through the spare-room door.

'Is that where you're sleeping? Lucky you – I'm on the couch.'

They carried their plates into the living room.

'Your mate's gay too, right?' said Shelley, checking out the tasteful décor. 'It's kind of like where I'm staying minus the tribal death masks.'

'Your guys sound intriguing.' said Tony. 'Where do they live? Maybe Geoff knows them.'

'Doubt it.' She took a bite of sandwich. 'They don't go out round here much. More your Soho queens.'

'That's what I mean. Geoff works on Greek Street. Knows all the bars. And all the bar boys.'

Shelley was bewitched by the giant acrylic that dominated the room: an arc of surf breaking on a beach that felt as if it was surging towards you.

'I like that,' she said. 'Reminds me of home.'

Tony hauled her back to Clapham. 'So, what did you want to ask me?'

'Oh yeah, no ...' She finished chewing, shielding her mouth with her fingertips like a bunch of crocuses. 'All it was – I wondered if you'd mind calling me on my mobile about nine o'clock tonight?'

He shrugged. 'Sure. Why?'

'I'm meeting this guy on Sloane Street at half-eight. He mailed me his photo and he sounds fine on the phone, but – well, you never know, do you? If it's not going well, I can always pretend you're my best girlfriend having a crisis and I've got to rush to your rescue.'

'Good plan. Can't be too careful. But why not ask your housemates?'

Shelley raised her eyebrows. 'Ah, they're out on the razz tonight. And the way they put the voddie away, I wouldn't trust them to remember their own names after nine p.m.'

Tony smiled. 'I won't forget. Let me get my phone.'

His jacket was in the hall.

You had to hand it to her: she was a feisty one! Asking a guy she hardly knew to check on her date with a guy she hardly knew. She reminded him of Greta. He should get them together some time – what a night that would be!

He keyed in the number as she recited it.

'How many more dates have you got lined up?'

'Oh, don't worry – I'm booking them strictly one at a time, on a cuteness-and-brains-first basis. Tonight's guy does triathlons and runs his own data-processing business.'

'Nice. Send him my way when he's done his duty.'

They finished their sandwiches.

'Hey,' said Tony. 'I didn't offer you a drink. What can I get you?'

Shelley considered. 'Have you got any OJ? I felt a bit snuffly this morning. Just my luck if I come down with a lurgy when I'm trying to look all fit and fertile.'

'Ah, we do usually, but Geoff finished it. I can pop out, though!'

'Oh look, I've put you to enough trouble—'

'No worries. We need some anyway.'

'And I should to get back for Ethel.'

'She can cross her paws a bit longer! Anyway, I want to hear about the other contenders for your maternal master plan.'

He nipped into the hall for his wallet and keys.

'Back in five …'

Tony shut the door of the flat behind him and galloped down the two flights of stairs. The convenience store was a block away, on the main road by the estate agents. And he needed time to think.

Something was troubling him – had been since the day he met Shelley on the Common. Something half-formed at the back of his mind, that evaporated when he tried to look at it.

He turned onto the main road. And as he did, he saw it, clear as day.

I want to stay in London. And I want to help Shelley have a baby!

The two notions launched as one; buoyant and seaworthy, if surrounded by a flotilla of post-rationalisations.

Number one: he hated his job in Auckland. Number two: his relationship was going nowhere. And number three: Jarvis was the latest in a long line of no-marks.

There was a number four, too: his family and friends.

It didn't much matter if Tony and his ma were separated by streets or continents, just as long as they were apart. And his brother was halfway down the aisle, en route to the Babycity superstore.

As for his friends – Greta was in New York, Nell was in Cape Town, and neither of them was heading home soon. That left Don and Ricky, his occasional clubbing buddies; but since they broke the cardinal rule of single-boys-about-town and started dating each other after years of platonic indifference, even that wasn't the same any more. They were the only ones Tony called close friends. Everyone else was just someone he knew; a comfort in the way they rubbed along together in the same groove, but not exactly special.

And then there was the baby. *His* baby. Or at least the idea of one.

The bell clattered as he went into the Indian supermarket. He'd thought about it before; they all had. Any gay guy who told you he'd never thought of adopting or fostering or growing-his-own was a liar. He and Greta had even bounced around names for their hypothetical offspring. Just a joke, far as he was concerned, though that email made him wonder ... But they were too close; having a child with Greta would be too much like the real thing.

Tony scanned the shelves of the ancient cooler cabinet, hoarded high with processed cheese and energy drinks.

So why was it any less real having a kid with a total stranger?

It wasn't philanthropy that was driving him, he knew that.

The idea of being there for a baby every day, of a new little person at the centre of his life – that wasn't for him. But he wanted to do something. Support a kid, as he or she grew into whoever they were meant to be. Hell, the amount he frittered away on clothes and shit, he could afford it!

He picked up a carton of freshly squeezed with extra pithy bits. Counted out two pounds and ten pence, and waited while the old girl in front paid for her fags.

Shelley could have her baby in Wellington and he'd be here!

He could help her provide for it, deposit a bit of money every month. Tony would do well from renting his apartment – two beds on the Harbour fetched $3K a month … Of course he'd end up back home eventually. They all did. And yeah, Shelley was right; maybe he would want to see the sprog. But chances were there'd be another dad on the scene by then. A proper, lifts-to-school, bury-pets-in-the-backyard dad.

And that was fine too. Tony would know. That was all that mattered.

'I want to give something back!'

In his head he'd only thought it. The counter guy in a red and yellow sweater was giving him a patient stare.

'Sorry, my friend. No receipt, no refund. Sorry ...'

He paid up and practically ran home, juice carton sloshing in his hand like a liquid baton. Tony was elated. His life looked clearer than it had in years! He knew what he wanted to do, if not exactly how. And Shelley said she was all for doing it the old-fashioned way, which presumably didn't involve anything as labour-saving as a turkey baster, but—

HIV test!

She'd expect that from whoever she picked, wouldn't she? Tony's last one was eighteen months ago, and he hadn't done anything dumb since so he probably had less to worry about than plenty of straight guys.

Hang on, he was getting ahead of himself! First he had to dissuade her from her quest for an English Einstein with Olympic-standard fitness. He puffed down the path, past the dustbins – and nearly barrelled right into her.

Shelley looked flustered as she snapped shut her mobile.

'Sorry, Tony, it's the bloody dog! Bloke next door called the boys. She's only got out and jumped in with his ornamental carp!'

She was bright red as she hared through the gate. Tony stumbled after her, holding out the orange juice.

'Don't forget!' she called over her shoulder. 'Nine o'clock, yeah?'

'Sure,' he panted. 'I'll call you ...'

Back in the flat, his dream dissolved. He slumped at the table in the kitchen.

Did that really just happen?

Had he decided to jack in his job, move to London and ask a woman he'd only just met to have his baby?

He opened the fridge and slotted in the juice behind the railing with the milk. Then something caught his eye.

Oh, cheers, Geoff! What sort of sadist goes away and leaves his roommate a box of éclairs from his favourite cake shop?

Tony slammed the door and looked down at his belly. Gene-pool wise, he was hardly up there with your entrepreneur triathletes. Shelley might also think he was too hairy – but what had he got to lose? He'd arrange to meet her for a chat when he called tonight. She could only say no.

Whatever happened, it wasn't going to influence his other decision. And if she did turn him down, at least it would save him breaking it to Greta ...

That evening, Tony watched TV with one eye on the clock. At twenty to nine he imagined Shelley arriving on her date, a few minutes suitably tardy.

Five minutes later, his phone rang. Her at a guess, to tell him it was over before it started, or the guy had stood her up.

His mobile didn't recognise the caller.

'Tony speaking ...'

'Hi darling, it's me!'

Geoff.

'Hello, matey. How's it going in the Big Apple?'

'Oh, so far so glamorous ... Listen, got to be quick, I'm on someone else's phone. I need you to do something for me. I've been really, really *stupid—'*

He was stressed and gabbling.

'—There's a bike courier coming round to pick up an envelope tomorrow morning, so you've got *to make sure you're in.'*

'Right. An envelope containing ... ?'

'Two grand in US dollars. Cash.'

'Blimey. I hardly dare ask.'

A snort came down the phone. *'Don't worry, it's nothing sordid. The agency's hired some local performers to liven up the pitch tomorrow – jugglers and whatnot – but the deal was, we pay them cash.'*

'Which I'm sending across the Atlantic on a motorbike? Hang on, where am I gonna get two thousand dollars?'

Cue tongue-clicking in Manhattan. *'You're not – I did! Work got me the money but I forgot to bring it. Now the MD's being arsey, and if I don't get it back to his secretary ASAP, I'm in major shit !'*

Tony was still two steps behind. 'So ... where's the money?'

'On my chest of drawers! I forgot to pack it!'

'Oh, gotcha. It's in an envelope.'

'*No,*' said Geoff. '*You need* to put it *in an envelope! Do you think you can manage—*'

A blaring Tannoy cut him short.

'Okay, keep your hair on! I'll sort it ...'

Jeez! For a guy with his fingers in advertising pies worth millions, Geoff was a ditzy queen!

As usual, his bedroom door was open. The chest of drawers was just inside, with its wrought-iron mirror and a pair of candlesticks wittily fashioned from engine parts.

But no money.

Geoff was wrong. He must have packed it. Tony's urge was to call him back, but he didn't have the number.

Then he saw the alarm clock on the bedside table.

Nine o'clock.

A nauseous seeping rose in his stomach as he fumbled for his mobile and speed-dialled Shelley.

A pause. A click, then a tone like two glass beads landing in a bowl.

'*Sorry. That number has not been recognised... Sorry—*'

Tony didn't remember going into the kitchen. Didn't feel much at all except a sense of utter impotence. Ironic, in its way.

He realised how rarely his ordered little life ever got out of control. Being late for a meeting, losing his favourite sneakers – that was as anarchic as it got. He pulled up a chair at the table and suddenly felt a long way from home.

He laid his head on his forearms, eyes open like a toddler pretending to nap. Found himself staring at his trusty old rucksack, hooked over the opposite chair. His eyes were drawn to one badge in particular.

It was a woven emblem, three inches square. A blue-and-gold shield, with a red book at the centre and the date 1991:

his graduation crest from the University of Otago. Beneath the coat of arms, virtually illegible in the script of a sweatshop loom, was the uni motto: *Sapere Aude*. Dare to be wise.

No damn wonder Shelley's guy didn't ring any bells!

A top-heavy magnet of the Leaning Tower of Pisa clattered to the floor as he flung open the fridge door. Tony had no idea how he was getting out of this, but he knew one thing for sure. Those bloody éclairs were going first.

IV

The hammerheads were out of town.

It felt like rubbing it in, telling him he'd missed killer whales too. But, judging by Adam's expression as he came out of the shower, it was worth a try.

'... and then he spotted a baby one!' said Mari. 'He was just pointing it out when you got there.'

Adam dried himself and said nothing. Wrapped his Man United towel round his waist so the red devil of the crest stared fiendishly from his bum. Umbrage wasn't his style; Mari knew there was something on his mind besides catching her in the wheelhouse with a pint-size sailor.

She unwedged herself from the bottom bunk. Slid her fingers over the top of his towel in her very best display of spontaneity.

'I did miss you this afternoon ... I'd have come along if you hadn't been looking for horrible old sharks ...' Her fingers moved slowly over his belly, a manoeuvre guaranteed to get his attention in any circumstance short of a penalty shootout.

Adam looked at her hands. Then he kissed her on the forehead.

'You seen my Rooney number-eight shirt?'

Whether it was the beer and paella or Paloma's preview of the lava-strewn delights of tomorrow's island, Adam's mood lifted with the dinner plates. Ten minutes later, it was all Mari could do to kick shut the cabin door before his passion overtook them both.

She wriggled out of her shorts and knickers. His boxers stayed at half-mast, though happily nothing else did. This floor was not designed for lovemaking; her head was resting on the guidebook and Adam's feet were in the ensuite. Mari winced as her buttock found an earring that had gone AWOL the previous day. She flicked it away and tried to relax into the undulations of the sea and her spicy-breathed beloved.

As passion was joined, ribald snores rumbled through the wall they shared with Heike and Klaus. The giggles it provoked in them both made for tricky kissing. Out of decency, and as the moment intensified, Adam tried to match his signature gentle grunts to the rhythm coming from next door – causing Mari to crack up completely.

Afterwards, as they lay in a heap, she fondled the back of his neck and kissed a familiar mole; drew back momentarily to check it for changes in size or colour.

Nothing to worry about.

Nothing at all—

She listened to the mechanical pace of Adam's breathing. True to form, he had nodded off on her shoulder. In a minute or two his weight would give her cramp, but for now she let him sleep.

Mari sighed. So what if she was curious about other men? She was only human, and curiosity was all it was. She wouldn't swap Adam for anyone; they both knew that. He had a nifty instinct for what she liked in the bedroom department; their love life wasn't bad at all, even after all these years. Frankly, if she went to bed with a man who didn't grunt like Rafael Nadal, she probably wouldn't know where to put herself.

Or him, come to that.

Twenty minutes later, they nipped back to the bar for a nightcap. But less than halfway down his drink Adam was quiet again. He was no great shakes at the emotional stuff, which was another family trait. His mother had told her as much, one Sunday as they dried the dishes.

'*Cosgrove men are all the same,*' she said, scraping at the tarry bottom of a roasting tin. '*My Howard's not shed a tear since he dropped the zapper in the fish tank during the Cup Final.*' She swapped the washing-up brush for a scourer. '*That was, what – two tellies ago ...*'

Mari was used to it. And having a partner who didn't believe in emotional baggage had its advantages; it left more room for hers. She might end up sorting things out on her own, but at least Adam was always there; strong, silent and uncomplaining, like the best sort of porter.

That was what made his current mood so odd. He wasn't the jealous type. Hadn't she seen him just now, nod a cheery 'All right, mate' to Jorge Luis as he sloped off for his post-coital fag?

Inscrutable sod.

She left her glass on the bar and followed him up to the deck.

The boat was sliding through the waves at full tilt, on course for their next island. Adam was by the railing, looking beyond the ever-moving halo of the deck lights into a darkness so dense you could almost touch it.

'You're still quiet,' she said. 'Sure there's nothing the matter?'

His neck was flushed above the white collar of his footie shirt.

'Nope. Nothing.'

His fag hand rested on the railing, letting the breeze scythe the ash to a molten cone. Before she could say more, Paloma appeared with Heike and Klaus. They walked towards the stern and stood, eyes down at the churning wake.

'*There's one!*' barked Paloma.

Mari and Adam followed her finger to where the hull cut the water and frothy brine shimmered like a welding torch. A tiny shape swooped into the circle of visibility and dived into the phosphorescence.

'Swallow-tailed gull,' she explained. 'The world's only nocturnal seagull!'

Heike cooed appreciatively and went below to fetch her camera. Presently the others followed, smiling to Mari and Adam as they passed.

'Beautiful night, no?' said Paloma, twinkling like the wonder never palled.

Klaus touched her arm.

'Tomorrow's island. What did you say it was called?'

'Fernandina. One of the youngest in the archipelago. Still volcanically active, and just about the most amazing place you will ever—'

She was cut off by the saloon door. Leaving Mari and Adam alone on deck as the *Beluga* slid through the night, trapped in its very own spotlight.

Next morning, he asked her to marry him.

Two days later, Mari was eating ice cream outside a café in Puerto Ayora. It was the only place in the archipelago where the shoe wearers outnumbered the clawed and flippered. It was also home to everyone who worked on the boats.

More importantly, it was the only place to shop. Three days from now they'd be back in England, adventuring done. Barring a rug she had already shipped home, they'd avoided buying anything bigger than a tennis ball that they couldn't eat or wear. But it wouldn't feel right, turning up to her parents in Hove without a bit of indigenous art.

She was shopping alone. Adam and the others had

opted for a tour of the Charles Darwin Research Station, with its breeding programme of giant tortoises. Mari's day pack was laden with carvings of iguanas, sea lions and more. She'd even found a killer whale with *GALAPAGOS* etched on its flank, which she was debating giving to Adam.

On the next table two Australian girls were emailing home, and she felt a pang of guilt. Mari had posted one or two snippets on Facebook when they were at the language school. But what might sound exotic at home felt like a slog in Quito, so her online reporting dried up. Now, in the islands, there was so much to tell she didn't know where to begin. And that was quite apart from their other news.

She checked her watch; two hours till she had to meet them back at the boat. Once they were home, it would take her weeks to catch up with everyone. She had left her phone in the cabin, but she knew she ought to do the decent thing – find a cyber café while she had the time. Tiny as it was, Puerto Ayora had a police station, two hairdressers and a traffic island; there had to be a cyber café too. She asked her waiter for directions as she paid the bill.

It felt odd, crossing streets again, even after a few days. The town was infinitely quieter than Quito, but oddly more cosmopolitan. And there was less of the grinding poverty – the beggars and the shoeshine boys, the women in shawls and strange top hats, with numberless brats clinging to their skirts.

The little shop was by the youth hostel on Calle Santo Domingo. Mari handed over her dollar. The only spare machine was right by the window in a patch of baking sunlight. The action of slipping a newspaper between her bare legs and the plastic chair took her back to childhood: climbing into the back seat of her dad's scalding parked car.

The PC looked surprisingly new. The keyboard ran

smoothly once she'd poked out the chewing gum from under the space bar. It took a few minutes to access her email, trawl for the relevant contacts, but her money had bought an hour. Plenty of time for the edited highlights.

The sun was stifling. Mari wilted against the window as she typed. She had got as far as *Day Five: The Curious Incident of The Boyfriend-Stroke-Fiancé on Fernandina,* when she was startled by knuckles rapping on the side of her head.

Outside was a smiling face.

She had returned the expression instinctively before she registered who it was. Jorge Luis, brawny arms bare in a basketball vest. And he was coming in. That was all she needed!

He high-fived the guy at the counter and pulled up a chair beside her; swung one muscular leg over the seat and sat back to front.

'Hey,' he said, with the wholesome grin of a high-school teen at a soda fountain.

'Oh,' said Mari. 'Hey.'

She carried on typing. It piqued her to have her train of thought derailed. She clamped her elbows to her sides, acutely aware of the dark patches forming in the underarms of her cotton top.

'Everyone go to see the baby tortoises,' said Jorge Luis. 'Why you don't go?'

'I've seen tortoises already,' said Mari briskly. 'Plus I've got shopping to do. And emails to write. Home.'

Now his smile looked familiar. All it needed was a damned toothpick.

'You could have visit – *cómo se llama en inglés* – Lonesome Jorge?'

Mari missed a beat, inadvertently switching to caps.

'Sorry?'

'He very sad, because he don't have wife. He all alone, the only one left in the world.'

She looked at the screen and found she was yelling in print. She held down the backspace key until her fingernail turned white.

'Only what left?'

'Tortuga de la Isla Pinta ... To you is 'Lonesome *George*', no? We say him *Solitario Jorge* ... He live at the Research Station. If they don't find him wife to make babies, when he die – *pffft* – all gone.'

Mari laughed. *A tortoise!*

She stopped. Extinction was nothing to laugh about.

'I got the panga,' said Jorge Luis, nodding towards the harbour; a movement that drew attention to the pleasingly sulky outline of his lips. 'You want I take you for ride?'

Now that smile of his was revving like a Harley, and it reminded her of someone else ... James Dean? Marlon Brando? Or was it Joey from *Friends*?

Wrong. *Cousin Harry!*

Mari shifted in her seat, obliging the newsprint to choose between the paper or the back of her thighs. Inside her top, a droplet of sweat rolled all the way to the bottom of her spine.

She leaned forward and pressed delete.

There was something utterly decadent about being chauffeured over the open ocean in unbroken sunshine. She felt like Cleopatra on the Nile, give or take a motorised orange lilo.

Lying back against the bow, Mari pondered this image; rather than the wisdom of leaving port without telling a soul, and with a man she hardly knew. But then Jorge Luis had to be back at the boat the same time she did. Why worry?

He was standing at the stern, black hair blowing back from his face, that smile still on his full, soft lips. With one hand on the outboard motor he was stripped to the waist, framed against the sky like a mini Colossus. She closed her eyes to the sun's glare. Relaxed into the sublime sensation of a warm wind lifting her hair—

... *Ooof!* She must have dozed off!

Silence.

The boat was at a standstill. The engine was out of the water, propeller tilted into the air like a resting egg whisk. Mari sat up straight and looked around. They were bobbing on a lagoon fringed on three sides by the densest mangroves.

'Where are we?'

Jorge Luis sat cross-legged in front of her.

'East,' he said.

His elbows rested on his knees. Mari couldn't help noticing how the slab of his stomach stayed vertical, instead of drooping over his waistband like any normal person's (her, Adam; especially Adam).

'Why have we stopped?'

Jorge Luis flicked a smooth hand at an invisible airborne something.

'I want show you my little friend.'

God, not another blooming tortoise! She looked round again, but there was no sign of man nor beast.

Unless he meant-

'There!' he said. 'In the trees!'

Mari's confusion amused him. She followed his gaze to a fallen trunk, cradled in a tangle of mangroves growing right out of the sea. She felt uneasy, being alone with a man who counted dead vegetation among his friends.

Then something moved. Something small and glossy, perched halfway up; an elongated ball of fur.

She squinted into the shadows. It was – what, a giant squirrel? Mari wondered if they had beavers in the Galápagos, then thought better of asking; just as a snout rose into view on the tip of a flexible spine.

A fur seal!

It was little more than a baby, roosting in the low branches like something off *The Muppet Show*. The creature turned its head, sniffed in her direction, then looked away with customary indifference. It was one of the most adorable things Mari had ever seen. Her heart sank at the thought of the pigeons and pitbulls of her own jungle back home.

'He always here in middle of the day,' said Jorge Luis. 'Keeping out of the sun. I come here with my girlfriend every week when I am home.'

She felt relieved.

'Why didn't you bring her today?'

His chin twitched. 'She not my girlfriend any more. She go with sailor from other boat – *Look there!*'

Now he was pointing at something in the shallows. Mari looked over, steeling herself for a shark …

Sure enough, a pale-edged fin was breaking the surface, barely an arm's-length from the panga. She shuddered, panic rising in her throat as she realised it was one of a swarm of fins, stretching far to starboard. Mari wanted to look away but found herself peering closer. Yet beneath the water were none of the torpedo bodies that chilled her to the core. Just fins and fins and more fins, with nothing much attached.

'Golden rays,' said Jorge Luis. 'Beautiful, no?'

They were the colour and shape of fallen sycamore leaves, oblivious to the boat in their slow-motion fly-past. Mari's mouth ran dry as they skimmed around her, fleshy wingtips emerging from the water on the upward sweep. As creatures went, they were intriguing more than frightening; hardly had heads at all, let alone teeth. The shoal had the effortless geometry of the starlings that wheeled over the old pier near her parents' place. She wished she had Adam's camera – there was nothing like this on his DVD ...

A minute later and the golden swarm had gone, gliding out to sea, dragging their wire-thin tails behind them. The water returned to mirror calm.

Mari was searching for another spectacle below the surface when abruptly the panga jolted. Jorge Luis was striding up the craft towards her …

In a moment they were side by side, snug as twins in a buggy. A mark had been overstepped; she was unnerved, but tried not to show it.

Her foot found her day pack under the seat. Inside was the mace spray Adam made her carry in Quito. If those hands of his went anywhere, she would-

What? Blind him? Tip him overboard – the only person who knew the way home?

What had she got herself into!

A warm, caramel-coloured leg was pressed against hers. It was disconcertingly hairless, like hers only almost certainly natural.

'Did you hear the *es*-story of the Baroness?'

Mari wondered if she was in for a rustic Ecuadorian joke. She turned to face him, to show she wasn't scared – and found herself staring into a gaze as glassy as the water.

'She live on Floreana Island – sixty, seventy years ago. My

grandfather, he remember her. Say she appear one day, on a donkey with her boyfriends – *two.*' He made the point with an appropriate number of fingers. 'Nobody know where she came from, but she was European. A fair-hair lady. Like you.'

Mari wasn't sure where this was going. She was quietly trying to snag her bag strap with a big toe.

'Only three families lived on Floreana, trying to make a beautiful world. But when the Baroness arrive, she say God has made her queen of the island. Her boyfriends build a hacienda, and they treat everybody like shits. But then Baroness, she make a even bigger' – Jorge Luis fumbled for the word – '*es*-scandal. Every day she bath in the only clean water of the island. Then she walk around naked. In just boots, with a whip and a little gun like a cowboy's, er ...'

His right hand made the shape of a pistol; the left a spinning motion.

'A r-revolver?' Mari inched the bag forward under her seat.

He nodded. 'And all the time, she is make sex with her two boyfriends. Until one day there is argument and she try to kill one man. She beat him nearly to death, throw him out of hacienda. But the next morning, when the people wake out of bed, Baroness and the other man have disappear.'

He was looking down at his feet. Or was it *her* feet?

'Nobody ever see them again.'

Playing for time, Mari scratched an imaginary itch.

'What ... what happened to them?'

Jorge Luis's eyes found hers. He shrugged.

'Some people say they sail to Tahiti. Or that other boyfriend kill them, bury them some place around. My grandfather he say different. He think they go for swim and feed the sharks.'

Mari felt nauseous. Her throat was dry.

'Well, well. Poor old Baroness!'

He was shaking his head. 'But me, I don't think the world miss a bad person. Do you?'

The question hung over them in the hot, dry silence.

The baby seal had disappeared. There was no sign of any living thing; not a ray or a frigatebird to break the meniscus of the day.

It was all Mari could do not to scream.

'Shouldn't we ... Isn't it time we were getting back?'

Jorge Luis didn't hear. 'And you. How many boyfriends *you* have?'

Something surfaced off the side of the panga with a plop. It was gone before Mari could glimpse it.

'One, of course! How many do you think I have!'

She remembered the thin gold chain tucked down the front of her top. She hauled it out, holding it between them.

'Look!' Her engagement ring spun like a talisman. 'Adam and I are getting married!'

The single blue stone glittered on its band. Jorge Luis looked puzzled.

'And why you don't wear it?'

'It's too small. The sun makes my fingers swell and—'

'Let me see,' he ordered. 'Take it off the chain.' He was holding out his hand.

Mari could hear the panic in her own voice. 'I can't. If I lose it, Adam will—'

'Then I help you!'

Jorge Luis lunged, pushing back the hair from her neck. She froze, powerless, as he found the clasp.

Seconds later, the ring was cupped in his palm. Tauntingly, he held it away from her, balancing it on the tips of his fingers, watching as it sparkled in the sunlight.

'*Zafiros*, no? How you say in English?'

Mari willed herself to keep calm. 'Sapphires.'

How could this be happening!

He nodded, resting an elbow on the side of the boat.

She made a grab for it. They tilted alarmingly, Jorge Luis laughing, pushing her away with his free arm as Mari tried again. He was still too quick, parrying her with a hand, an elbow. As one arm snaked, the other remained motionless, suspending her engagement ring over the side of the boat like a hapless mutineer.

Then he turned away, making a wall of his broad back. Circling four fingers round the tip of his thumb, he placed the ring on the tiny platform. As if he were about to—

'No!' begged Mari. '*Jorge Luis, please!*'

'So!' He was laughing again, colder this time. 'And me, I didn't think you even knew my name ...'

And with a referee's aplomb, his thumb flipped the tiny payload into the air.

High, high into an empty sky, above an empty sea. Too bright to look at, too ridiculous to believe, like a flying saucer hovering over the bottom of your garden.

THREE

I

Agnes was still laughing as Ian accelerated out of the Windmill car park. He could see her in the driving mirror, hands on hips, shaking her head.

This was just a game to her!

His first instinct was to follow the other car, but the snapper's Renault was long gone. As he turned the wheel the other way, slow-motion replays crowded in on him like thugs in an alley ... *Ian Newton and a girl half his age, caught in a clinch against the Windmill's whitewashed brickwork!*

His mind's eye tormented him, but his hands and feet slipped into autopilot. Before he knew it, he was home, pulling up on the gravel beside the van.

Jasper trotted up the hall as he went in. The stairs were empty; Carla had finished her stream of calls. The Westie sniffed him about the ankles, then returned to his basket. If he detected the odour of vile charlatan, he was keeping it to himself.

Ian popped his head round the sitting-room door. The misaligned armchairs indicated tai chi. Carla was executing a posture on the hearth rug, motionless.

'Did you get any?' she asked.

His face froze.

'Milk!'

'All gone,' he lied. 'And at Sainsbury's. Actually, I thought we'd eat out …'

They had dined at Faraday's the night before she went on the boat. Six weeks passed in an instant as they were shown to the same table by the unlit hearth. White tablecloth, silver cruet, tiny white vase.

The waiter nodded to Carla as he gave out the menus. 'Nice to see you home safe,' he said with a wink.

He handed her the wine list and disappeared. This particular chap had worked here so long that customers thought they knew him, even when they'd never caught his name. Tonight, his usual tone – informal, bordering on garrulous by last sitting on a Saturday night – had a deferential edge.

'Get used to it,' said Ian, catching Carla's eye. 'My wife, the icon of happy marriage ...'

She sniffed. 'It takes two to tango. You'll be in the spotlight too, you know, as long as it lasts.' She scanned the dry whites. 'Are you all right with that?'

Ian's gaze rested insensibly on the starters. *Bit late asking me now!* But then they'd hardly drawn breath all day.

'Why not?' he said. 'Like you say – chance of a lifetime.'

This was it! If he was coming clean about Agnes, it was now or never. Better she found out from him than some exposé on their 'perfect' marriage. He was fairly sure she would take it without histrionics. Carla wasn't the plate-throwing type. She might even think of a way out.

On the other hand, was it kinder to wait till they got home?

He ordered for them both, including a bottle of sancerre – the last in a long day of decisions. She was starting to relax. Might be best if he just dived in—

'Mad, isn't it,' said Carla. 'The way things turn out. I said I wanted a new direction and look, I've got one ...'

Ian sat back. She was in ruminative mode; he'd have to bide his time.

'Being on the boat soon palled, but it was fun at first. You know, getting to know everyone, all mucking in. It's funny, you end up talking about the most intimate things with complete strangers, people you'd never normally ...' She finished with a shrug and unwrapped a breadstick. 'You never forget about the cameras and the mikes, or I didn't. But eventually you think: what the hell! To thine own self be true. Then, one night, I was talking to Mitch …'

The Geordie Mong.

The starters arrived. She put down her breadstick.

'… I know he probably came across as a twit, but he was a nice guy underneath. Been through a lot for twenty-six. Mum died of cancer, Dad on and off the wagon … And he had a girlfriend. Cindy. Been together since they were fourteen. Mitch bought her flowers every single Friday. Said she was his *canny lass*, that she was the only thing in the world he loved more than football. Then one day, Cindy turned round and told him she'd been sleeping with his best mate. For a year and a half – Mitch didn't have a clue!'

She paused to unpack a prawn.

'He told me this when we were on lookout one night, watching the headlights slip by Castle Urquhart. And he said the nicest thing I've ever heard anyone say about a heartless, two-timing bitch. He said, '*Carla, I wouldna done owt even if I'd known she was putting it aboot. Cindy was my daily pint of sunshine …*' She wiped her fingers on the serviette. 'In the end, she went off with the other fellow and that was that. Mitch spent six months smoking dope and applied for the show.'

Ian didn't appreciate being humbled by a badger-haired idiot. He felt the urge to confess sinking away like a leaky life raft.

'And it made me realise: I'm *so* lucky! When I think of all I've put you through … Buying and selling properties, trogging up mountains on my spiritual quests, and that ridiculous fling with the Malteser ... There I was, looking for more, when I had what I wanted all the time!'

She caught his expression over the single gerbera.

'You, Ian! *Us*.'

He nodded and toyed with his soup. 'So, why a baby all of a sudden?'

'For us! It would be something, *someone*, who's part of both of us! I know I sprung it on you out of the blue – it's only an idea. But I want to if you do. You always said you did.'

'That was years ago! I got used to it. I also said it was your choice. Your body, your life – I'm just the breadwinner.'

'You are not just the—'

'I know. I'm being funny.' He held her fingers across the tablecloth. 'You've never deprived me of anything, I promise you. But the rule still applies. It is up to you.'

The waiter appeared and took their plates. He returned with a platter of assorted entrées – olives, tiny crackers, dates – placing it between them with geometric precision.

'On the house,' he said.

He asked after the wine, made a great play of refilling their glasses until the other diners had noticed the lady from the telly in his restaurant.

'Well,' said Carla when he disappeared, 'the answer's yes. I'd like to try. Of course it may not be easy. I might not be able to.'

'*I* might not be able to!'

She shrugged, smiling. 'You know what, Ian? You still amaze me after all these years.'

He sipped his sancerre.

'Nothing fazes you, does it? Everything life throws at you, you just take it on the chin.' She laughed suddenly. 'Like poor old Mitch's mate!'

'Eh?'

'Didn't I say? When Mitch found out he was screwing his girlfriend, he broke the guy's jaw in three places.'

She helped herself to a date. 'Never laid a finger on *her*, though. Quite the gentleman.'

Ian watched her pass the stone back through her lips and place it neatly on the side plate. It looked back at him like a petrified cockroach as Carla helped herself to another date.

That night, it took him two minutes on the net to track down Maisie O'Grady, freelance journalist for News Direct.

He waited till Carla was running a bath, then hitched Jasper to his dreaded lead.

'Shan't be long!' he shouted up the stairs. 'Just taking him round the block …'

He shut the front door before she could comment on Jasper's renewed enthusiasm for walkies. The little dog lumbered down the steps in the warm darkness. Wrong-footed, he stumbled at the gate as Ian turned away from their usual route to the Common.

'This way, boy ...'

Time was of the essence. He waited till they were two streets away, an avenue of big Edwardian conversions. Then he speed-dialled Maisie O'Grady.

It was a landline, presumably her office. A long shot at this time of night. But then what were the hours for a position like 'Tabloid Rottweiler'?

Two rings … Answerphone. Then a familiar rasp:

You're through to Maisie ... I'm not at my desk, so leave a message. If it's urgent, try my mobile. If it's not, try a Bacardi and a bloody good shag, works for me! My mobile is oh-seven-five …

She spat out the numbers like a Donegal fishwife. Ian dialled before he forgot them or thought better of it.

Five rings. It'd be another answerphone. If only he had—

'Maisie! Hang on!'

She clicked off an orchestrated riff that might have been Meat Loaf. The rock music was replaced by traffic. She was driving with the window down.

'Yeah, who is it?'

The challenge rooted Ian to the spot. 'Good evening. My name is Ian Newton.'

'Can't hear you! Going hands-free …' A pause, then the sound of shuffling. A pelican crossing beeped in the background. *'I hear you now – Ian who?'*

He looked round for eavesdroppers; the well-lit street was empty. 'Newton! Carla's husband, from *Hell in a Houseboat*.'

Another pause, which grew into a silence. For a moment he thought he'd been cut off. She was winding up the window.

'Well, well, Mr Newton ... And what would you be wanting at this time of night?'

His mind raced. He couldn't be certain what she knew; about the imminent press on their model marriage, or the potentially disastrous photos. But her tone said she was in charge. Ian leaned against the bricks of somebody's garage and tried to banish the image of a blindfold and last cigarette.

'It's about your photographer. I think he may have – misconstrued something …'

'May he?' fired back Maisie. *'May he, indeed? Well, Ian, isn't it a shame we didn't get the chance to chat yesterday? See, there's nothing gets my old snapper Dan's curiosity like a shut front door …'*

Jasper looked up through snowy eyebrows. His master was preoccupied so he chanced a lie-down.

'Yes, sorry. Mad day yesterday. You know what it's like, I'm sure.' Of course she did, the hard-bitten cow!

'Look, Maisie – *Ms O'Grady* – I don't know what you're planning to do with those pictures, but they could make things very awkward. For my wife.'

A four-by-four sailed past, headlights blazing. Jasper's eyes followed the slipstream without stirring a hair.

'Well, that'd be a shame, wouldn't it, Ian? What with your wife being a heroine and all ... A little bird tells me we can expect quite a splash on her in the next few days. On the two of yous, in fact!'

Bollocks! She knew it all. So much for newspapers keeping their plans under wraps ... What happened if Raj's mate filed a story of minor-celebrity monogamy in SW4, and another tabloid torpedoed it? Would he and Carla still get paid? Would they get sued? And how did you get through to someone whose only motivation was their byline and other people's anguish?

He was about to make an appeal to Maisie's humanity. Then he had a better idea.

'Thing is, nothing's signed and sealed – not really ... Carla's still humming and hawing over the detail, and I dare say she might change her mind if, er ... Would you still like to chat? There is *one* thing we haven't told anyone. Yet.'

'No need, love!' snapped Maisie. *'I've got me scoop – you and your lady friend, courtesy of Dan and his trusty trigger finger. Unless you're telling me the canal-boat queen can top that? Don't tell me – she works for MI5? She's having an affair with Bono?'*

'No,' retorted Ian. 'She's just pregnant, that's all!'

Silence.

An emergency vehicle swept past Maisie's car with the throb of a startled turkey.

'Pregnant? You shitting me?' He had done it – he'd pierced her armour-plated heart! *'Hang on, would this by any chance be a* waterborne *conception?'*

'A what?'

'Are you saying she was at it on the boat? Jesus, Mary, a fine picture of marriage yous two are! Out of each other's sight for five minutes, then leaping on the next available body like a cat on a kipper!'

Ian was aghast at this twist on his own fiction. 'It's MY baby!'

'Yeah? Is that what she told you?'

Bitch!

'Maisie – I said, it's mine! That's why she ran out on the show. We've been trying for years and … Look, this means everything to Carla!'

A cough at the other end of the line. Then a sigh, or was it a hiss – the sound of a pondering dragon? He struck again.

'Please – let me deal with this. My wife left the show to be with me and this means more to us than anything. All right, I know I'm no angel. I've got stuff to sort out and I'm doing it – but if you print those pictures, we're finished! Let me talk to her, tonight, and you've got an exclusive.' He was warming to his theme. 'You know: PLUCKY, PREGNANT CARLA JUMPS SHIP FOR LOVE!'

'Cool it, smart-arse! I do the headlines …'

A click, then another sigh. Maisie was lighting a cigarette.

'All right. I can't do anything now, but I'll call you tomorrow lunchtime. And I want you and her singing off the same hymn sheet, ready to sign on the dotted, terms to be advised ... And I want exclusive access and *an option on your baby photos. Clear?'*

She dragged on her fag. Deep, into the dark place.

'Yup, clear as day! Thanks Maisie, I can't tell you how—'

'And Ian?' When she blew out the smoke he could almost smell it. *'Let me down, and I'll have you and your floozy on every newsstand faster than shit off a shovel. Got it?'*

'Absolutely! I—'

The line went dead.

Ian's entire body drooped. The phone fell from his ear with the weight of a dumbbell.

Jasper looked up from the pavement. He sensed walkies were about to resume.

II

There wasn't a soul about as Glory turned into the quadrangle. The blocks felt different at dawn on a Sunday, without the throb of music from parked cars and open windows. The only movement was the flutter of clothes drying on balconies; and the stir of pigeons huddled on the ridges where one concrete tier slotted onto the next, as if by a mighty hand.

Inside, the flat was just as quiet. Mercy, Sam and Sherelle would still be asleep. But the children's body clocks had no respect for the day of rest; they'd be up at any moment, bright as buttons and clamouring for TV and Krispies.

Glory threw off her bag and made herself a cup of tea. She slid onto the couch where she customarily savoured the peace before going to bed. But for now her head was too full of the night's events, of Mrs Molyneux's ridiculous theory and its implications. She had suspended Glory on full pay, pending an investigation into the case of the shoe that went walkabout. There was even talk of the police.

Glory didn't trust that woman and never had. Got a bad feeling about her from the day she walked in. Miss Saville, her predecessor, had sung her praises: how Mrs Molyneux was going to make all the changes at the Hall that she had tried to and failed. It saddened Glory, to see her old manager sitting on the sidelines, smiling dutifully as this new woman addressed them. Short as she was, there was an air of simpering triumph about her that reminded her of someone. It came to her, weeks later on this very spot, as she flicked through the channels for something to watch with her cocoa.

Margaret Thatcher, waving down to the crowds from her bedroom in number 10 Downing Street.

The next day, Miss Saville had gone, earlier than expected. It was soon apparent the changes Mrs Molyneux had in mind had more to do with raising fees and adding duties than buying a ping-pong table for the staffroom. Extra tasks sneaked onto the rota for no extra pay, driving away staff with years of good service. And Glory suspected Mrs Molyneux would be glad to see the back of her, too. For while the little woman was happy enough to milk the families of the Hall's few ethnic residents, she seemed less than eager to recruit black people to her staff.

She recalled that clipping on the senior manager's pinboard: a piece on last summer's garden fête. She remembered returning with the glass of water she'd been sent to fetch for the man from the local paper – to find Mrs Molyneux, surrounded by the staff she had picked to be in the photo. All quite random and all quite white. That day, as today, Glory seethed in silence.

The peace was broken by footsteps outside the window. The front door creaked on its hinges ...

Mercy! Slinking in without a care in a cloud of her usual perfume ... Smoking again!

As she passed the front room, Mercy caught her sister's eyes, wide as searchlights. She jumped back with a start.

'What you doin' home so early?'

'Never mind what *I'm* doin'!' snapped Glory. 'Have you been out all night?'

Mercy rolled her eyes. She slouched up the hall without a word; looked in on the kids and came back, the better to get it over with.

She closed the door and lowered her voice to a whisper.

'Before you start, I left them me mobile. Sam knows if he wakes up and Mummy isn't there, he press star-star-one and I answer.'

Glory was incensed. *'He's six years old!'*

Mercy tried to shush her, to no avail.

'What you thinkin' of, you idiot woman! If the social find out you been leaving them alone to go smokin' the night away, they'll take them away! You could go to jail! How many times you done this?'

'Keep your voice down!' snapped Mercy. 'It none o' your business.'

'You're making it my business! By the Lord, Mercy, if Ma was here she would say you're no daughter of hers!'

'An' it none o' her business either!'

The weed had lost its calming influence. A moment later, they were both on their feet, chins up and fingers waving, bickering like the teenagers they used to be.

'You want to live like an old maid,' bawled Mercy, 'that's up to you! Spend your life clearin' up the shit an' piss of old white folks – *that's up to you!* But don't tell me how to spend mine!'

'I couldn't care how you live yours!' yelled Glory. 'Swan around playin' the village ho if you want to! Drop on your back for any man who'll have you ... But that's my nephew and niece in there. Lord knows, they might as well be *my* kids, for all the providin' I do!'

Mercy had had enough. Her hand was on the door.

Then she changed her mind.

'An' what about me? What about me, when you're out all day? I'm the one that feeds them an' takes them to school! Washes their clothes – washes *your* clothes, you forget about that! Keep this place clean and tidy so you—'

'Clean?' Glory exploded. 'The last time you had a

mop in your hand, you were chattin' up the brush man. An' if I hadn't come home, it woulda been more than his mop!'

Mercy threw her arms in the air. 'Aye, you're a bitch, Glory! You always were!' She snatched at the door handle. 'A jealous, uptight little—'

The door swung open. Sam and Sherelle stood frozen to the keyhole in their fleecy pyjamas.

'What you doin'?' snapped Mercy. 'I'm talking to your Auntie Glory. Get back to bed!'

She chased after them.

Glory's body was quivering as she slumped on the couch, her face in her fingers. She heard Sherelle ask Mummy why she and Auntie Glory were fighting. Heard Mercy turn on the portable TV as Sam said:

'*Mummy, what's a village ho?*'

The next thing she knew, there was a hand on her shoulder. Mercy's voice was a worn-out hush.

'Come on, don't cry now. I didn't mean to make you cry ...'

Glory looked up, tears about to burst their banks.

'I'm not cryin', you idiot woman! *They're just like you and me!*' She snorted with laughter, pulling a tissue from her pocket. 'Remember how we used to listen at the door when Ma was rowing with Grandma? An' that time she left us in the vestry at choir practice? Caught us peepin' through the screen as the vicar got changed, trying to see what he had on under his cassock!'

Mercy cackled and lolled on the couch beside her.

'*Reverend Watkins!* Sock suspenders and paisley boxers!'

Now they were both laughing. Rolling on the cushions like fallen skittles, at memories of days when they were young enough to be friends as well as sisters, when the only pressures were homework and school reports.

'I need a cuppa tea,' said Mercy when her eyes uncreased. 'You wan' another?'

The TV murmured from the bedroom as Glory followed her into the kitchen.

Mercy filled the kettle. 'I know I shouldn't o' stayed next door. An' I know you won't believe me, but we was only talkin' … I told Alfonse I can't go to Trinidad. It ain't fair on you, or the kids. He never should of bought those tickets, but he thinks his half-sister'll buy them off him, so it not the end o' the world.'

Glory tutted as she rinsed the mugs. Even yesterday seemed an age away. *Lucky old Mercy, fallen on her feet again!*

'I got something to tell you. You can go on your holiday. I'll look after the kids.'

'No!' insisted Mercy. 'You'll be running a marathon every day, gettin' them up and out before your work. An' I don't even know this half-sister o' his he says'll mind them. I'm not trustin' 'em to a stranger.'

'I said: you can go! I'll manage on me own. I'm not working for a while, so it's not a problem.'

'Wha'? How come? If you take all your holiday, you'll—'

'I been suspended.'

Mercy stared. 'No! What they say you done?'

Glory's chin fell to her chest.

Her sister put her arm round her. 'Hey, you can tell me. What is it?'

Glory puffed out her cheeks in a giant sigh. The tears were back again.

'There's been trouble with one o' the old ladies. They reckon I been sleepwalkin' again.'

Mercy leaned against the worktop as she explained about Pearl.

'… I could shoot meself for fallin' asleep in that chair. I never should o' done it, but that doesn't make it true!'

Her sister shook her head. 'It's lies! All rubbish and lies. You ain't sle'pwalked since you was a girl!'

Glory took the kettle off the heat and poured. 'Seventeen … You were staying over with Beula Pomfret. Ma found me in your bedroom, goin' through the wardrobe.' She couldn't hold back a smile. 'I said I was looking for cheese. Made her promise not to tell you …'

Mercy did the sums. 'But that's twelve, thirteen years ago. How come they know about that?'

Glory grimaced. 'When I went for that cleanin' job, I had to fill in a form. Medical conditions, allergies, all o' that. Well, I had nothin' to put, and I kept thinking about what they said in school exams: *Never leave a blank space* … So I put about the sleepwalkin'. Must have been mad.'

'But if you was asleep in a chair, someone coulda whipped your shoe an' put it in the old woman's room! It's a fit-up!'

Glory shrugged. She hoisted out a teabag, leaving the other in to stew.

Her sister was on a roll. 'Wait a minute. How many o' them knows about your sleepwalkin'?'

'Only Mrs Molyneux. But it's on me records.'

'An' where they kept?'

'In the filing cabinet. In her office.'

Mercy nodded sagely. 'So she's the only one who could know.'

'But she leaves her room open half the time. Jan and me been in those files once, when one o' the girls was bookin' too much holiday.'

Her sister looked disappointed. 'So what she gonna do? Did she call the pigs?'

'Said she might. Said she had to speak to Pearl's son about it. Mind, he's a streak of sap – he'll do whatever she tells him.'

Milk splashed into the mugs. 'I don't like it. You got a union. You got rights!'

Glory had precious little faith in unions. 'They're a lotta hot air an' take forever. Maybe it won't come to that if—'

'Mummy! Can we come out now?'

Sam's voice chimed out across the hall. The bedroom door was open a crack in case the torrent still raged outside.

Mercy squeezed her sister's hand. She picked up her mug and went to see to her children.

Two days later, Mercy and Alfonse were packed and gone.

Her sister's beau had kept out of Glory's way since she kicked him out like a mangy tom. Though in fairness, he'd made an effort with the children, taking them next door to paint in the afternoons to keep them out of her hair. Mercy had been supportive, too; she'd done a bit of shopping for the fridge, and was careful not to appear too cock-a-hoop at leaving the world behind for sixteen nights in paradise. And the children were as happy as ever, believing time with Auntie Glory was a treat worth the price of being without their ma.

Glory tried not to worry. There was nothing she could do. She'd get her wages at the end of the month whether she worked or not. Only her basic, mind. She was missing out on the extras for nights and weekends that made the money liveable. She had never asked much out of life, and, sure enough, life had obliged. But hadn't Ma always taught her not to waste her time on pointless dreams?

'Keep yourself to the here and now. Leave to the Lord the when and how.'

So she had said whenever her daughters' feet left the ground. It was the creed Ma lived her own life by, right to the end. Probably just as well.

Ma's only dream was to see her girls married, and to live long enough to see her grandchildren. The cancer deprived her of the second part; Glory suspected Ma could have outlived Methuselah and not seen the first.

Like Ma, she believed in letting things take care of themselves. She sensed an orderliness in her current situation that made her wonder if it was meant to be. Whatever she thought of Alfonse Bidman, he cared for Mercy well enough. The fact he was taking her to meet his folks out of his own pocket (strictly speaking, Lambeth Council's) counted for something. Maybe they would get hitched, or at least move in together. And since Alfonse had the flat next door and Mercy had this one, maybe Glory would have her own place sooner than she thought ...

But for now, she had enough to do, on hectic days and peaceful nights with her nephew and niece. Children she was deeply fond of and who, compared with a lot of kids, were no trouble at all.

She worried about Sam. He reminded Glory of herself at that age – always the responsible one. He did his best to look after Sherelle, who was a little minx at times. But he was getting to the age when Glory had started sleepwalking, and she prayed family history would not repeat itself. It was an unsettling thing for a child, though she had never come to harm. Her biggest mischief was playing with the lights on the landing – off and on, off and on, like a lighthouse ... Ma never made her feel bad, just led her quietly back to bed. Then a neighbour told her about a cousin whose boy climbed down the drainpipe one night and disappeared. A nightwatchman found him on a building site, fast asleep at the top of a crane. Ma fitted locks to all the windows after that; but as it was, Glory's sleepwalking petered out around puberty, with just the one occasion after that.

As far as she knew.

Right now, her biggest problem was keeping the children occupied, particularly on sunny days. In Glory's opinion, they were too little to be left outside alone, even on the walkway of the block. She and Mercy had been forbidden to play out till they were ten years old. And they'd lived in a respectable little terrace over Peckham way, with none of the graffiti that turned up in the stairwell at night, like messages from the devil. In those days, even a dog's business on the pavement was a stain on the neighbourhood. Ma kept a plastic bag under the doormat in case she should ever open up to such shamefulness.

No matter what Sam and Sherelle got up to at school and that crèche, it was never enough to tire them out. So most afternoons Glory took them swimming at the local recreation centre. Sam was a hearty swimmer in a splashing sort of way, and Sherelle was fearless in her pink armbands. Glory liked the water least, tolerating the chlorinated murk as long as there were none of the bigger boys around. Boys who defied the posters and delighted in jumping in, narrowly missing her head.

The following Wednesday, they had finished their swim and were getting dressed in what the rec called a 'family cubicle'. Glory was tying shoelaces, and caught her back on the nappy-changing shelf as she answered her mobile.

'Hel-*ow*! Hello?'

'That you, Glory?' It was Jan. *'You all right?'*

'Jus' nearly crippled meself. We're at the baths.'

'Well, I won't keep you. Listen, can you come and meet me tomorrow, in me afternoon break?'

'At the Hall? You know I'm not supposed to show me face. An' I got the kids, so—'

'I know, I know!' Jan sounded flustered. *'Meet me by the swings on the Common. I got something to tell you ...'*

Next day, Glory and the children took her usual bus to Clapham Common. Those roadworks were still there, grinding away further up the road outside Carson Hoggart. Half a dozen men in yellow jackets and hardhats leaned on their machines, watching another man do a bit of work. Glory couldn't see the danger from above in laying an electric cable; she assumed the hats were for keeping the rain off.

The light drizzle didn't stop Sam and Sherelle. Once they were over the zebra, she let them run on the grass, hard and free. They'd be out of breath long before they reached the playground. In the porch of the old boathouse skulked a knot of boys, hoods up and lighting fags, acting tough till a bit of rain sent them bolting for cover like rabbits.

When she caught up with the kids, they were panting happily, sweaty inside the anoraks she had made them wear.

'I'm going on the roundabout!' yelled Sam.

'Auntie Glory, can you ride the seesaw with me?' pleaded Sherelle, who hadn't even her auntie's grasp of physics.

'Best you play with your brother,' said Glory, ignoring a whine of little-girl protest.

The playground stood behind a low fence in the shadow of the Windmill pub. A handful of children were already there, young enough to take the rain as part of the game. Two or three women stood under umbrellas, buggies idling, watching sullenly or talking into phones.

Sherelle made a beeline for the slide. Sam went for the roundabout, then changed his mind at the swings. As the shower eased to a spatter, he wrestled out of his anorak. Glory tucked it under her arm while he sat on a swing, begging her to shunt him higher.

When the rain passed the sunshine returned, bringing others with it. Squirrels scuttling between the trees; crows shuffling like sand-dancing pallbearers. Glory left Sam to himself as she reluctantly helped Sherelle onto the tiny seesaw. She took the other end in her hands and hefted it up and down, in the manner of a silent-movie star escaping a train. She could only keep it up for a minute.

A little white girl appeared at her side, watching solemnly.

'Want a go?' puffed Glory.

'No, thank you. I want to sit on it.'

Glory said nothing as she moved aside and let the girl climb aboard.

Sam had found a playmate, too. The boy was smaller than him, wearing a blue football strip and red rubber boots. He was trying to whirl the roundabout singlehanded. Sam jumped off and gave it an extra push.

'Auntie Glory!' he yelled, holding her eyes for as much of the rotation as his neck would allow. 'Come and help!'

Still out of breath, Glory took a grip on the rail and gave the roundabout a heave. The other boy tried to match her, and the more they pushed the more Sam egged them on – till a mighty shove sent the smaller boy sprawling on all fours.

Glory froze, waiting for him to bawl … Before she could help his nanny appeared, all stringy red hair and daisy-button jeans. She bent to scoop him up, putting half her backside on display as she comforted him.

Foreign; another Polish, and too skinny for her own good.

The nanny twitched her chin at Glory, then led the boy away without a word.

As she carried on spinning, Sam lay back on the roundabout with his head at the hub, looking up at the sky.

'You'll make yourself sick,' she warned. 'You'll—'

Then she spotted them. Two figures at the edge of the Common, crossing the track joggers had worn into the grass. Jan's narrow shoulders and swinging hips were unmistakable. The other was a male, with hands in his pockets and a limp that looked affected.

That mouthy caretaker's boy!

Jan was in her uniform, minus the tabard. The boy, whose name Glory could never remember, was carrying a knapsack and umbrella. She could read Jan's mood even at this distance – she was pleased about something. Glory remembered her theory that the boy had designs on her. She wondered at the news they had come to break.

Jan gave her a wave, but the boy looked as moody as ever, head bobbing away to an imaginary beat. He flipped the umbrella behind his neck, furling a hand over either end like an old-fashioned dairy maid with a yoke. As he got closer, Glory sensed something more than just his usual cockiness.

An ice-cream van had appeared with the sunshine, parking enticingly near the playground with its music-box tune looping gaily. Glory felt in her pocket for change. The children were happy for now, but lollies would be a distraction if the grown-up talk dragged on.

''Allo, Glory,' said Jan. 'How you keeping?'

She managed a smile. 'Gettin' on with it, you know.'

They chose an empty bench from where she could watch the children. Jan sat in the middle. No touching between her and the caretaker's boy, Glory noticed. He tried to loll back casually, then remembered his knapsack.

'Mustn't be long,' said Jan. 'Molyneux's on the warpath.

The Hall only got a B from the inspectors – course it's everyone's fault but hers. Anyway, listen. We think we've got to the bottom of your little mystery …'

Glory's eyes widened. The caretaker's boy smiled at last, bouncing the umbrella between his kneecaps as Jan explained.

'I been keeping an eye out while you're away. Day before yesterday, I was working with the new girl. Lesley-Anne – you know, with the big fat hips?' Jan disliked her body shape, particularly on other people. 'And twice I had to tell her off for the way she was lifting. Grabs the old dears like she's loading a dustcart! Anyway, yesterday I'm taking Daisy to the toilet, and I see these bruises on her arm – *just like the ones Pearl had!* They were right where Lesley-Anne had been manhandling her!'

Glory took it in. 'Well, that makes sense, but …' It explained the bruises, but not why Lesley-Anne would go around frightening old ladies in the night; the last time, she hadn't even been on duty. 'Have you told Mrs Molyneux?'

'I was gonna. But then I got talking to Errol, and he told me something else.'

She sat back.

The boy took his cue without looking over. He tossed his head in the direction of the Hall.

'I been workin' round the back, tidying the garden. Them bushes by the terrace ain't been pruned in years – some of them's high as your head.' He swung the knapsack off his shoulders and slid open the drawstring. 'An' I found this ...'

Inside was a supermarket carrier bag. When Glory went to take it out, he pulled away.

'*Uh-uh.* Evidence!'

Errol hooked the handle of the umbrella through one polythene handle and teased it apart. Inside was a bale of clothing, mismatched and crumpled: blouses, a slipper, ladies' underwear – and something in lilac wool that looked familiar.

'That's Pearl's cardigan!' said Glory.

He smiled, his crucifix slapping gently against the knapsack.

'I been through it all,' said Jan. 'With rubber gloves. It's all the stuff that went missing!'

'But how did it get in the garden?'

'Aye,' said Errol leaning back, 'that was the mystery …' He ran his arms along the back of the bench. 'I been watchin', watchin' all the time. An' yesterday, while I's tidying the shed, I sees him through the window.'

He was loving the role of the great detective. Glory played along.

'*Who?*'

'Old Archie. Come to check on his treasures. *Him a knicker nicker!*'

He chuckled, stretching out in his mucky boots.

Glory was lost for words.

Jan was off again. 'Now, what I reckon is, Archie's been helping himself to the ladies' bits and pieces in the night. You know how quietly he wanders about!'

Errol nodded. 'He pinches your shoe when you're asleep in that chair. Then he go lookin' through Pearl's smalls – she calls for help, an' he drops it on the way out.'

That was his theory and he was pleased with it.

It was possible, at a push … Poor, confused Archie; who knew what went on in his head while he was drumming on that wall?

The boy's eyes were smiling. 'So I'll put this back in the bushes,' he said. 'Then you can go see Molyneux, an' if you want, we can show her together.'

He was excited. Glory chided herself for judging him hastily.

Jan looked at her watch. It was time she got back.

'*Auntie Glory!*'

Sam was at the top of the climbing frame. Sherelle was swinging from the low bar, scuffing her trainers.

'Can we have a' ice cream?'

Glory turned to Jan. 'Wait – I can't come now. But I'll find someone to mind the kids and come tomorrow, okay?'

The others nodded.

'Thank you for this ... Thank you, both of you!'

She gave Jan a hug, then realised the caretaker's boy might expect one too. But he was shrugging on the knapsack, his cool, moody self again. He read her mind:

'I don't need no hug, Glory.' He nodded to the pub across the playground. 'But you can take me for that drink one o' these days ...'

III

'Do you think you might have taken her number down wrong?'

The policeman was standing at the mantelpiece. His voice was deliberate, as if he was addressing a kindergarten class.

'I doubt it,' said Tony.

'Worth trying a few combinations,' said the policewoman. 'Very common to reverse the last two digits.'

They had told him their names and he'd forgotten already, not least because he'd hardly slept last night. It was nearly lunchtime, but Tony wondered if he should offer them tea. The English always did in Agatha Christie.

The male officer flipped back through his notebook and scanned the statement again. 'So, Mr Torrence … You let a lady you don't know into a flat you don't own. Where she helps herself to two thousand American dollars you didn't know you had.'

'Yeah … no,' Tony floundered. 'See, it's not my money. It belongs to the guy who owns the apartment.'

'Who's in New York,' finished the policewoman helpfully.

She was looking round at the living room from the couch, for clues or just out of nosiness. She was ridiculously young, wearing too much makeup. Tony wondered if the careers adviser had pushed her into the police force away from hairdressing. Her colleague was older and smelt of fags. His belly peeped out under his regulation bulletproof in a white cotton smile.

'And according to what the young woman told you, she's a New Zealander like yourself, a singer, staying with friends locally. Anything else?'

Tony racked his brains.

'They've got a dog.'

'Who has?' asked the policeman.

'The guys she's staying with. It's called … Ethel.'

The officer's Biro didn't budge.

'Have you got any photographs?' piped the policewoman.

'She means *of the lady*!'

His tone wasn't necessary.

'No,' said Tony, 'I haven't. I only met her twice. I asked her in for a sandwich while we talked about her – love life.' (Jeez, he wasn't getting into all that!)

The officers exchanged glances until the policewoman's radio crackled like a talkative corsage. She walked to the window and mumbled as the policeman said:

'Do you normally … Does *your mate* normally keep large amounts of currency lying around?'

'I don't know. I don't think so. He had to pay people in New York.'

'Oh?'

'Business associates.'

'*Oh?*' His pen was moving again. 'And what's the nature of these business associates, if you don't mind me asking?'

He was enjoying this a little too much.

'Actually,' said Tony, 'they're jugglers!'

It came out with more force than he intended.

The lady PC swung round. 'We're only trying to help you, Tony. There's no need to—'

'No, look: they really *are* jugglers! It's for a business presentation. He's—'

'I see.' The policeman snapped shut his notepad. 'I think we've got all we need. I presume the householder's insured?'

'I guess so.'

'Won't do him any good, because there hasn't been a forced entry.'

Shit.

'Best thing he can do is see if his employers are covered. Obviously we'll keep an ear to the ground, but our best chance of catching this young woman is if you keep an eye out yourself. Presumably she's local, and only you know what she looks like.'

The female PC picked their helmets off the couch and passed the bigger one to her colleague. 'Now, we're not asking you to apprehend anyone. If you see her, give us a call and we'll take it from there ...'

They were halfway down the hall before she finished speaking, heavy boots tapping on the laminate with an echo you didn't get from Nikes.

'And when your mate gets home from his meeting with P.T. Barnum,' said the man, 'tell him to keep his wad out of sight in future. Seventy per cent of burglaries are opportunistic.'

He opened the front door, unable to stop himself making way for the lady. As she stepped through, the policewoman fixed Tony with a reproving stare that looked wrong on a twelve-year-old.

'But, of course, it's not burglary if you let them in, is it, Tony? If I were you, I'd get to know your lady friends a bit before you let them loose on your worldly goods.' She popped on her helmet like something from a dressing-up box. 'Sort of thing we usually have to warn the gays about ...'

Tony watched from the curtains as they got into the squad car. The roof lights fired up as they pulled away.

He should get himself together. Get out there, start looking for her. He hadn't a clue how big Clapham was, but surely he could cover it in a day? He'd start at the Common, or maybe the banks on the high street. Maybe she'd changed the dollars into sterling. He could run round the exchange desks, ask if they had served a woman of her description. He could—

Fuck! What was the point?

What he really needed to do was get in touch with Geoff, but how? The bozo had left his phone charger here, too, so he wouldn't be getting voicemail.

Email!

Bollocks: no computer. Tony would have to call his office, get them to break the news. Or maybe he wouldn't need to. He was due back tomorrow.

Pulling on his comfiest walking shoes, Tony reflected on how he'd decided to resign, live abroad, father a child *and* become a crime statistic, all in twenty-four hours.

Some bloody holiday this was turning out to be!

'Did the police seem hopeful?'

Geoff's head was in his hands, his elbows splayed on the kitchen table.

'Not exactly.'

Tony didn't know what else to say. It was Wednesday morning. Yesterday had passed in a blur of pavement pounding and awkward phone calls. He had even tried spotting Shelley in old INXS promos at The Glow Room, squinting so hard at YouTube the foxy waiter asked if he'd forgotten his specs.

Geoff had arrived at quarter to eight. His Diesel suitcase was by the door, handle festooned with airline tags. Neither of them had touched their muesli. Geoff was so quiet, for a moment Tony thought he'd nodded off.

Abruptly, he sat up, arching his spine till it clicked.

'Right: shower. Got a meeting at eleven.'

He detoured to the fridge, sculling the orange juice straight from the carton.

'You polished off those éclairs, I see.'

'Oh. Yeah.' (Great – more guilt.)

'Doesn't matter.' He closed the door. 'I only go in there to ogle the guy on the counter. Gives me the cream horn, just looking at him ...'

And off he went, trailing his designer-pitted suitcase.

This does not feel good, thought Tony. Accepting the hospitality of a guy you didn't even know that well, then landing him in the shit. He wondered how Geoff's agency was taking it. The MD's secretary was understanding when they spoke on the phone; had agreed, with a chortle, that they may as well cancel the courier.

The sound of sloshing drifted in from the bathroom.

'By the way,' yelled Geoff, 'Greta sends her love!'

Tony jumped at the chance of a diversion. 'You saw her? She didn't think you'd have time.'

Gel squirted from a bottle with squeaky flatulence.

'I met her for lunch while everyone else was schmoozing the clients – my name was mud over the money thing, so I was keeping out of sight.'

Tony was munching a mouthful of muesli. He slopped the rest in the bin.

'How is she?'

'Cool. Had enough of her job – needs a man, so pretty much same-as ... And she took me to this great little place in the Village. All papier-mâché dinosaurs and funky Indian music.'

Tony had introduced them in Auckland all those years ago. They'd hit it off in a needling sort of way, and met up another time when Geoff was in New York. In Greta's words, he was like Tony *'with the guard down and the volume up'*. Great in small doses, but long-term she said she preferred the original.

Tony wandered into the hall. 'No sign of her finding a beau in New York?'

'Seems not,' replied Geoff between splashes. 'Says they're all married or gay, yadda yadda. I told her: she'll meet a man in Manhattan just as she's heading into the sunset.' He reappeared in a waft of steam with a towel wrapped round his waist. His torso was skinny, with broad knobbly shoulders you could hang a hat on. 'What you doing today, anyway?'

'Keep looking for Shelley, I guess,' said Tony. Having fun while this was hanging over him would feel like getting a grope at a funeral.

Droplets flew off Geoff's chin as he shook his head. 'Don't be daft. Needle in a haystack. I know people round the corner I don't see from one year to the next.' He went to untuck his towel, then thought better of it. He seemed remarkably resigned. 'Leave it to the cops. If she makes a habit of it, they'll get her in the end.'

Habit?

Was that what she was – a serial swindler? Tony prided himself on a nose for bullshit: account execs with recurring dental problems, clients with no intention of walking-the-walk to the corporate wallet. His head must have been seriously on holiday when Shelley came along.

Geoff disappeared into the bedroom. Tony followed him halfway up the hall, putting together the question he'd been avoiding.

'Geoff – does your agency say you're liable for this? I mean, if the money was their property, maybe they can ...'

The clonk of an opening drawer.

'Doubt it. They didn't want me carrying cash in the first place. I had to twist our MD's arm. I booked the performers, so I signed for the money. My responsibility.'

The drawer shut with the hint of a slam. Tony paused a few feet shy of the bedroom. A rhomboid of sunlight falling through the door framed Geoff's shadow, arranging itself into underwear in a sequence of Charlie Chaplin knee-bends.

'It's my fault, mate. I'll pay you back.'

'We'll see,' he said breezily.

It wasn't *no*.

Geoff emerged, threading a panther-head belt onto his jeans. He hooked the metal canine through an enviably short hole.

'I reckon I can get them to dock my salary till it's paid off. Listen, Tony – I know you've got your travels to go on and everything, but we're an account director down on the BT team. Plus, if we win the Pit Stop pitch, we'll be even busier. How do you fancy a bit of freelance? I could put a word in. And if you're staying here rent-free, you can pay me back in no time!'

He was trying to sound like he'd just thought of this.

On Tony's dream itinerary, running a major telecoms account was one up from a blood transfusion in Kabul. On the other hand, paying up out of his savings would leave his travel plans dead in the water. And now he thought of it, if he was serious about settling in London, it wouldn't do any harm to make a few contacts.

'Possibility, I guess. But I'm only on sabbatical, remember. Legally, I don't think I can—'

'Don't worry about that,' said Geoff. 'Our personnel department know all the tricks. I'll have a chat with them this morning.'

And with that he went in search of aftershave.

Tony screwed up his face as the mist from a homoerotic atomiser seeped out of the bathroom. Something citrus with woody top notes ... It hung around the flat for the rest of the day, like the stench of captivity.

***g.daniels@shermansumnerinc.com* 03:13**

Hey gorgeous.

Thanks for the e! Blimey, no flies on old Geoff!! I heard about Christina Aguilera running off with his millions over brunch. So much for your sabbatical – how do you feel about working in London again?? Return to commuterville!

Personally I won't be sad to see the back of the New York subway. I always get jammed against the guy with the Christian Coalition pamphlets and the nervous leg!! Hey, how ironic is this: I go travelling to work, you go travelling to play, and as I jack my job in, you start one! Remember, don't let them sign you up for aeons and DON'T sell yourself short. Freelance means they save on sickies and holidays, remember, and that old Kiwi twang always goes down well with clients.

Anyway, drop me a line. And tell Geoff that waiter from the restaurant hasn't stopped talking about him. Tween you and me, it was only because of his T-shirt. It had fake powder burns, and military chic is SO passé in the Village, the waiter thought he was on manoeuvres!!

Luvya

Gret xxx

It was the following day. Geoff had taken the laptop to work, so Tony was back at The Glow Room. He dunked another biscuit in his blackcurrant tea. Not strictly on his diet sheet, but when he spotted Griffin's Candy Squiggles behind the counter, there was no resisting a taste of home, even at three pounds a pack. His health regime had taken a dive, though trudging the streets must have burnt a few calories. It had certainly given him time to think.

TTorrence1010@hotmail.com 14.15

Hi there sweetheart.

Yep, can't tell you how thrilled I am to be returning to paid employ. Geoff skipped in last night like a man who'd well and truly passed the buck. Said he'd cleared it with the agency and I start next week. British Telecom here I come :-(

And you're right about the irony, but fasten your seatbelt, there's more … Just as you leave the big city, I'm thinking of staying! Right now I don't know what I'd be going back to Auckland for. You're not there. Nell's on the Cape. Jarvis is off the scene, and I've had a bellyful of playing gooseberry to Don and Ricky. Time for another crack at London?

I'm working under the radar for now, but Geoff thinks they'll need a board account director soon. So I'm thinking I might nip home in a month or two, resign and rent out the apartment. And break it to Ma, of course – who'll say I'm crazy and sure to get blown up by terrorists ...

What do you reckon? Needless to say I've got all the wrong clothes, so I'll have to go shopping. Hey, shades of Geoff in NZ, remember? Stormy November and all he had was spray-on tops and ripped jeans that let the water in! Saying that, he's offered to lend me one of his Vivienne Westwood jackets, but methinks the diamanté buttons would protest too much.

Diet and exercise still on the agenda ...

Big squeeze babe.

T x

He hesitated a moment, then pressed send.

No point leaving the last Candy Squiggle … He

coaxed the crumbs from the wrapper with a wet finger.

And no point sending an email when you hadn't said what you meant …

TTorrence1010@hotmail.com **14.22**

PS BTW if you do get bored of hanging out for Mr Immaculate, I want you to know I'm ready to help. Give it a while, eh – he could be in Bali or Honolulu or wherever you land next ... But I'm just saying, I'm ready to step up to the plate (or whatever the correct crockery) if required.

T x

That evening, Geoff was in an excellent mood. He regaled Tony with tales of Prague as they flicked through his well-thumbed copy of *Spartacus*, the gay guide to the world.

'… then there's Charles Bridge which is *gorgeous*. All wooden and Gothic. It's decorated with statues of saints or kings or something. That takes you into the big square with the clock, where these little figures come out and bong the quarter hour like on *Trumpton* ...'

'On what?'

'Then there's the bars.' Geoff inhaled through his teeth as he scanned the listings. 'This one's good. Matrikks. Old bierkeller with industrial décor and drag on a Friday night. The men are fab, too – cheekbones you could chip your nails on. Half of them are rent, mind, so you leave those to the fat blokes in suits. No offence.'

'None taken,' deadpanned Tony, sipping a glass of water.

'I'm getting another beer. Sure I can't tempt you … ?'

A minute later, Geoff bounced back from the kitchen, launching himself at the couch like Jean-Claude Van Damme's little sister. He settled his glasses on the bridge of his nose and snatched back his book.

'By the way,' he said. 'Either my laptop's being attacked by a viral cowbell or you got *loads* of mail.'

Tony went to investigate. Sure enough, he'd been instant-messaged a dozen times. They were backed up on screen like a deck of cards stretching to the horizon. The alert tinkled every twenty seconds till he opened the last one. He clicked respond.

<OK OK babe, I'm here!! You still there?>

No reply. The most recent message was twelve minutes ago – Greta had probably left the office. Then suddenly:

<FUCK TONY WHERE YOU BEEN??? And why's your mobile off? It's like asking a girl to marry you, then buggering off before she can answer!!>

He frowned. Was it?

<Sorry babe. Didn't know there was a rush. What you thinking?>

<List of what I'm NOT thinking's shorter! I thought you thought we'd spontaneously combust if we had a baby together! Presume you ARE talking co-parenting? Not the full-on wedding bells & Sunday mornings washing the car in Northcote Point?!>

<That's about the size of it Matron. All I meant was, if you decide to go it alone, I'll help.>

He clicked respond again:

<In every way I mean. Money and stuff.>

Another pause.

<Wow. Dark horse! What brought this on?>

<Long story. Partly turning 40 I guess.>

<And a certain light-fingered songbird by any chance??>

<Possibly. Hey, sleep on it. No rush. My sperms ain't going anywhere. Specially at the moment.>

<Okay. Yeah, lot to think about. Everyone's popping them out like peas these days. Our Head of HR brought her baby in today. Slept under the fax machine in his Moses basket good as gold, while she sat there badmouthing the kid's father till home time. What's that about??>

Tony smiled.

<You'd be a brilliant ma, babe. Anyway, offer's there. I better go, Geoff's planning our tiki tour to the fleshpots of Prague.>

<Hang on, we haven't talked baby names!!>

<Girl's job!>

<Or schools!!>

<Plenty of time for that when you're laid up like a beached whale ...>

<And how are we gonna – you know – DO IT???>

Uh-oh. Those kind of details could definitely wait!

<OK, ducking out now to drool over Czech go-go boys. Night, babe.>

<Appreciate this, Tony. Just knowing that – well, just knowing.>

<Luvyalots! T x>

<You too (Daddio!!) Gret xxx>

That night, as he clambered onto the air bed, Tony switched on his phone. Sure enough, there were voicemails and a raft of increasingly frenzied texts from Greta. With a bit of luck, a less fiddly mobile would come with the job. He put it on the floor and switched off the lamp.

On the laptop, Geoff's screensaver of line-dancing twinks cast a friendly glow. The rash of sequinned posing pouches was still there when he shut his eyes, streaming by like a comet's tail.

Daddy Tony! What a concept!

In his head, he was cryogenically frozen at twenty-one; but for a first-time dad he was positively ancient. The guys you saw pushing prams around malls these days got younger all the time.

Doubts invaded his head under cover of darkness. Was it fair, what he was suggesting? Bringing a kid into a world where the only fatherly influence was a monthly draft in the bank account? Who would he be doing it for, anyway?

That was easy. Greta, of course; rescuing her from a life where the lofty apple of motherhood hung out of reach while every other woman munched contentedly. Behind the ballbreaker façade, she was the kindest, funniest, most dependable person he knew. The next generation needed genes like that, and he'd do anything to make her happy.

The questions kept coming. Tony turned them over for what seemed like hours; till he started to wonder if those sausage rolls were still in the bread bin. He was about to investigate when his mobile rang. The fluorescent display showed a name he wasn't expecting.

'Hello, mister …' he said warily.

'*Hi. How you doing?*' Jarvis didn't wait for a reply. '*I need to see you.*'

The guy's tone could be as clipped as his scalp. Tony did his best to sound cool.

'Well, tricky one, cos in case you've forgotten, I'm in London. Do you know what time it is?'

'*I'm at the airport.*'

'Auckland? Where you going?'

Jarvis tutted. '*Heathrow, you idiot. I just got in.*'

Tony's mind was churning. 'What? Why didn't you tell me?'

Breath exhaled into the mouthpiece. '*I'm en route to Madrid with some guys from work. We've missed the connection and we don't go till tomorrow night. I've meetings at the Hilton all morning, but I can see you after lunch.*'

Jarvis had a way of making the most inconvenient invitation sound like he was doing you a favour. Tony resisted the urge to rip out the phone battery and lob it at the wall.

Jesus! What now?

On the laptop the dancing boys disappeared as the screen tripped into power save. The little room plunged into darkness.

'OK. When?'

IV

The property was on a leafy side street in Stockwell, a perennially up-and-coming area of South London. A good-size ground-floor flat, well-proportioned with one and a half beds.

No one was home as Mari and Adam looked round. It wasn't one she was familiar with, though a safe bet the owners were gay. You developed a nose for that sort of thing in the property game. Nothing overt in this case; no muscle-man prints over the bed or half-hidden sex toys. But the décor was *minimalist with a flourish;* that mosaic splashback at the kitchen sink was straight off a makeover show.

Adam was inspecting the second bedroom.

'Nice,' he said. 'Nice and snug for a little 'un.'

He tickled the flesh over Mari's hips through her linen jacket, in the way that made her jump. 'This the bathroom?'

She followed him, consulting the Carson Hoggart spec: *Integral shower and designer radiator ... Overhead lockers in brushed aluminium ... Frosted sash to side return.*

He shoved the door, hard enough to rattle the aftershaves. Gave the room his cursory corner-to-corner glance.

'Cool.'

It was the same blanket approval he'd given every bathroom so far. Swiping the pages out of Mari's fingers, he made for the lounge.

High ceiling and cornicing, door through to the kitchen. The stereo was tiny and wall-mounted, like art. As was a TV the size of a pool table, with speakers dotted round the room for the full, cinematic effect.

'Very nice,' he said, running a finger along the telly's chamfered edge. 'D'you think they'd leave it?'

Sometimes, Mari wondered how much he saw beyond the fixtures and fittings. Adam didn't care where they lived. In fact, his commitment to finding them a home was like his commitment to their wedding: total and unquestioning, without ever dipping below the surface. His mantra since the day she said yes on Fernandina was '*Whatever you want, babe …*' Such benign disinterest was flattering in its way, and meant Mari could fix things the way she liked. But it also implied their wedding was a little treat she and her mum were arranging for themselves. Fine by Adam, as long as all he had to do was turn up on the day.

Mari had another peek at the master bedroom. The fitted wardrobe would make hers redundant, though it might squeeze in the guest room. Not 'nursery'; they wouldn't need one of those for a while.

Adam flipped to the front of the details. 'Three ninety-nine, nine-fifty. You can talk 'em down, though, eh?'

The financial side was her province too. The broker at work would do them a deal.

'Is that your way of saying we should make an offer?' asked Mari.

He shrugged. 'S'all right, innit? Parking for you – near the tube for me. Do us till we move to the sticks. How many more are we seeing?'

She sighed. 'There's that one near the Common. Three blocks from my office. Remember?'

'Oh, yeah.' He didn't. 'Whatever you want, babe ...' He looked at his watch. 'Got to get back. Meeting at half-two.' He handed back the spec and kissed her on the cheek. 'What time are you home?'

'Sevenish, if I go via Sainsbury's. Unless of course you could, er —?'

Fat chance of that!

As she pulled away from the kerb, Mari watched Adam's retreating back in the mirror. Naturally it was easier if she did the shopping. *Her having the car.*

On the face of it, living together was working out well enough. Life had resumed pretty much as before they went travelling. They had both wheedled back into their old jobs – him on a new contract at Transport for London, her behind her old desk at Carson Hoggart. This, despite Mark-James's doom-laden warning he would have Mari's shoes filled before she took off from Heathrow. It was hard to see how jacking in her job had been the big mistake he promised it would be, considering the relief on his face when she walked back in three months on.

And since they were engaged, moving Adam in had seemed the logical next step. His flatmate Phil had given notice; and though Adam made noises about finding a replacement, she knew his heart wasn't in it. He was in her place within a fortnight, lock, stock and bachelor habits.

To be fair, he'd done as she asked and ditched a mountain of junk. They managed the move in a single trip, including his precious crate of rap CDs, now consigned to her communal loft. It was a perk of having a scruff for a fiancé that accommodating his entire wardrobe meant her sacrificing just twenty centimetres of hanging space.

She was hard on him sometimes, she knew that. But Mari liked to think she was not the kind of girl you could manipulate. She'd let Adam move in for the same reason she was marrying him: it felt right. For her.

She had learned two things, that faraway day on the

panga with the creepy sailor. For all his faults, she felt safer with Adam around. And that niggling voice at the back of her head was wrong; she was done with other men. Why bother, when exploring further afield only led you into a mire of uncertainty? Mari only had to look at people she knew with exotic, quick-fire sex lives to know that settling down spared you endless emotional conundrums.

The traffic was moving fast on the main road. Past Clapham North station, the Carson Hoggart *For Sale* signs were holding their own. For her branch this was their manor, though that new block by the gym was bristling with competitors' boards. It was a sign the market was tight, but also a good time to buy, even for first-timers like Adam. And when they did, Mari had already decided she was keeping her flat as a little investment. He might not like it, but it made sense. To her.

Clapham High Street had long since lost its way. It hardly deserved the name any more. It was all takeaways, bars and charity shops; nowhere you could buy a watch battery or a blouse without three previous owners. As she drew up at the lights, she spotted that wino she used to see every day. Propped up against Wok-World noodle bar in his filthy old jacket. Same stringy old dreads and that bird's nest of a beard. He was one bit of squalor she'd been pleased to leave behind on their trip of a lifetime. Now she was back and he'd never been away.

At the end of the high street, the first slivers of green appeared. Her office had an uninterrupted view of the Common, or did from the top floor where the lorries and double-deckers passed unseen. Carson Hoggart occupied the middle of three units, between an Asian convenience store and a tandoori. Mark-James enjoyed telling anyone as un-PC as he was they were surrounded *'like Kitchener at Mafeking'*. Mari was fairly sure Mafeking was in Africa, and always meant to check Wikipedia.

Approaching the office, she drummed her engagement ring on the steering wheel. Made a mental note to book them a viewing of that flat up the road. It sounded hopeful and Adam would love it; this was even nearer the tube than the last one.

She sighed again as she parked the car. Under any other circumstances, such an undemanding client would be a dream come true.

A row of backs greeted her as she walked in. The full complement of Carson Hoggart staff were gathered at Mark-James's desk, with the exception of Melissa, his PA, who was in the back, manning the switchboard audibly.

A dozen faces turned her way as Mark-James sniped, 'There you are, Mari. We've started without you ...'

Her boss's pernicketiness had gone up a notch since she got back. Not even a rise in sales, for which she took much of the credit, was enough to please him. He was making one of his announcements. The all-staff memo had been on her desk that morning: *Team Talk 2 p.m.* How could she have forgotten?

Mari mugged an apology and waved the car keys, implying some blameless mechanical setback. Mark-James was perched on the desk, left buttock achingly close to a drawing pin.

'As I was saying ... We're under the cosh from Head Office and it's not just us. I'm talking the entire South-East sector, Reading to Maidstone. Punters aren't biting and year-on-year figures are down. So – *consequently* – I've had a fight on my hands to get this appointment approved, but get approval I have.'

Nodding from the front row.

'Now, some of you may see this as reason to panic.' The nodding stopped. 'Since it also means another knife to cut the cake with. But – and this is the point – it's a cake we have to *grow between ourselves* …' Mark-James could string out a topic like a lonely widow. 'So, ladies and gentlemen, without further ado I give you Felix! Think of him not as another knife – but as *the yeast*!'

These final words he delivered with a wobble of incipient jowls. Mark-James was the very image of a young Churchill, had he ever addressed Parliament in a Cecil Gee shirt and rowing-club braces. Mari craned her neck to see the subject of this drum roll; he was hidden by the filing system until he leaned forward and said:

'Actually, it's pronounced *Fey-leece*.'

His voice brought a shudder to the pit of her stomach; it was warm and unmistakably Hispanic, if at odds with his appearance.

Mark-James didn't care to be corrected. For a long moment, the only sound was the unseen Melissa, munching crisps. He wavered on the edge of his desk.

'Right. Well, I think we all got that! Now, *Fee– Fe-leez* – comes to us from Keenlyside & Gupta on Battersea Bridge Road, where he's been heading up their Lettings division with great success. I'm sure he won't mind me saying *that*!' Each man's eyes flickered in the other's direction without making contact. 'And while he'll be filling the gap left by our good friend Derek Brady, experience tells me that a man of his ... *experience* can take on a bit more of the load than dear departed Derek.'

People were bored. Half-eaten tuna niçoise baguettes were receiving longing looks.

'So with this in mind, Felix joins us as deputy branch manager, with a particular remit to grow the lettings side of our business.' He scanned the room for appreciation. '*Bigger cake*, you see … Good. Well, I'm sure you all want to introduce yourselves to the new boy. Don't get too excited ladies, he's engaged! Lot of it about at the moment, Felix!' Mark-James fired a Mr Smoothie-wink at Mari. 'I'd get your honeymoon on the holiday chart sharpish if I were you. Right, that's all … Phones, everyone. *Thanks, Melissa!*'

Mari sat at her desk. She checked her diary, even though she knew her schedule to a T. She watched the office junior take out a nail file and set to work on a troublesome claw, one eye on the incoming-call lights. Saw Mark-James unhook his slate-grey blazer from its hanger and slot it over one shoulder. Looked everywhere, in fact, except at Felix.

Melissa was back in her seat and taking him through the database, managing to be flirty and superior all at once. She was over-enunciating, as if the only Spanish speakers she'd ever met were nannies and cleaners. The sensation in Mari's stomach had risen to her chest, where it hovered like an obstinate burp. She caught his handsome reflection in the window display. His hair was fair and wavy, skin more almond than olive. Down on his haunches for a better view of the screen, Felix took up the slack in his well-cut trousers to reduce the risk of knee-sag.

Melissa switched from aloof to perky; the new boy knew his stuff. He also had an easy way with questions, holding her gaze as she answered and he learned what he needed to know. Soon she was doing that thing with her head: turning away slightly and resting her chin on her collar bone, her default posture when asking Mark-James for time off to go shopping. Felix nodded, his elbows spreading along the edge of the desk as he hung on her every, burbling word.

It was only when he stood that Mari realised how tall he was. Six-four at least, the top end of off-the-peg sizing. And that petrol-blue suit fitted him very nicely indeed … He moved on to the next desk, the junior with the nail file, and took her hand. For a moment, Mari thought he was going to kiss it. He introduced himself politely in the unlikely event she had forgotten him. The office desks were arranged in the shape of a horseshoe; or, if you believed Mark-James, a magnet, with prongs open towards the door to draw in waverers. Two desks to go and he'd be round to Mari.

Her anxiety mounted. It was like waiting to meet the Queen at the London Palladium. She wondered if she should pop to the loo.

The door opened with a two-tone bleep. A middle-aged woman who'd been scrutinising the window was braving the threat of being sold to. But before anyone could greet her, Felix broke off his conversation, engaging her with a smile so genuine it looked out of place.

Mark-James was at Mari's elbow, admiring Felix's style.

'Lovely opener! That's my boy,' he whispered, like he had taught him everything he knew. 'Free for drinks tomorrow night, Mari, yes?' Her heart skipped a sickly beat; he saw it. 'We're *all* going! I thought we'd pop to the Windmill about seven. Bit of a double-edged bash. Give Felix a proper Carson Hoggart welcome, plus it's my birthday at the weekend. Which I'm sure you haven't forgotten ...'

'I'd love to,' blurted Mari, 'only Adam and I are—'

'Don't worry, you can bring 'im indoors. It's karaoke – he can give us his Emin-Ad!' He guffawed, shuffling into his jacket. 'Right, I'm out for the afternoon ... Melissa, on my BlackBerry if you need me!'

His PA mumbled, still agog at Felix's customer care.

The door bleeped behind Mark-James. He strode across the paving, briefcase swinging, and flipped the locks of the Audi.

Mari rummaged for the spec she needed for her three-fifteen. She checked her watch. The house was on Brierley Road, Balham, and she was meeting the viewers there. Traffic was picking up, so she would be as well to —

'And you must be Mari!'

She swivelled her chair and stared directly into a petrol-blue crotch.

'Very pleased to meet you,' said Felix, offering his hand. It was warm and eggshell smooth. 'How is your day going?'

He dispensed with the full introduction, perhaps in deference to her status. Mari was the obvious choice for deputy branch manager, a matter she would be raising with Mark-James at the earliest opportunity.

'Oh, busy, busy!' she said pleasantly, letting go of his hand. 'Actually I've got to pop out again. I hope everyone's being helpful.'

Felix nodded. 'I'm sure I'll soon be in the swing of things.'

His grasp of English was as confident as his handshake. According to the memo, his name was Felix Martin, which didn't sound that Spanish at all. There was nothing very Hispanic about his appearance, either.

Mari found herself prolonging the conversation out of politeness. 'How long have you been in London?'

'About five years. Since I finished my degree. I was staying with my mum's family – never went back.' The next question he fielded before it passed her lips. 'I'm from Buenos Aires. Have you ever been to South America?'

Mari smiled. *'Por supuesto. Estuve recientemente en las Islas Galápagos ...'*

How ironic was that!

Mari was sipping a rum and coke under the big screen in the Windmill annexe. Adam wasn't a karaoke person at the

excuse to sidestep a night out with her office lot. He'd be on the settee with a lager right now, little knowing he could be watching it here in wall-mounted glory. If she called him, it was only ten minutes in a cab. Then again, he wouldn't get changed, and Mark-James would have a field day over his trackie bottoms.

She slipped the mobile back in her bag. It wasn't eight o'clock yet. The karaoke began at half past. Barring two eager beavers who'd snapped up the chance to do the evening viewings, everyone from work was here ... Melissa was holding court on a torn banquette, filling in the girls on her holiday plans (seven nights in a spa hotel in Borneo, plus bolt-on to the orang-utan sanctuary). As if they didn't know; she'd made all her arrangements from the office, with a running commentary loud enough to drown out the roadworks.

A familiar laugh drifted in from the bar. Mark-James, carousing with the lad trainee. It was girls over here and boys over there, just like school. To give him his due, the boss was generous with the rounds, and he always sloped off as soon as everyone was too drunk to notice.

Felix reappeared beside him. To Mari's disappointment, he'd been outside for a fag. He looked too clean-cut for a smoker. Lovely skin, though – for now. And, as she'd observed through the window as he took his coffee break by the post box, a cigarette did rather suit him. He looked like those men in adverts from the 1950s. She wondered if he played polo too. Argentinians did, didn't they? And he had the legs for jodhpurs.

She smiled to herself; she could look at him now without feeling a thing! The flurry of yesterday had gone, whatever that had been about. Jorge Luis had cured her of any grumbling desire for Hispanic manhood. And now she looked closer, there was something a bit *inbred* about

Felix ... Weak chin, her mother would say, letting down his otherwise fine bone structure.

Mari tutted. Just as well, really; troublesome eye candy was the last thing she needed as she embraced her future with Adam. As she sipped her rum and coke, she looked around – and immediately averted her eyes from the bar.

The three of them were looking over. Mark-James was saying something, probably vulgar and at her expense. He lurched abruptly, slopping his pint as someone jogged him from behind. The culprit, a gangly student shouldering an amplifier, received his best rowing-eight-on-the-start-line glare. The boy nodded an apology as he eased past, followed by two more grungy types either end of a mixing desk they were manoeuvring into the next room.

The karaoke had arrived.

Mark-James dried himself on the drip mat. Then the male contingent came through to join the ladies. He and the trainee slid in beside Melissa; Felix took the chair next to Mari, pausing to take the cigarettes from his back pocket and put them on the table. His knees wouldn't fit underneath and he angled them towards her as he spoke.

'So, the local pub. Do you come here often?'

Mari scrutinised him for irony. There was none.

'A few times a year. We sit outside if it's nice. Except when Mark-James insists on serenading us.'

Felix laughed. His aftershave lent the taint of cigarette smoke a sophisticated edge. 'Will you be doing a number?'

She exhaled sharply, making her ice rattle. 'You must be joking! That's only for very special occasions.'

'Don't tell me – your hen night, right?' He looked down at her engagement ring. 'Nice. Sapphires, no?'

Mari swallowed, though her mouth was empty. *Talk about déjà vu!*

She gathered herself. 'I hear you're getting married, too.'

'Yeah, six weeks. August fifth.'

'Oh, not long. Your fiancée must be in a state!'

Felix looked surprised. 'Actually, I'm doing the arrangements myself.' He sipped his drink, something tall and tawny red.

The urge to compare notes was irresistible.

'How long have you been engaged?' asked Mari.

'Three years. She was my English tutor.' He turned the pack of Silk Cut end over end like an egg timer.

'*More drinks!*' brayed Mark-James. 'Another rum, Mari? And one of those poof's drinks for you, Felix?'

He pronounced it *Fleece*.

Felix nodded without turning round, raising one eyebrow to Mari.

'I did an English course when I came to London. Language school in Islington. Got good grades in everything except conversation, because every time I spoke to Sandra I clammed up.' His words had the rhythm of an oft-told story. 'I asked her out after the last exam and she's been giving me marks out of ten ever since …'

Mari laughed politely. She wondered what score he was getting these days. She was about to relate her own experience of language teaching when he asked:

'And what about you? How did you meet your fiancé?'

She told him; though eyes across a crowded uni canteen didn't have quite the glamour of meeting your soulmate on the other side of the world.

'What does he do?' asked Felix.

Mark-James interrupted as he returned with the drinks: 'What does who do – Adam, the rapping homeboy? *Literally* now, isn't he, darling? I hear you finally moved him in.'

Mari ignored him. Mark-James was a lightweight for booze, a quirk he ascribed to his near-Olympian fitness. He tottered back to the bar for the rest of the round.

Felix sighed. 'Sometimes I think Sandra and I moved in too quickly.'

'Really?' She leapt on this new strand of conversation like a kitten.

He nodded. 'It was all my idea. I had to move out of my aunt's place and she didn't like where she was living, so ... We got a place together and that was that.'

There was something bitter about the way he gazed into that glass. Mari tried to make light of it.

'Well, you wouldn't be getting married if you had any qualms. As in—' She floundered for an equivalent word in Spanish. It wasn't necessary.

'We're having a baby in December.'

'Come on, you two!' bellowed Melissa. 'Time for a sing-song!'

The backing track to 'Tainted Love' throbbed through from next door. Everyone else was on their feet, with varying degrees of reluctance.

'You too, Felix!' wheedled Mark-James. 'I know for a fact they've got "La Bamba".'

Felix cringed. For the first time, Mari thought he looked out of his depth. 'We'll be through in a minute,' she said, holding up her drink. 'Just finish these.'

The boss took Melissa's arm, muttering: '*Effing wedding bores ...*'

Mari watched them go, spinning the ice inside her glass like riders on the wall of death.

'Baby not planned, then?'

He shook his head. She wondered if he'd still be wearing that expression in August.

Felix knocked back his drink. 'We should be in there.'

'No hurry,' she said. 'We're safe till Melissa does her "Happy Birthday, Mr President". If you're not there to clap, you won't get a cream cake tomorrow.'

He looked bemused. He might have picked up the database, but Carson Hoggart's birthday rituals would take a little longer. Mari was secretly delighted he hadn't looked at the football once.

'Can I have a cigarette?' she said.

Outside, the white lamps along the path painted fish scales on the pond.

On warm summer nights, the terrace at the Windmill was young Clapham's watering hole of choice. There was one table left, but instead Mari led Felix to the fence of overlapping planks that partly hid the bottle banks.

'What are you afraid of?' he asked. 'Paparazzi?'

She blew out a plume of smoke. 'I don't want that lot seeing me smoke. Mark-James is a fitness nut. Only dates women who spend half their life on a treadmill.'

He smiled. 'Not jealous, surely?'

She almost choked. 'Mark-James? Give me a break.'

Felix laughed. '*Give me a break!*' His stab at Yankee intonation made him sound more out of place than ever.

Mari looked up at the sky. It had rained that afternoon, but the night was clear and alive with stars.

'You in tomorrow?'

Felix shook his head. 'They say it's going to be a hot one. Are you?'

She caught his eye again. Another innocent slip.

'Second shift. One o'clock start.'

They watched as a plane rumbled overhead, night lights flickering like a faulty Christmas star.

'So, I guess Adam doesn't smoke?'

'Oh no, he does! Ten a day, regular as clockwork. He has to go outside since I had the curtains cleaned.'

Felix rolled the cigarette thoughtfully between his fingers; not cupped away from a nonexistent breeze.

'Don't you ever smoke with him?'

'Nope. Gave up when we left uni. I'd never hear the end of it if he thought I did.'

He nodded. 'Sandra smoked until she got pregnant. Now she looks at me like I'm injecting heroin. But why don't you, if you want to?'

Mari took a drag on the shrinking stub, conscious of the metallic tang on her fingers. Soap and mints before she got home …

'Dunno. Adam wants to give up. I guess till he does, I've always got one over on him.' She'd never said it out loud before. 'Does that sound terrible?'

But Felix was looking away.

'*Over there!*' he said

He was pointing over the fence. Past the bottle banks, to where the wheelie bins were lined up like drunken soldiers.

'Where am I looking?'

He put a hand on her shoulder. Brought his face close to hers, one eye shut against the jet stream of his smoke.

'*There!*'

Mari felt his breath on her ear.

A skittering sound, as the beam from a car's headlights slid over the bins, then a gleam of brownish red.

'Foxes, see?'

She framed her hands over her eyes to block out the glare from the street lamp. Sure enough, two shapes were skulking in the overflow of rubbish. One had something white in its mouth – a bone or a bit of bread.

Felix was entranced; more than it warranted to her mind. (Didn't they have foxes in Argentina?)

He clenched her shoulder suddenly.

'And look – *a baby!*'

His voice was soft, quavering with excitement. His other hand rested on her arm. Mari felt the pressure of his lean torso against her shoulders. She snatched a breath; it was fetid and reproving.

Bad girl! One cigarette was quite enough ... This was all distinctly weird. Surreal, and not helped by the fact this cigarette was making her feel a bit sick. Any more to drink and she'd end up making an absolute-

'Nice one, Felix! You should hear the grief I get when I ask her to take the rubbish out ...'

The fag butt leapt from Mari's fingers like a smuggled ruby. Behind them, Mark-James's lips twitched with a smile he couldn't quite keep in check.

'Come on!' he said, 'Melissa's up next!'

TWO

I

Carla was pressing the off button on the cordless phone as Ian came down for breakfast. He was wearing old jogging bottoms, his second-best loafers and a faded T-shirt.

'That was Raj,' she said. 'All go on the boat, apparently. Mitch is making hay before he gets ejected. He and the understudy hit it off immediately and spent the night on the top bunk; Suki slept in the galley under the fibreglass fire blanket, which has brought her out in hives; and Mitch concussed himself trying to put a sock over one of the cameras.'

Ian went to make toast with his wife in pursuit.

'And to cap it all, the doctor paddled out in a canoe, capsized and didn't roll up again, so the new girl jumped in in her underwear! Now she's making cow eyes at the cameras, rubbing herself all over with Deep Heat. No fool, obviously.'

He detected a hint of jealousy.

'Raj won't say how they're explaining me away, so we'll have to watch. Mind you, I'll be old news if the scandal quotient's up, so the quicker we get in the papers the better.' She handed him the butter dish. 'Which reminds me, they're sending round the contract at half-eleven. Talking about teaser pieces tomorrow, an exposé on Sunday, then the full-on feature in the midweek lifestyle section ...'

She frowned suddenly, looking Ian up and down. She ran her fingers through his hair like a nit nurse.

'You need a haircut. We've got an interview this afternoon and they're bound to want photos. I wonder if Plush can fit me in for a body scrub while we're at it – I still stink of peat, can you smell it?' She waved a wrist under his nose. 'And a manicure …'

She went to fetch the phone again.

'Carla, we need to talk.'

'I know, just let me—'

'No,' said Ian, taking the receiver and putting it back in the cradle. 'Now!'

She let him shepherd her to the sofa and looked irritated as he stood at the mantelpiece. He launched in before she could say another word.

'Look, I don't think we should be rushing into the first thing Raj proposes. I've had a chat with another journalist. You only get one bite at something like this, and—'

Her spine jolted to attention. 'Other journalist? Who?'

'Maisie O'Grady.'

Carla's eyes narrowed. 'The one Raj calls the Rottweiler? Are you mad – why did you do that?'

'Well, I just … I think we should explore our options.'

Five minutes ago, he had his argument pieced together. Now he couldn't even find the corners.

'*Ian!*' she squawked. 'Raj is talking about eight and a half grand for an exclusive – life on the boat, and how yearning for my husband pushed me overboard! Then there's the follow-up on the secrets of our marital passion – it's all right, someone else is writing that – and maybe my own column! Why the hell would I want to talk to another journalist?'

He thrust his hands in pockets and looked like he was trying to touch his chin with his bottom lip. This was going to be tricky … Carla's hands were neatly folded. She was waiting for whatever he was holding back.

Which meant it wasn't tricky at all.

'Maisie's got pictures.'

She took a full five seconds to react.

'Go on.'

He swallowed hard. 'I met someone while you were away. A woman. Nothing major, I was going to tell you … It was just – one of those things.'

'Oh? One of what things?'

Her voice was soft and measured, the way he hated. Tai bloody chi had a lot to answer for.

'One of those things we talked about. Like you and your Malteser!'

'*My* Malteser?'

'Well, who else's is he?'

Her body sagged, as if someone had pulled the plug.

Ian's words tumbled out. 'Carla, I'm not excusing myself, but I swear: I never meant this to happen. It could've been either of us, any time – couldn't it? For some fucking reason it was me, and it was now, and I'm really, really sorry! I—'

'Where did you meet her?' Her voice had decayed to a whisper.

'Eh? It *doesn't matter*, it's finished! Anyway, somehow this bitch journalist has got hold of photos.'

'What sort of photos?'

'Not that sort! Just pictures of the two of us.'

'So?'

'We were – embracing.'

Carla took a breath. And held it.

'And what's this Maisie woman going to do with them?'

Oh God. Straight to the gaps in his knowledge, as usual.

'I dunno; we didn't get that far. Hang onto them probably, till your marital-bliss piece hits the newsstands, then print them so it looks like a sham. That's what they always do, isn't it? Build 'em up, knock 'em down ...'

Carla nodded slowly. She was back on form, icily cool in a crisis.

'But she won't if I talk to her instead. Is that it?'

'Yes. Sort of. It's a bit more complicated than that.'

Her eyes were asking the question for her.

Ian cleared his throat. 'I told her you left the boat because you're pregnant.'

Her mouth fell open. 'Christ, you *are* mad! What happens when she finds out you lied?'

(Calm, Ian. Stay calm!)

'Well – she doesn't have to, does she?'

Her jaw dropped even lower in a silent laugh.

'What, you mean I fake it? Start throwing up all over the place?'

'No. Well, yeah, but only for a week or so. Till she's run her bloody article and the cheque's in the bank.'

Carla was speechless; he ploughed on.

'Then we say you lost it ... Look, you want a baby anyway, so in the meantime we keep trying. With a bit of luck you'll get pregnant, and if we keep her interested she gets another story and you get paid again!'

Still she said nothing. Ian was getting desperate.

'Carla, it's still a way into the papers! Maybe she can get you a column, too. We can talk to her about—'

'Just like that?'

A trickle through the floodgates.

'Eh?'

'Fake a pregnancy, fake a miscarriage, make a baby, sell pack of lies to the tabloids. *Just like that?'*

Ian's attention drifted through the French windows; that magnolia needed pruning ...

'You say it like you've found a way of dodging VAT on the fucking compost! How could you be so stupid? And why now, eh? I thought affairs didn't interest you!'

'They didn't. I mean—'

'You've had all these years to punish me, but oh no – you have to go and do it now!'

'I was not trying to—'

A second later, Carla was standing in front of him.

'What's this really about? Is it sex?' She was turning nasty. 'Feeling your age, Ian – or did you just fancy a bit of an adventure? Get your own back on old Carla for gallivanting off on the telly!'

They were toe to toe; her chin was up as she looked him in the eye. Ian was framing a reply as another look passed over her face. It was very nearly delight.

'You're sure it *was* a woman.'

He drew back.

'That you've been dallying with? As opposed to …' Her eyes dropped to the front of his jogging bottoms with an insolent little smile. 'Well, don't look so surprised. You know I've always had my suspicions … God, wouldn't the papers love that!'

She laughed.

And there it was. The old insinuation, the refrain of their married life. It had followed Ian around like a ticking crocodile; no matter how much of her shit he put up with, or what he did for her in bed. And, as she stood there with that taunting smile, Carla lifted the dust-sheet on a memory that had lain in darkness for all these years:

Russell Shipton in the playground!

Pinning him to the breezeblock wall of the chemistry lab as a dozen faces crowd in, pushing, shouting, goading them on! Class Sissy v. Class Fatty, in a fight to the death or humiliation …

'QUEER!'

'POOFTER!'

'BUMBOY!'

The words ring in Ian's ears as he breaks the tussle, struggling free of the sweaty fingers … Shipton draws back a podgy knee, poised to drive it into his bollocks at the next volley of taunts. But Ian catches him off balance, twisting his right arm free ... He draws back a fist with alien vigour, teetering on the brink of a brutality he's always forsworn – then he strikes the fat lad on the side of the head. The blow sends him reeling across the tarmac …

He's got him – he's going ... HE'S DOWN!

It's all over!

The crowd are cheering victory, slapping Ian's blazered shoulder and backing off one by one. But not before they egg him on to a celebratory kick of that great, beached battleship-grey arse ... Shipton squeals as Ian's battered winklepicker makes impact; begs for mercy as the laughter rings out around them, and tears trail down the scarlet pillows of his cheeks.

With sweet relief, Ian is hailed a hero – one of the gang for the first time in his eleven years! With a bit of luck, it'll last till home time …

He felt it now. Not the relief; the humiliation, a seeping powerlessness in the face of suspicion that never, ever went away. Thirty years on, the stinking irony of it was that the only person who could bring on the feeling, was also the only person who could hurt him with it.

It was all he could do not to laugh. There he was, confessing to his wife he'd been screwing another woman on the side, and what does she do?

She accuses him of being queer!

There was no escape. Gently, Ian put his hands on her shoulders. As he pushed her to one side, he whispered:

'Sign what you like. I'm only your fucking husband.'

He was out of the room and out of the house before she could say a word. He needed air … No, he didn't; he needed to drive. But the front door slammed before he remembered the car keys.

What the hell – the sky was clear and the sun was warm. It was a lovely day for a walk.

Christ. What a fucking disaster!

As he turned the corner into Haverill Road, Ian felt sympathy for any man who'd murdered his wife … Carla could – *screw herself!* He didn't doubt she'd be very good at it.

He hadn't a clue where he was going, but the reassuring pound of feet on concrete was the best legal antidote to her poison he could think of. Half of him felt an overwhelming urge to contact Agnes (no prizes for guessing which half!) He had a good mind to go straight round there. Walk into old man Wallace's house and sweep her up in his arms, like Richard Gere in *An Officer and a Gentleman.*

The other half knew he was better off just breathing. Breathing and thinking … Trying to relax before he rushed into any more complications. He wandered up the road, past the whitewashed houses with their self-important front gardens. Turned into the parade of boutiques and restaurants where three prim dress shops stood all in a row, companionable but austere, like sisters who never spoke. He paused at the window of the internet café. The one that sold the kind of cakes he never allowed himself ... Those meringue nests looked particularly enticing – high-sided and swamped with cream.

Sod cream cakes! He needed a drink!

Until his gaze drifted to the girl behind the counter. Her crop top was exposing a pierced belly button and more flesh than was strictly hygienic. It also failed to disguise her exceptionally fine breasts.

Tits, you see! Ian liked them, all right – always had!

It was just that he'd put his interest on hold while he applied himself to the thankless task of loving his wife. She of the chest of a teenage high jumper!

Perhaps he should have a cake. Line his stomach first. He looked down at his jogging pants and saggy loafers. Hardly dressed for café society … He peered in again. The computer stations were empty, but the tables were chocker, with well-bred mums resting their Jimmy Choos in a break from shopping for deli staples. Oh, two of them had just stood up … They dropped a tip in the saucer on their way out. Ian stepped back from the doorstep as the women and their armfuls of designer carriers negotiated the exit.

He was about to go in when a bearded man emerged from the kitchen with a tray of pastries. His hair was a crew cut except for a thick plume at the back. The girl smiled as he slipped behind her. He winked, saying something as she brushed icing sugar off his bestially hairy forearm.

Hussy! thought Ian.

His mobile rang. If that was Carla, she could bloody well-

'Ian! Raj Sinatra. You alone?'

He froze.

'Raj—'

'Is the wife wiv you?'

'No, she isn't. Look, whatever—'

'Whoa, mate! Hear me out first. I got a proposal …'

His tone was smooth and controlled. Ian pictured him, trainers up on a Perspex desk, surrounded by fawning bimbos with their underwear on show to the world.

'No beating round the bush. How d'you fancy nipping up to

Scotland and joining the Houseboat?'

Ian took a step back. 'Me?'

'Yeah, you! Don't worry, it ain't for long. Powers-that-be have pulled the final week. They've moved the live finale to tomorrow, so this is our last chance to give the show a kick up the ratings … And I know all about your deal wiv the tabloids, but don't worry – this way, everyone wins!'

Ian doubted he knew about all of it. He had a sudden sensation of his surroundings engulfing him, of shrinking like Alice. He closed his eyes and tried to put a meaning to the idiot's words.

'In what way would everyone win, Raj?'

A sound like a snapping G-string was probably a tut.

'Double whammy, mate! By the time you and 'er indoors have got your story in the papers, you'll both *be media babes! Twice the publicity sells twice the copies! You could end up wiv your own gardening show – how about that? I know for a fact a certain prime-time, green-fingered goddess is on her way to the Cactus Channel, courtesy of being outed as a raging lezzer … Play your cards right and there's a big opening there.'* He gurgled gratuitously. *'No pun intended. Look, fink about it – you and Clara could be the next Posh 'n' Becks!'*

'It's Carla.'

'Who is?'

'Hang on – I thought you told her everything on the boat was fine now the understudy's shagging everything in sight?'

Raj grunted. *'Uh, yeah. You rumbled me there. Look, you gotta keep this secret-squirrel, what wiv her being knee-deep in journos … Truth is, the understudy's a total drip. All she does is sit round the galley drinking tea, trying to get the others to debate the effics of organic farming. Might as well ask Mitch and Suki about the Large Hard-On Collider … And plus she gets changed under a towel with the light off, which ain't cricket in my book. Like I told her, it's only her rack got her the gig in the first place.'*

Ian was staring at the pavement. He had one foot either side of a paving crack like hopscotch, until a double buggy made a step in the gutter inevitable. It felt rather apt.

'But why me? I'm not exactly Daniel Craig, am I?'

Raj hesitated. Again Ian wondered how much he knew.

'Trust me! The bosses know what they're doing. Besides, all the research says the audience don't give two fucks about them lot! You got furty-six hours to dazzle 'em, and you could still win that seven-star cruise!'

A paper bag blew over Ian's shoe.

'I don't know, I—'

'And I didn't tell you this, but the final-night challenge just might *involve repotting ornamental heather, followed by a quiz about veggies … It's right up your alley!'*

'I'd have to—'

'Fuck's sake, Ian!' Wherever they were, Raj's teeth were clenched. *'Three grand – cheque for – on helicopter! But you've got to go now!'*

Helicopter?

Ian watched the bag bowl away on the breeze, snagging on the display board outside the beautician's. This was madness – he couldn't do it! Someone was coming to interview them this afternoon – him and Carla, all blissed-up and marital. He couldn't just zip off to Loch Ness, leave her to fend for herself like-

Like she did to him?

Three grand. It was a lot of deadheading.

'When you say now, Raj …'

'I mean now, *mate! I've got a chopper on standby at Battersea*

Heliport. Soon as I give the nod, he picks you up and it's next stop Bonnie Scotland … Where are you?'

'Just – out for a walk. Other side of Clapham.'

'Cool. Nearest open space is the Common. Head over there pronto and he'll do the swoop-and-scoop in fifteen.'

'Hang on – I need to nip home first. Grab a few bits. If I drive to Battersea, I can be there in an hour.'

'NO TIME! The flight takes free hours! I need you on the boat by five p.m. for the online feed.'

'I—'

'And listen, Ian: not a word to Clara! You're both Hell-in-a-Houseboaters now! She's still under contract whether she likes it or not … I'll give the pilot a buzz – find out where he's gonna be, yeah, so keep your mobile on. Don't make or take any calls unless it's from this number. Got it?'

'I don't think you're supposed to land helicopters on the Common, Raj. By-laws and all.'

'Fuck by-laws! Leave it to me – I know people on Lambeth Council ... Right, any more questions can wait till you get here!'

'Here?' Ian felt like the slow sidekick in an impenetrable detective drama.

'Loch Ness! *Where do you fink I am? If* Houseboat *doesn't make the top twenty this weekend, I'm gonna be cutting clips for* Hundred Worst Chat Show Blunders. *And Christ knows there's no new angles on Parky snogging that Emu.'*

'Raj, I still—'

In a three-tone electronic sign-off, he was gone.

Ian closed his phone timidly, as if it were a Fabergé clam. He felt giddy and sick like he'd been picked up, shaken and put down again.

He looked at the sky between the rooftops on the other side of Haverill Road. It was that shade his grandmother used to call mockingbird blue. He had a sudden vision of

Carla, Agnes and Maisie O'Grady, all looking down at him from the clouds and laughing their socks off … The good, the bad and the bleeding ugly.

What the fuck would Alice do?

Turning on his heel, he set off for Clapham Common.

*

Luckily for Glory, the hair-extensions lady was waiting in for the plumber.

Too many strands down the plughole, was her theory. She had no appointments till two o'clock, and if the council's man didn't put her drain to rights, she'd be cancelling those too. Either way, she would look after the kids.

Sam and Sherelle needed no persuasion. They loved visiting the flat downstairs with its bottles of dye and scented fluids, and the hanks of coloured hair that hung in the window like carnival decorations.

All well and good for today, thought Glory. But Mercy wasn't home for another week; if Mrs Molyneux let her come back to work, she'd need to find a proper minder.

She called Jan. They arranged to meet at the Hall at one o'clock, when the senior manager would be eating her onion salad. Glory wanted to be sure she'd be there without making an appointment; with people like Mrs Molyneux, it was always better to catch them off guard.

She looked around the flat. The breakfast dishes were washed and tidied away. The bathroom was spotless. Even in Mercy's room nothing was out of place. Glory let the kids sleep in the big bed while their ma was away. When she'd peeped in last night, those two solemn little heads were on the one pillow, bedclothes up to their chin like Siamese twins in the manger.

Back in her own room, she helped herself to a dab of her favourite, orange-scented skin cream. Then she made herself a cup of tea and found a bag of crisps, left over from the lunch she sent downstairs with the children.

She sat on the couch. The postman had been. Still no card from paradise. Mercy had texted when they arrived in Trinidad, and again a day later, reminding Glory to record her soaps. Since then, not a word – but she didn't begrudge her.

You had to grab your chances in this life.

Glory had never been abroad, unless you counted Wales. One day, it would be her turn. The way things were going, it was her turn in lots of ways … She'd see how it was when they got back; but if Mercy was as serious about Alfonse as he was about her, then that might well be that. Being single never bothered Glory while her sister was making a hash of her love life; by the looks of it, you were better off alone. But she wasn't sure about them all moving out, even as far as next door.

She fancied finding a man of her own one of these days. Having a baby, too. There was still time ... Mind, he'd have to be a good bit older than that caretaker's boy – Errol. Have a proper job, too; not spend his days giving cheek and shunting furniture where he was pointed. Glory liked the idea of a man with his own business. One who would insist on her having a life of leisure if that's what pleased her. Like her sister, but without scamming the Social.

She finished her crisps. Folded the bag into pleats, knotted it and threw it in the bin. Perhaps today was a sort of crossroads: this way her job, that way the dole – or worse, if Mrs Molyneux really had called the police. And turning in the other direction: this way a place of her own, and that way the rest of her life sharing a shoebox with Mercy and the kids.

Leave it for the Lord; that's what Ma would say. *What will be, will be.*

As she rinsed her mug, Glory wondered if Ma was watching her now. If she could see how hard it was for her little girl to heed those words. Inside, she was quaking like a scalded pup.

It was time she got her bus.

*

Tony's phone said quarter to midday. He felt like he hadn't slept a wink.

In three days' time, it would be an early-morning fight for the bathroom. But for now, with Geoff at work, he could dawdle. His mind was buzzing with questions as he stepped out of the shower.

If Jarvis was only passing through, why did he want to see him – was he out to rekindle? Would he greet him at the hotel with roses and room service? Or had they just left too many loose ends for his logical lawyer's mind?

Whatever. Tony had moved on.

He studied his reflection as he loaded the toothbrush. Here stood a man of forty, about to embark on a new life. Maybe even create another one, with a little help from his best friend …

Jeez – what would Jarvis say about that!

He'd given it a lot of thought in the wee small hours, and come to the conclusion he wasn't just doing this for Greta. It was for him, too. Not to leave his mark on the world, or prove himself in any macho sort of way. You only had to look at the torpid mumblers, dragging their kids round the high streets of the world, to know it didn't take much to make a baby.

No. He was doing it because he could give a child a brilliant start. And a brilliant mum. *The best.*

One thing for sure, Greta would make a better go of it than his ma ever had. Tony had never forgiven her for the long years after his dad died, when he was in middle school and she was in her bedroom … While he'd made the breakfast, walked Chippy, dropped his bro at kindergarten. Years when Ma's silences and incessant smoking cast a pall over the evening, as he and Brad did their homework.

Her lack of affection drove both sons away; steering Tony away from the fairer sex, and his brother right at it. While his serial fumblings with a boy at school had stayed under wraps, it was Brad who brought shame on the family. His not-so-little brother's deflowering of Margaret Hawkins was the talk of Waitangi Avenue – and the final, inescapable proof that Ma had failed. It took the first of many prescriptions to get her back on track, round about the time she flirted with Christianity. A flirtation she'd shrugged off just as quick when doe-eyed Margaret's miscarriage left her thankful as well as aggrieved.

That was also when Ma discovered her flair for cookery of an unspectacular kind, turning out rivers of stew and cakes by the dozen. Cooking was a conduit for all her maternal concern, backed up in years of silence. Brother Brad worked off the stodge with vigorous activity; playing rugby and chasing after more besides, his disgrace doing nothing to discourage the teenage girls of the neighbourhood.

Tony, on the other hand, was no one's idea of a rugger hunk. Bar a few more experiments with his friend, his libido lay fallow till uni. In the meantime, aged seventeen and trapped between two worlds, he took the easy option – and ate his way out. Whether gluttony upset his metabolism or merely awakened the latent hefty within, his appetite had been a problem ever since, and particularly at times of stress.

Like in the last few days, as his anxiety coalesced into peanut-butter bagels, pastries and full English breakfasts.

Indulgences that were shamefully evident now, thought Tony, as he stood at the mirrored door of Geoff's coffin-sized vanity unit. He hadn't exercised in days and it showed.

He hopped on the scales.

Ninety-eight kilos! Up one and a half!

Tony didn't know what Jarvis wanted, or even if he cared. But he did know he didn't want his ex to see him fat.

They were meeting at three o'clock. The subway to Heathrow would take just over an hour. Tony had to decide what to wear, iron a shirt and pick up some groceries for Geoff. He checked his watch.

No worries. He had exactly one hour to lose weight.

*

The weathermen got it right for once. By half past twelve it was as warm as a morning in the Galápagos.

Mari was back on the Common, with just time to catch a few, reviving rays before she dragged herself into the office. At the back of her head was an ache like glass on a metal guitar string. She hadn't a clue how much she drank last night. Everything was fuzzy from when she and Felix went indoors, and she'd a suspicion they had done karaoke. At least she left the car at the office, sharing a cab with one of the girls. That was something.

Adam had let her sleep. When she woke, he had already gone to work. She didn't remember speaking to him, or even going to bed. Though judging by the beer cans, and the dog-ends littering the back step like trampled field mice, he made a night of it himself. Mari doubted he'd have smelt fags on her if she had rubbed her face in the ashtray.

She'd been tempted to lie in, but the stuffy bedroom made her head worse. A shower and fresh air were the best options; and now she felt an utter wastrel, lying on the grass like this in her work skirt and blouse, jacket laid out like a beach towel and her bag for a pillow ... The Common was quiet in the week even in the sunshine; empty but for a few needy sunbathers. The occasional pushchair trundled up the path, and someone somewhere was mowing the grass. Mari could see the Windmill through the trees; it would be a while before she set foot in there again!

A few more minutes and she'd have to make tracks. Her sunglasses shielded the rooks from her dark circles; more concealer was required before she braved the office. She fumbled in her bag but her fingers found sunblock instead.

Her nose was already tingling. Mari unscrewed the cap. Better safe than sorry ... She'd survived three months of South American sun; she wasn't about to burn up in SW4. She slipped off her watch, and her engagement ring, which put up a fight when the weather was warmer. Better have it altered before the big day!

As she applied the lotion, a shambling figure caught her eye, silhouetted against the fence two litter bins along. That skanky old tramp from the high street, rummaging for his lunch!

Mari settled back. High overhead two squirrels scampered along a branch that tapered away to nothing ... If Adam was here, he'd be taking photos. (What was it with men and even the most mundane forms of wildlife!)

She dreaded work and the inevitable dissection of last night, though she doubted she'd made a bigger fool of herself than anyone else. Mark-James and Melissa's 'Islands in the Stream', complete with winsome gazes and inappropriate pelvic thrusts, would surely detract from anything she'd screeched through. She wondered who else was in today – not Felix, she remembered that ... It was all right: nothing had happened. Booze or no booze, she would know if it had. Even so, the thought of him was making her uneasy again, raising questions Mari didn't want to answer.

Blooming Cousin Harry, all over again!

She checked her watch: gone quarter to one. Just five minutes' more release.

Even here, there was no escaping the growl of traffic. This was as far from the road as you could get, between the bandstand and that enclosure where the groundsmen kept their trucks. Talking of which …

Reluctantly, Mari opened her eyes, the dark lenses of her glasses muting the sky to monochrome. Sure enough, a Land Rover was coming her way, its mower attachment bouncing lightly across the camber of the path.

Ah, well. No rest for the wicked …

She sat up. Her head still hurt. She flicked a grass clipping off her calf and tried to remember her appointments. At a push, she could just about face the phones, or writing up property specs, but the thought of showing apathetic punters round dingy studios was too much today. She arranged her face into the Carson Hoggart smile, which brought the back of her throat up somewhere near her ears. Perhaps she wouldn't bother with that today, either.

Mari picked up her jacket. She slipped the bag over her shoulder and walked. Rounding the groundsmen's lockup, the playground appeared, complete with squealing toddlers on swings and a long-suffering mum dabbing at something in a pushchair.

She sighed. *That's me, one day.*

By the Windmill, the wheelie bins were free of the signs of scavenging life, four-legged or two. On the last stretch of grass, churned by endless kickabouts, a solitary traffic cone stood like a lighthouse on a faded green sea. And beyond the passing cars were the shops, including Carson Hoggart. She could just make out Melissa through the jigsaw of the window display, looking as sickeningly immaculate as ever.

Mari waited at the kerb for the lights to turn red. As she crossed, it dawned on her she hadn't eaten, and that the prospect of food no longer revolted her. She'd have missed the half-twelve sandwich run; she would need something.

She checked the window again. Melissa wasn't looking. Just time to get some chocolate from the shop.

Mari picked out a Twix and a KitKat, and took her place third in the queue. The man behind the counter was wearing his famous red and yellow pullover. He liked to chat, which was neighbourly, if a nuisance when you were in a rush. She took out her purse and scratched around for a couple of pound coins. As she looked down at her hands, she stopped.

It wasn't her nails and it wasn't the purse, but there was something wrong about ...

A moment later, she tossed the chocolate bars to one side where they landed on a stack of yoghurt-covered flapjacks. Powered by an energy that wasn't there a minute ago, she was out of the shop like a bullet.

Sod lunch and sod work! *She had to find that ring!*

II

Ian had never previously considered tarmac an aphrodisiac. He crossed onto the Common at the Windmill car park, which, despite being the crucible of all his current torments, still gave him the raging horn. He glanced at the wheelie bins – the very spot where he and Agnes had last embraced. If only he'd …

No time for that!

Eyes and ears trained firmly on the horizon, he carried on walking. Raj hadn't got back to him and he hadn't a clue where to find the best place to land a helicopter in two hundred acres of green space. Intuition was driving him to the centre, the groundsmen's lockup, setting for that one delicious night, the memory of which was making him hornier than ever.

Here and there, girls lay around in the sunshine and not much else. That wasn't helping, either … The sun was hot on the back of his neck as Ian rounded the corral. On the far side of the Common, Battersea Power Station jutted above the mansion roofs, like the legs of a dead art-deco cow.

Oh, to be a million miles from all this, he thought. *Preferably watching cricket!*

Good. An empty bench.

He took the weight off; sprawled the entire length of it, staring at the sky like a stupefied wino. Except he still hadn't had that drink, and he didn't know when he'd get one now. Hadn't had a pee, either, come to that. Or anything to eat since his toast this morning.

Raj said it was a three-hour flight. Ian had never been in a helicopter. Was an empty stomach wise? There was usually a burger van around here somewhere …

Pee first; he could nip in those bushes and— Hang on, this was Clapham Common: there would be gaylords everywhere! (Cameramen too, probably. Could it get any more complicated?)

Talk of the devil – there was one now. Hairy great specimen, mincing along in his too-tight sports kit ... Ian could spot them a mile off; why couldn't Carla?

To hell with Raj!

He had to phone her. The contrary bitch would get worried, sooner or later. Her confusion would turn into slow-dawning hysteria, as she realised he'd done a runner on her precious interview ... Then it struck him: Carla would see him on the box tonight! She was the one viewing figure Raj could bet his hair wax on. (Christ – the irony!)

Ian watched as a rook looked up from the lawn with a glassy eye. In a sweep of black it was up on the bin beside him, fearlessly inspecting the contents.

He let his head loll to one side. Rested his cheek on the flaking wooden planks of the bench.

And that was when he saw them.

*

Glory's mind was racing as she stepped off the bus. She had a thing or two to say to Mrs Molyneux!

The road works were deserted. Amazing, wasn't it, the way people could string out a job when it suited them? Like that lazy day duty manager with his muscle magazines. Took him half an hour to fetch a bit of laundry from the basement, just when he was needed on the toilet run.

And did Mrs Molyneux ever notice that? No!

But now, with Jan and Errol to back her up, she was

about to solve the little woman's mystery before her very eyes. She would have to reinstate Glory then – any fair-minded person would. The trouble was, if Mrs Molyneux wanted you out, you couldn't trust her not to wriggle. And no disrespect to Errol, but it was a pity it was him that found those clothes. To that woman, he was the lowest of the low …

Then again, thought Glory, Mrs Molyneux should be careful herself. What would the trustees say to her letting care assistants do the night-time drug run, all because she was too lazy to get off her bony backside?

She stopped and looked down at her T-bar sandals. It was hard to believe something so simple could get you into so much trouble … She switched her bag to the other shoulder and walked on, head bowed in concentration. Was it possible the caretaker's boy had a – what did they call it now? – *an agenda?* Some reason of his own to prove Glory was innocent? He was keen on her, she knew that. And if Mrs Molyneux knew it, too, she'd be even more hostile.

She tutted at herself as Cedars Hall came into view past the council lockup. As Ma always said, '*A suspicious mind misses the good in everything.*' It was another of her little rules Glory tried to live by. Though not to the point of recklessness …

She heard the footsteps behind her.

Who was this now?

Glory turned, half-expecting to be greeted by those famous words — the cause of so much amusement over the years, to everyone but herself. And as she did, she wondered for the hundredth time what on earth they found so funny about a flower as pretty as a morning glory.

*

The lights were on green as Mari reached the kerb. The far lane was empty, but a Peugeot was streaking towards her, fast enough to interest that camera on the corner. The driver must have seen it as he slammed on the brakes.

Heart pounding, she hurtled over the crossing, dipping under the railing and onto the grass.

Adam would kill her!

That ring had been trouble since the day it all but cut off her blood supply on the beach! As she passed the playground, nightmare scenarios flashed up in Mari's mind as if revealed by lightning: was it rooks or crows that picked up shiny things? What about squirrels? Or dogs?

Christ! The lawn mower!

She broke into a sprint at the lockup. Swiped off her sunglasses, scanned the ground …

Pointless. She knew exactly where it would be.

Then she saw the black woman up ahead carrying a holdall. Oddly, her eyes were also trained on the ground.

Mari slowed, trying not to look suspicious. She didn't have a racist bone in her body – prided herself on it – but no one was above temptation. A few metres more and that woman would be right where she had been lying … As she drew level Mari saw nothing else, so absorbed in her search for a telltale glint in the grass.

She saw nothing else, because nothing else mattered. Not the man stretched out on the park bench, watching her with a less than innocent eye; not the rook on a litter bin, tossing out an empty sandwich box bigger than itself.

Not even the red helicopter, swooping over the mansion blocks as it roared towards them.

*

Tony slammed the door as he left the apartments. Swung into power walk before he was even through the gate, elbows high for the maximum calorie-burn. He just had time for one full circuit.

Why had he let himself get like this? If he had to eat like a pig, at least he could have stuck to the fitness regime … Too easily distracted, that was his problem!

The sun was stronger than it looked. He'd already worked up a sweat by the time he could see the fishpond. Those lads were there again, more of them this time, looking bored over their rods.

Some fat guy mincing past in a litre of his own sweat – that'd be the best sport they got all day …

He decided to take a detour. He could still get a good forty minutes, which had to be worth half a packet of biscuits.

For a second, as he skirted the thicket by the footie pitch, Tony could have sworn he saw something ... A face maybe, watching from the bushes. According to Geoff, this bit of the Common was a mecca for cruisers – mostly by night, but you never knew your luck in the big city. He glanced into the foliage again as he crossed the gravel track.

Gone.

Eyes front, Tony, my boy! Now is not the time.

Talking of which, he and Geoff still hadn't done anything about Prague. He would need a bit of R&R when he started work again, and maybe even a massage or two. He could always pop back and see those charm-school graduates at the beauty parlour – when he'd lost a bit more weight.

A minute later, something else distracted him. A noise this time: squawking, up in the high branches. Familiar, but not a crow or any of the other English garden birds that watched him strut his stuff on the Common. As the cries broke out again, Tony allowed himself a pause. He looked up, squinting into the sunlight.

The culprit was invisible at first. Indistinguishable from the surrounding leaves till it took to the air with a flurried hop, alighting lower down.

A parakeet! Two of them, rustling around in the branches – bigger than a budgie, greener than a kea. Wild parakeets in London town! Who'd have thought it?

Tony smiled as he carried on, upping the pace to boost his heart rate. The wide open spaces were one of the nice things about London. You could soon get away from the bustle and the noise. Apart from the cars, the planes ...

Aye aye: there was one now ...

Hang on: no, it was a chopper, buzzing low over the edge of the Common. Police, maybe, looking for druggies or other miscreants in the bushes.

He kept on walking. From here to the road there was hardly a soul to be seen. Just a couple of girls up ahead, and some leery bloke on a bench by the rubbish tin.

Tony felt a sudden sensation needling his side. It was the beginnings of a stitch. Ah, well – no point doing himself an injury ... He eased up a little, swinging his arms in a less strenuous arc. And as he did, he wondered if he maybe ought to ease up on himself a bit, too.

Honestly, talk about fickle! There he was, all ready one minute to shoulder the responsibilities of fatherhood, say goodbye to the trashy side of life … The next, it was all forgotten – and off he went, waddling round the Common like a demented duck, trying to look hot for some guy he'd travelled half a planet to avoid!

Tony Torrence, sometimes you're just a bloody idiot!

Where would it all end?

ONE

I

One black one, one white one. *Just like in the rugger song!*

The two girls were crossing the grass a few yards apart. Both seemed to be looking for something. The white one, who was slim and fair-haired (rather nice, in his estimation) looked a bit out of breath. He wondered if she was the kind of girl who—

Helicopter!

Red. Neat little thing, getting not-so-little all the time. Should have seen it coming for miles but he didn't, what with that noisy mower, not to mention the other distractions.

The ringtone of his mobile was the last thing Ian heard above the roar.

Raj! He couldn't make out a word he was saying, but he could guess.

'Yes, I know!' he yelled. 'I can see it!'

Raj wouldn't hear him either; but he would hear the rotors pummelling the air, whipping the surrounding foliage into a frenzy. The helicopter was hovering a hop and a skip yonder, over that area reserved for softball. If Ian shaded his eyes he could just make out the pilot in his bright-yellow helmet.

He rammed his fingers in his ears and wondered what to do. Should he wave his arms about, criss-cross in the air like they did on aircraft carriers?

The noise was now excruciating; he kept his fingers where they were. The pilot seemed to be hesitating. Ian peered at the ground beneath the fuselage …

Christ! There was someone lying there, right in the bloody thing's shadow!

A real-life wino, all ropey dreadlocks and a mess of beard,

limbs flailing like a loon ... *Move, you cretin!* Ian looked on bewildered, as pilot and tramp engaged in a bizarre game of chicken.

The seconds felt like minutes. The pressure on Ian's ears was almost unbearable. Until the helicopter pulled up tail-first, like lifting a heavy saucepan, and executed a deafening arc over the pitch.

He had half a mind to go and give that wino a bloody good kicking! Instead, he watched the chopper as it slid overhead, banking slightly as it looked for a better place to land. The pilot appeared to be heading for the other side of the lockup. Ian scurried after it; when it came down, he'd need to get on board fast. (Or did you wait for the rotors to stop first?)

At the edge of the Common cars snaked by, occupants craning curiously from windows. Ian pressed himself to the fence around the lockup, his eyes slitted against the old dust and new grass swept up in the maelstrom. The pilot had found his spot: a patch of sun-bleached clearing between the plane trees that shaded the duck pond. It was empty, but for a wittily positioned traffic cone.

The chopper began to descend. The numbing beat of the blades was making Ian's teeth judder as he got ready to run. That thing wasn't coming down as squarely as it might ... Tail a bit near the trees, but then the chap would know what he was doing … Broken boughs from the storms last winter were still dangling here and there, left by the council to rot till they dropped on someone's head.

Careful – those rotors were a bit bloody close! Pilot better watch it or he was going to prune them himsel—

When the blades hit the branches, it sounded like gunfire.

*

The white woman was staring at Glory as if she was meant to know her. Glory stopped in her tracks; whatever was coming her way, she would face it head on.

Though dressed for the office, the woman looked dishevelled. She was panting, and her face was red where the edge of her sunglasses had been. Nervously, she held out her hands towards Glory, clasping one with the other. But whatever she was saying, it was drowned out by that infernal clatter.

Can't – hear – you! mouthed Glory.

A movement at the corner of her eye. The man was up off his bench, shouting into a mobile phone. Fine time for a chat!

When Glory turned back, the white girl was bent double, examining the grass like she'd lost something. If she could have made herself heard, she would have offered to help … Now the bench man was bellowing at a tramp, lying on the ground right under the helicopter!

What on earth was going on?

Police, probably, thought Glory. She'd seen them at night, hovering over the Common with their searchlights. Looking for men cavorting in the bushes – and proper thing, too. It wasn't safe for a boy to go walking his dog around here.

The helicopter changed its mind. Glory's hands stayed over her ears as it sailed overhead, wind whipping her jacket, blowing her hair flat to her head like poor old Pearl.

The bench man broke into a run – now he was following it! Perhaps it was him it had come for, thought Glory. Though he didn't look like the kind of gentleman who had his own helicopter …

*

Mari didn't know what to say without it sounding like an accusation. But the words were lost in the cacophony of engines – the grass cutter and that blooming helicopter that appeared out of nowhere!

Had the world gone mad?

She crouched and searched the lawn – still unmown, thank God! This was where she'd been, about three metres from that bench. She'd been facing the litter bin as she put on her damned sun lotion.

Reflexes sent her hands to her ears, blocking out the towering roar as she scanned the ground for anything gold and glinting … Over there a scrunch of foil from a chocolate bar gave a silvery wink – but nothing else. Mari leaned, to see if the light caught it at a different angle. If only that hideous thing would buzz off, she could ask the other woman to help.

Abruptly, the sunlight disappeared. A giant shadow swept over her. Good riddance!

When she looked down again, the black woman was heading for the edge of the Common. Mari was about to go back to her search when the woman turned. She shucked her chin once, asking her what was going on.

Before Mari could reply, the Land Rover trundled between them, blocking her eye line and tossing a confetti of clippings in its wake. She waved away the haze of particles, squeezing shut her eyes. She was fighting back a sneeze as an Aussie-inflected voice behind her yelled:

'Jee-sus CHRIST!'

*

Tony broke into a run at the edge of the lockup. His mind strained to grasp what he saw. The little chopper was barely thirty metres up as the tail clipped the nearest tree. Slowly, horribly, it started to spiral, chassis slumping on its nose like a roped steer … If the pilot didn't do something, it was coming down!

Must have heard him. The chopper broke its spin and lurched, regaining height in an upward swoop. Tony held his breath.

Almost. Nearly over the tree line …*No good!*

Horror wrenched at his stomach as the tail blades sheared off in a single piece, boomeranging towards the pond in a slew of branches. Tony didn't want to see them land ... This was too fucking surreal – an action movie without the thrills, unfolding before his eyes!

In a grind of agony the chopper's undercarriage spun like it was being sucked down a plughole. Tony's gut told him to wrap his arms round a concrete post before he was dragged into the descending tempest. With the force of a bullet, a traffic cone slammed into the fence beside him as he glimpsed someone from the corner of his eye. The scruffy bloke from the bench, clinging onto the next post but one. Worst of all, as the windscreen of the chopper hove his way, Tony caught a snapshot of the guy in the cockpit. Helmet, sunnies and a human grimace. Freaky but true: the smooth head and glasses made him think of Jarvis.

For elongated seconds the chopper dipped lower, the gyrations winding ever tighter. With one last turn it caught the ground, a quake that sent the fuselage spinning counter to the juddering blades...

The downdraft, the roar or the thunder of impact – whichever it was threw Tony to the ground with a force that all but tore the vest from his back. The blast rent his eardrums, crushing his face into the earth. The last thing he remembered was the shitstorm of debris, hotter, denser and sharper than the mulch of new-mown grass …

Tony thought he was dead. Turned out it was just the bliss of silence.

A second later, or a year, he raised his head. *Voices!*

People were running across the Common. Somewhere in the traffic, two distracted bumpers socked each other with a plastic crunch. He realised he was looking directly into the undercarriage. The carcass of the helicopter was on its side; the severed tail a distance from the chassis and slightly at an angle, like a mechanical take on a Damien Hirst. All around him the ground was peppered with shrapnel. One giant rotor blade had sheared clean off and stood in the earth, half buried and shivering.

Tony hauled himself to his feet and staggered towards the wreckage. Incredibly, his body was still working. Being alive this close to such devastation felt like a fucking miracle.

No bodies that he could see ... If you had to crash a chopper in London town, a big old empty park was the place to do it. Good on the-

Jeez! The pilot!

He picked up the pace and ran. The scruffy bloke had the same idea.

Tony was shocked at his own calmness. The stench of oil and roasting engine took him back to a mundane childhood afternoon ...

Peeping through the fence at Frank McLagan's rotavator; their neighbour's new toy had short-circuited as he dug his spud beds and bloody nearly killed him...

As he reached the cockpit, the other guy was right behind him. The windscreen was intact, but by the side window diamond shards crunched underfoot. Smoke rose from the joystick and miniature blue flames danced on the dash like – cold irony – pilot lights. For a moment Tony

thought the cockpit was empty, until-

'Get him out!' bellowed Scruffy Bloke. His hand was on Tony's shoulder.

Sure enough, the pilot was in there, twisted under the bank of leather seats, his face and clothing blackened into camouflage. His feet were pointing their way, but his body was in a shoulder-stand, putting all the weight on the back of his neck.

'Is he ... ?' Tony's words were choked by the acrid mist.

Was it safe to touch him? Touch anything? What if the whole wreck was live?

More footsteps. The fishing boys from the pond, mouths agape like guppies. Scruffy saw them too.

'You lads, keep back!' His plummy voice didn't fit his appearance. 'And call an ambulance!'

'Is he alive?' yelled a woman out of nowhere.

She was black, with a bag over her shoulder. She dropped it as she ran towards them.

Scruffy was leaning in the shattered window.

'Can you hear me, old chap? Can you move?'

The three of them stood, silent but for their own breath. Listening, watching for a sign.

Nothing.

Tony pointed at the dashboard: 'We gotta get that fire out!'

There had to be an extinguisher in there somewhere. He couldn't see it.

'Let's get some water from the pond ...'

'No!' said the woman. *'Foolish!* You can't throw water on a 'lectrical fire!'

A groan from inside the cockpit. A flash of yellow as the pilot turned his head. Where his helmet had been lying, the plastic was still bright and clean. He tried to speak.

'Guh ...'

The window was too small to climb through. The woman made a grab for the door. Tony and Scruffy winced, afraid to touch anything metal. Their hesitation was noted.

'Help me!' she snapped. 'If the whole thing was live, he'd be dead, wouldn't he!'

They squeezed their fingertips into the gap between the frame and the buckled door and tried to prise it open.

The pilot coughed; he was spitting up something thick and black.

'Guh ... Guh ...'

'We're getting you out, mate!' said Tony as the door budged a fraction. 'Don't move!' (Bloody stupid thing to say!)

Another woman appeared from behind the lockup. She was fair-haired and frowning, wearing a business suit. She inched closer, daring herself to look.

The door was coming. One more pull ...

It was stuck solid at thirty degrees. Not wide enough.

'You!' yelled the black woman. 'Help us!'

The fair-haired girl hitched up her skirt and ran to the door. She slipped her fingers in beside Tony's, adding what strength she had. On a count of three they heaved together.

Again.

And again.

This time, Tony and the other guy got their weight against the underside. Scruffy's neck was cording like a vascular diagram ... Until, with an unoiled groan of protest, the door creaked and gave, falling open in a cloud of fumes.

'Get him out!' barked Scruffy. He had one loafer up on the fuselage, ready to spring inside.

'Leave him!' ordered the black woman.

Scruffy stared. 'What, let the bugger die? Are you mad?'

But the woman's eyes were wide with disdain.

'You can't move him! Don't you know first aid? We got to wait for the ambulance!'

The man looked at Tony. Tony looked at the black woman.

Another groan from the cockpit.

'*Please …*'

Scruffy took his foot off the chassis. 'Not long now, old chap! Ambulance on its way, but you've got to stay with us. Keep talking – what's your name, eh? Tell us your name!' He yanked his head out of the door and spotted the fishing lads, rooted to the spot. '*Where the fuck's that ambulance?*'

The younger lad was shaking. He nodded to his mate: 'He f-forgot his phone, mister …'

Scruffy swore as everyone scrambled for their mobiles.

The fair-haired girl was first to dial 999. But a dozen calls had already been made. More now, as new faces arrived; joggers and dog walkers, rubberneckers from cars abandoned on the pavement; that Asian guy from the shop who Tony knew by his sweater … All of them wanting to get close but not too close, to see but not see, held three paces back by a force field of dread.

The pilot was still moaning.

'What's he trying to say?'

'Maybe it's his name,' said Scruffy. 'Are you saying your name, old chap? Gary? … Graham? ... *Shit!*'

He pulled his head out again to yell at the surrounding horde.

'*IS ANYONE HERE A DOCTOR?*'

'What's up?' said Tony

Scruffy swallowed, taking a breath before he whispered.

'Something's gone through his arm. I think it's one of the blades.'

Tony nerved himself to look through the windscreen. The interior was unfathomable, bright sunlight casting the darkest of shadows. He pressed his hands to the glass to make a tunnel for his eyes. Traced the line of metal guillotining through the cockpit ceiling.

He was right. The blade had sunk into the pilot's arm where the sleeve of his pale-blue flying jacket had soaked to black. Worse was the other thing, sticking out through the fabric of the sleeve where it shouldn't have. It was a spindle of bone, deathly white.

The fair-haired girl had finished her call. She was right beside him, her face bloodless. Tony tried to push her away before she saw, but it was too late. Two breaths later, she was wailing like a baby.

'Calm yourself!' tutted the black woman. 'You're no good to anyone like that!'

But the girl shook her head and backed away, wails turning to full-blown, billowing sobs.

The angle of the rotor blade meant the end was hanging free, a metre inside the cockpit. With an agility that was news to him, Tony found a foothold and clambered up onto the chassis.

'He's bleeding bad. If one of you pushes the blade from inside, I'll try and pull it through the ceiling ...'

Scruffy shook his head. 'She's right. We should wait for the medics.'

The first shriek of a siren sounded in the distance, an ambulance or a fire engine, fighting the frozen traffic.

On the roof, Tony lay down on his belly, stuck his head through the window.

'They're here, mate! You'll be right. Hang on in there!'

The guy looked like he was losing consciousness. His foot was only touching distance away. Tony leaned in further and squeezed the end of his boot ... Metal toe cap. He tried higher up the instep.

The pilot wiggled his foot. He was still trying to speak. Tony strained to make out the words. Then, in his calmest voice he saved for babies and nervous pets, he said:

'What you saying, mate? What you telling me?'

The guy was trying to shift his weight onto the other shoulder.

'I'd stay as you are, mate. You're better off ...'

Then Tony heard it. Thin and high-pitched: the seep of escaping liquid.

It caught his nose as it caught his eye, trickling in from the back of the cabin, pooling in the recess behind the concertinaed seats.

The poor bastard was lying in a trough of diesel!

Idle rivulets were spreading to where blue flames had taken hold of the dashboard. The plastic fascia fizzed with spurting sparks. The pilot was breathing harder, twisting his neck, trying to lean closer to Tony. From the deep grooves around his nose and mouth Tony realised he was older than he thought. Fifties, maybe sixty.

'Geh ... gehhh ...'

In a string of fume-choked coughs the words came at last:

'*Get – the fuck – AWAY!*'

Tony's foot caught Scruffy's thigh as he hurled himself off the fuselage, landing right on top of him on the turf.

'What the hell are you—'

'Back off!' bawled Tony. 'It's gonna blow!'

He shoved him away. Shoved the black woman, too, whose mouth was wide in horror. Which only left—

The fair-haired girl was slumped by the tail, legs splayed in front of her like a discarded doll. She was plucking at something in the turf.

Glass. Her fingers were bleeding as she picked at splinters of glass.

Someone else was with her. Another woman, kneeling, talking quietly. All Tony could see of her was the back of her T-shirt and soles of her sneakers. The fair-haired girl wasn't responding. She was trying to shrug the other woman off as he ran towards them.

'Get her away now!'

Still the girl wouldn't move. He grabbed her under the arms himself, tried to haul her up, a dead weight. Her shirt was soaking. The woman helped him lever her upright as at last, with aching slowness, she wobbled to her feet. The heel of one of her shoes had come away. She was looking around forlornly.

'Come on,' said the other woman. 'You gotta go!'

Her voice was cajoling, oddly familiar. With her arm round the fair-haired girl's shoulders, they started to move. Tony thrust them away like a pushy gameshow host – and for the first time he noticed the other woman's hair. Pulled back in a ponytail.

Blond.

Their eyes met as she turned. His mouth fell open.

Shelley!

He froze, until-

'Just get her out of here!'

Tony gave them a final shunt. Then he ran back to the wreckage.

II

'Hello. Is that Maisie ... ?

'Maisie, it's Carla. Carla Newton.

'I understand you've been speaking to my husband … Well, I know you know *exactly* what I'm talking about, because he's already told me …

'Look, I don't know what your angle is, but as far as we're concerned those photographs don't change a thing. My husband and ... *Ian* and I are very, very happy, and the portrait the papers are going to paint of us will be a fair and accurate representation of our marriage—

'Well, frankly, your readers can view it anyway they like. Though I've no doubt that all comes down to how you manipulate them …

'Maisie – no, Maisie, I am Ian's wife, not his keeper. We have our own rules for making our marriage work and I think we're doing a bloody good job. How many people can say that these days? Are you married?

'Divorced. Surprise …

'Oh, isn't it? Then why the hell is mine any business of yours? That's stumped you, hasn't it?

'Look, all I'm saying is – and God knows why I'm telling a total stranger – I love my husband, Maisie. So whatever you've got on him won't make the slightest difference. It'll end up making *you* look stupid in the end. Is that what you want?

'Well, I think you do care – you should …

'All right, I've said my piece. I can't stop you doing what you're going to do. What is it they say in your business? Publish and be – *JESUS CHRIST, WHAT WAS THAT?!'*

*

'Come on, Pearl. One last spoonful ...'

The problem with Fatty Ginger was, she didn't have the patience of some of the other girls at this hotel. Always looks sulky, too, thought Pearl, with stains down her front like she can barely feed herself, let alone anyone else ... *And I'll have a spoonful in my own good time, thanking you!*

The sooner that nice coloured girl came back, the better. Glenda ... Gloria? They always had such pretty names. Now *she* knew how to treat a lady.

'Last chance,' squawked Fatty Ginger. 'Open up, or I'm telling Mrs Molyneux!'

Good Lord! Pearl gave what she hoped was her best frown. Was that supposed to frighten her?

The girl had parked herself on the edge of the bed, her enormous buttocks dragging the crochet bedspread halfway to the floor. She reminded Pearl of the orang-utan at London Zoo – or was it Whipsnade? – sitting in the corner of its cage with a face just like that, playing with its own doings.

Pearl looked down at the girl's fingernails. Perhaps she wouldn't eat any more after all.

'Right!' snapped Fatty Ginger, dropping the plastic spoon in the bowl. 'That's your lot!' She hoisted herself off the bed. 'Don't blame me if you don't get your cocoa ...'

Pearl sighed when she was gone. Alone again; that was the last she would see of anyone until they sounded the gong for dinner.

Thank the Lord!

A beam of sunlight danced on her bedspread, waking the fairies in the woollen squares. They often came out to see her at this time, and at least they didn't expect her to answer back. They were all the company Pearl needed these days. Till Ernest rolled up.

And anyway, they could keep their cocoa! It was the worst thing about this establishment. Always tepid, and they never got the sugar right. What made Pearl laugh was the way they used it as a threat, like it was meant to leave her shaking in her boots. Didn't they know she'd lived through the Blitz? Survived the Luftwaffe when they levelled Protheroe Road?

But Glenda, now – she was all right. Always a smile for Pearl. And a hug, though that had taken a bit of getting used to. Not quite what you expected from a chambermaid!

She could be sneaky, too, mind you. Poking around in her room at night like that. Pearl had played dumb – but she knew it was Glenda all along. She would know that lovely orange smell of hers anywhere.

She meant no harm, and anyway Pearl liked a girl with a bit of mischief. It reminded her of herself at that age-

Goodness!

She woke with a start. The room was shaking, so violently she could have fallen off her chair. The rolling *BOOM!* seemed to go on forever; it was still there when it wasn't, making Pearl's head buzz like a hive full of bees.

There were screams outside. Shouts from upstairs, and not just the usual ones. Footsteps clattered down the hall, the front door crashed open …

Pearl checked herself over. Still in one piece, she was pleased to report. She peered through the window: surprise – that blessed bird table had been felled to the ground.

Typical Ernest! Never there when you need him. Probably making a nuisance of himself in the laundry again …

She waited, but didn't make a sound. Just held her head high. Any minute now, and one of the maids would be along to wheel her down to the shelter.

*

Half an hour later, Adam was still at his desk. His belly told him it was time for a sandwich. Or chips.

He checked his pocket for his new mp3 player. *Sausage, chips and Urban Gangsta Crew*. Music to his ears. He was half out the door when Trev called across the office.

''Nother late lunch, Ad? She got you looking at flats again?'

Adam didn't rise to it. His boss was old-school Transport for London. The kind of guy who thought any woman with a bit of initiative had to be trouble. It was one reason why he firmly intended to be sitting in his chair this time next year.

'Here, Adam – look at this!'

Alison. Trev's secretary. She was another.

He sighed. Whatever it was, it was going to keep him from his lunch. He leaned over her shoulder as she stabbed at the keyboard, avoiding any contact with her peachy soft skin. As he always did, in office hours.

Him and Alison had been off and on for eighteen months. Still managing to keep it under wraps. (Who says office romances always end in tears?) The work lot were too dozy to cotton on. Alison's hubby was only home two nights a week. And Mari-

Well, Mari didn't think he had it in him.

Mr Cake-And-Eat-It, that was what Alison called him. And he had every intention of helping himself to a few more slices yet.

She clicked at the ticker tape on the BBC News homepage. So far there was no link, just the headline:

1.25pm GMT. Reports of helicopter crash on Clapham Common. Casualties unknown. More soon.

Adam swallowed. He reached for his mobile.

*

Three messages. All ignored.

Then that's that, thought Jarvis. He could take a hint.

He slipped the phone into the breast pocket of his blazer and sipped his tea. The Heathrow Hilton wasn't exactly Raffles, but they knew how to brew a pot of Earl Grey … Tony had had his chance and he'd blown it. Which was odd; he was a reliable sort, all told. Or he had been in Auckland.

But then living abroad did funny things to people. Jarvis had a cousin who spent a year in Reykjavik and came back believing in trolls. And, of course, some people never came back at all.

He'd been looking forward to their afternoon tea. It seemed just the right sort of atmosphere to break the news about Simon. Cordial and a bit refined; classy enough to dissuade Tony from a display of anything too embarrassing. Jarvis had colleagues around, after all.

Now he would never know.

The woman on the next table had left her iPad open on the *Evening Standard* website. The headline blared: *CLAPHAM COMMON AIR CRASH – Unknown number dead.*

Christ. That was all he needed. One more whiff of air-traffic chaos and they'd never get to Madrid.

Jarvis sighed. He should find the others, prepare them for the worst. He should find some of this excellent Earl Grey, too, to take home to Grandmamma. It was always a good idea, keeping her sweet – and a gift from the Old

Country never did any harm ...

First, he lifted the pot. Gave it a swirl. Still another cup in there, and he wasn't about to waste it. What was it they said in England?

Everything stops for tea.

FIVE MONTHS LATER

I

'Auntie Glory, will you wave to me when you're on the telly?'

Sherelle was belted into the back of the black cab beside Mercy and Sam. She was wearing her best shoes and a coat with furry purple trim.

'Foolish!' said Mercy. 'You don't need to watch Auntie Glory on the telly. You'll be there in the studio with her!'

Sherelle's tiny brow furrowed. She still wasn't sure what this morning was all about.

'Will I, Auntie Glory?'

Glory nodded. 'Aye. 'Long as you're a good girl and sit nice and quiet now.'

Sherelle put a finger to her lips to show how quiet she could be. Mercy rested a hand on her daughter's knee; Sam reached over and put her other hand on his.

Quite the happy family, thought Glory in the jump seat. All scrubbed up and smiling ... She peered over her shoulder at the meter. West London was not her part of town. Men and women in suits and raincoats poured into an unfamiliar tube station, picking up newspapers to read with their cardboard coffees.

She looked at her watch. Took the call sheet out of her bag for the tenth time today. At the top was the title of the programme and the date. She wasn't due at the studio for half an hour yet, but for once they'd all been ready in good time.

So nice of Mrs Molyneux to give her the day off. The little woman hadn't even made her swap shifts, but then they were positively matey these days. Amazing what a difference it made – being called a heroine in the newspapers.

Mercy was eyeing a department store with tastelessly early Christmas windows. 'How long it gonna take, all o' this?' she asked peevishly.

'Why? What you rushin' home for?'

Her sister sunk back in her seat and said nothing. Just toyed with the hair weave she'd had done specially: ruby-coloured rhinestones and matching streamers. Glory's lips pursed involuntarily. *And as for that blouse …*

She checked her own top button and smoothed her smart new slacks. Credit where it was due: Mercy was improving. Getting better with money, and she was doing more of the shopping these days. Since Alfonse took off to live with that half-sister who turned out to be nothing of the sort, she was making an effort with the kids, too. Breakfast, bathtime and bedtime, she was there as she should be. There was even talk of a diet.

Sometimes, Glory caught her sister looking at her with something more than her usual indifference. It hadn't been easy for Mercy, grasping what she went through while she was away in Trinidad. By the time she got home, the horror of it had been and gone. And there was Glory in last week's papers, with the football scores and soap stars falling out of nightclubs. By then, she was tired of the whole thing – which Mercy took to mean she didn't want to talk about it, shushing the children when they asked about the man in the helicopter (*He's in heaven now; there's no more to say*). Soon, the papers were thrown away, with nothing kept except a few cuttings. But Glory had heard her sister on the walkway, chatting to the hair-extensions lady as she kept an eye out for Alfonse sneaking back for his post:

'Typical Glory. Always there for anyone in trouble. Just like Ma woulda been …'

The words touched her deeply. Though she wondered how long they would last.

The taxi turned into an alleyway between what looked like deserted warehouses. Beside each doorway were the nameplates of companies Glory had never heard of. They pulled up at one that said *FloatYaBoat TV.*

'Here you go,' said the driver.

Sam was gazing up through the window. Like Sherelle, he was dressed for best, in his little black bomber jacket.

'Mummy,' he said, 'are all telly programmes made in factories?'

His mouth was still open when they walked into reception. It had the look of a spaceship. The boy behind the desk wore an earpiece like a silver beetle.

'Hey there – Raj will be with you in five. Do take a seat ...'

Everyone who came out of the lifts looked sixteen years old, just like the girls who had interviewed Glory at home. And they all wore T-shirts. She wondered if they were going to make her get changed, after all the trouble she'd gone to.

She'd only spoken to this Raj Sinatra on the phone; he sounded like he thought he was in a movie. While Sherelle hauled herself on and off her auntie's knee, Glory tried to spot him whenever the lift doors opened.

Easy. He would be the one in the sunglasses.

As Raj jogged over his stare bounced from one sister to the other.

'Glory, yeah?'

Glory put him out of his misery by offering her hand. The sleeves of his Superdry T-shirt were rolled over non-existent biceps.

'Great to meet you – you're the first! Hey, who's this little lady?' Raj patted Sherelle's head like a basketball.

'This is Sherelle,' said Glory. 'And that's Sam.'

'Cool. Yours, yeah?'

Mercy let Sam slip to the ground as she stood to hold out a hand. Her fingers were freshly armed and lacquered.

'They're mine, Raj. I'm Mercy. The younger sister.'

Raj laughed. 'Glory and Mercy! Like it ...'

He stopped short.

'Okay. Green room's up on third, studio's on second, so if you'd all like to follow me ... Walk this way, as they say!'

He laughed again and offered his hand to Sherelle. The little girl's face said she remembered what she'd been told about strangers. She took Glory's instead.

As they waited for the lift, Raj shouted to the boy on reception: 'Send the rest straight up, Chas!'

Inside, Mercy manoeuvred her chest so that Raj had to lean over, under or actually brush against it in order to reach the buttons. She was still smiling.

''Scuse I,' said Raj, peering over his specs.

'Why, whatcha done?'

She giggled flirtatiously and tossed a jewel-tipped weft.

Glory squeezed Sherelle's hand as she watched the numbers change ... She was going to miss these kids.

*

'Ian, Carla – great to see you!'

Carla got a kiss. Ian was luckier.

Raj looked different; new hairspray or something.

The green room had custard-coloured walls with over-designed sofas in navy gabardine. The art, an intended touch of class, was sub-hotel standard – a trio of seascapes, possibly rendered by foot. On the other wall was a row of photo portraits: a firmament of FloatYaBoat's brightest stars. One Ian recognised as Jake, winner of *To Hell in a Houseboat I*. But while the council housewives' choice grinned from a plastic clip frame, there was noticeably no one from this year's show.

The corporate upholstery had sea-green cushions. The winking tugboat logo was on every notepad, as well as the T-shirts of the skinny minxes swanning about with trays. Ian slouched gratefully on the sofa. His left leg was still a bother, from when the big chap landed on him as they bolted from the helicopter.

Small price to pay.

Across the room, he spotted the black woman from the crash. She was with two children and a scary-looking fat woman, probably related and making short work of the biscuits. He raised his hand in a wave. Glory nodded back.

Raj spotted it. 'Right, I'm sure you all wanna get together, chew the fat. So to speak. So I'm just gonna give you a quick briefing before we start.'

Carla sat forward. 'Raj, one thing. While we're here, I was wondering if I could have a word with someone. About *Houseboat*.'

Ian sat back. May as well get it over with ...

Raj looked irritated. 'What about *Houseboat*?'

'Well ... re: any opportunities arising therefrom. I know at the time there was talk of a reunion show. Maybe a match-up with last year's crew?'

The top half of Raj's face didn't move. 'Carla, as I fink you know, all future *Houseboat* projects are on hold.'

'I realise that, but—'

'The day after the tragedy wiv the helicopter, the board suspended the show. They sent the last free contestants on a cut-price cruise off Haiti wiv a Ouija board, two chickens and a cameraman who does Tarot cards. It's being edited as we speak.'

'It sounds great, I just—'

'It's not; it's bleeding awful. There's footage of Mitch on the cutting-room floor the RSPCA could have us in court for … Now, I'm sorry you lost out when the publicity got canned – but you could say, if you hadn't scarpered off the boat none of this would have …' He steadied himself. 'Well, we wouldn't be making this show, would we?' He looked around for his notes.

Carla was stony-faced. Ian put a hand on her arm and squeezed. For the last five months, she'd been an emotional fireball, waking him in the night with *what ifs* and *why us's*; scheming one minute, screaming the next, running the gamut from guilt to bitterness. He wondered if it was her old restlessness returning … Though surely she had enough to focus on now?

His musing was broken as a corporate temptress with a dragonfly tattoo leaned down to serve him coffee.

Whatever … One walk on the wild side was quite enough for him. The truth was, he was only doing this for Carla. With the legal enquiry still pending, the very idea of making a documentary revolted him. Plus his fee was paltry, and he didn't care if he never saw any of these people again. But she seemed to relish it all: the negotiations with the TV bods, choosing what shirt he should wear ...

'My wife's not been feeling too good, Raj,' he chipped in. 'In fact, we—'

'Heavy times, Ian, I know. And for me, too. But let's just remember why we're all here …'

Ian waited. Was he about to invoke God, or Mohammed? Or that thing with the head of an elephant?

'See, here's how it works. I interview all you have-a-go-heroes, one at a time. Ask you the same questions – more or less – then we top and tail it wiv a bit of background. There's no live footage unfortunately, but we've got a wicked CGI of the chopper coming down. I tell you, the geeks in the basement have done us proud. I'm keeping the wireframes for me den.'

Ian fought the urge to bludgeon him to the corporate carpet.

'We *was* hoping to have input from the pilot's daughter, but she declined.' Raj raised an understanding hand. 'Which is cool – telly's not for everyone.'

'What about, er – the other one?' asked Carla. 'Did you get hold of any relatives?'

'We did,' nodded Raj. 'Oh, hang on ...' He plucked an instant message from his iPhone. 'Okay, nearly ready to roll. Last one's on the way up.'

*

The motion of the lift was barely perceptible. Mari still felt giddy as the doors slid open on a dozen pairs of eyes.

She very nearly hadn't come. She'd had more than enough of the media at the time, and the two preliminary meetings with researchers had all but finished her off. She'd put her phone on divert when the calls from this Raj Sinatra person started driving her mad.

That would be him: too much hair wax and sunglasses on his head. Not quite how she'd seen him in her mind's eye – no turban or tuxedo – but he looked the part.

'Mari, mate!'

The backward lean of her torso told him not to come closer. She smiled weakly and looked around; people she faintly recognised were positioned like chess pieces around the room. The gardener man was there, looking anxious with his reality-TV wife. The black woman was in the other corner.; brought her entire clan, by the look of it.

As Mari understood it, they were being interviewed one at a time. A relief, if odd given the name of the programme. She felt no connection to any of these people. How they fitted a documentary series called *Bonded By Tragedy* was anyone's guess.

'Don't get too comfy, Mari!' Raj cajoled, pulling up a chair. 'You're on first. If you had a look at those questions we mailed you, you know what's coming. There'll be a bit of background about yourself – could be captions, or a voiceover. I leave all that to the tech boys – just do me Jonathan Ross!' A truncated laugh. 'I'm not on camera, though. They won't pay for me suit.'

The gardener's wife and the black women were watching. Everyone was dressed to the nines, whether they were going on air or not. Except for her; Mari was going straight into work afterwards.

'There is *one* little fing,' said Raj ominously. 'We've got a surprise for you.'

She blanched.

'No, nuffink to worry about! But I don't want to spoil it, cos if I tell you we won't get a proper reaction ...'

It sounded like exactly the kind of thing she hated.

'Raj, I am not about to—'

'Trust me, Mari! You got my word: if you don't like it, we cut it. Scout's honour.' His fingers made a ridiculous little salute, inadvertently putting a gun to his head.

A studio girl appeared.

'Cool!' said Raj. 'Okay, everyone – wagons roll! We're gonna take our free stars down to makeup, then into the studio. Starting wiv Mari. Ladies first!'

One of the black women made a noise through her teeth.

'Er, swiftly followed by Glory! *All* the – ladies first ...'

He fiddled with his iPhone. Mari made it to the lift without looking at anyone. Was it too late to back out now?

The chair was on a plinth in front of a blue backdrop. The padded-leather arms were warm from the lights. Mari felt like she was on *Mastermind.*

Raj was sitting cross-legged on a table out of shot, a clipboard balanced across his calves in a display of casual authority. Either side was a TV camera; behind him, half a dozen T-shirted teens milled about at monitors. From where she sat, Mari could see three screens running the same picture, like a hall of mirrors. It was footage she remembered from the news: two boys with fishing rods, giving eyewitness accounts of the crash. As Raj twiddled with his regulation earpiece, she felt the ghost of Adam's arm around her.

One screen flicked to something else. Her stomach did a somersault. It was a slow-motion reconstruction of the helicopter spinning down to an apple-green lawn, switching direction at the last moment then slumping on its side like a felled elk. The caption read: *12:55pm.*

'Okay, Mari?'

She closed her eyes. Opened them and nodded.

'Going for a take!' shouted one of the T-shirts.

The throng of bodies froze. All eyes were on Mari or the monitors, including everyone from the green room, now filling the chairs at the back. A grown-up hand was clamped firmly over the little black girl's mouth.

'*Bonded By Tragedy: Chopper of Doom* – take ONE!'

'Mari,' said Raj. 'What was on your mind just before the shocking events occurred?'

She looked blank. 'I can't remember.'

'Was there any particular reason you were walking on the Common that day?'

'No.'

'Nuffink out of the ordinary?'

She cleared her throat. 'No.'

Raj looked quietly thrilled at being on the studio floor. If he had lapels, he would have clutched them.

'So it was just an ordinary summer day, yeah?'

'Yes.'

'Strolling on the Common, not a care in the—'

'*What are you getting at?*'

Mari's glare was vicious. Raj shrank visibly.

'Okay, we'll leave that one … So, tell us, how's your life changed since the tragedy?'

This she considered. Waking up in sopping sheets at least once a week, from dreams of the scalding blast and that numbing roar as the cockpit blew itself apart ... She pushed the thought away and made the mistake of looking up into the lighting rig. When she spoke, all she could see was stars.

'I wouldn't say it has, really. Not because of the crash. I'm still me. Still work at the same place across the road … I often used to go on the Common in my lunch hour. I haven't done that yet, but I will.'

Raj tried another. 'Has it been difficult, adjusting to people seeing you as a heroine?'

'They don't,' she said tersely. 'I know *I* don't ...'

'But you were portrayed in the press as—'

'Exactly: a portrait. Someone else's idea. No one wants to be in that situation! I bet if you ask any of us, we'll all say we wish we'd stayed home that day.' Her eyes flicked to the back of the room which was deep in shadow. 'You get caught up in something like this and suddenly you're fair game. I had reporters at my flat, hanging round the office. Journalists turned up at my parents', wanting my baby photos! What's that about?'

Raj looked baffled. Mari watched his hand fly to his ear. He was receiving comments from the gallery; critical ones, judging by the way he just flinched. His other hand was in his trouser pocket, fiddling with his underpinnings. Something high-cut and fussy, she thought. He was the type.

The hand fell from his ear, upsetting his clipboard.

'Mari, if you want to take a break, we can—'

'No, you're all right. Let's get it over with.'

Raj's eyes were watering. He regrouped.

'Fing is, people love a golden girl, don't they? It's human nature. I'm finking Katie Price, Paris Hilton … Hillary Clinton-'

Mari snapped.

'If you want a golden girl, Raj, try the one who pulled me away from the wreckage before we all got blown to hell! She was blond; you'd have loved her!'

Raj goldfished. Mari found her composure as she stared straight into the camera.

'The papers never found her. She walked me to the edge of the Common, then vanished into thin air … But if she's watching now, I'd just like to say thank you. You saved my life.' She wiped her eyes. 'Thank God for decent people like you.'

Raj managed a respectful pause; he wasn't good with tears. 'Smart. Fanks, Mari. We'll leave it there.' Something inaudible knifed him in the head. 'Sorry, no — one last fing!'

He slid off the desk and approached the plinth. Mari watched suspiciously. He was avoiding her eye as he dug around in his pocket, tense as one-legged lion tamer.

'Mari, one other fing that *didn't* make the papers is why you was on Clapham Common that day … A little bird tells me you were looking for somefink you'd lost. Am I right?'

Her face was rigid. She nodded once.

'Well, our researchers couldn't help noticing that you haven't replaced it, so' – he held out his palm – 'on behalf of FloatYaBoat TV, I'd like to give you this.'

She could scarcely bring herself to look as he prised open the box. Screwed her eyes shut, as a trio of technicians stepped in to fire flashguns, implying a surging mass of cameras … When she opened them, Raj was back on his table, making '*Give-it-to-me-baby*' gestures with his fingers. All Mari could manage was her weakest smile.

At the back, someone started to applaud, a little too slowly. They were shushed by the soundman.

'And *cut*!' shouted a T-shirt.

For a second there was total silence. Till a cameraman said: 'Glare off your shades, Raj. Can we go again?'

II

'It was only what anyone woulda done.'

Glory wasn't enjoying the spotlight. It reminded her of being in trouble at school. And they'd made her get changed. Not into a T-shirt, thank goodness, but they'd swapped her new turquoise blouse for a pink one. Something to do with the cameras and the blue wall behind.

By the looks of him, Raj's day wasn't improving either.

'So, Glory – you've never felt you were hero material or anyfink? Heroine, I mean.'

She didn't flicker. 'If it's heroes you want, you should be talkin' about that man who died. The one who tried to save the poor pilot.'

Raj sighed, consulting his notes.

'Oh yeah, Terrence – no, Tony Torrence … Look, don't worry about him, yeah? We got a nice montage for the credits – his passport photo over a fluttering New Zealand flag. And his mates have done some pieces to camera, though God knows where we're gonna slot them in …' He was finding it hard to keep still. 'Anyway, back to you! It must have changed you – *somehow* – being in that tragic situation? Even a little fing … ?'

'Oh no,' said Glory decisively. 'It changed *everythin'*!'

Raj brightened. 'Yeah?'

She nodded. 'It's made me value every single day.'

'Right. How's that, then?'

'Well, I was goin' through a particularly difficult time when it happened. At work.'

'Which is?'

'Cedars Hall. It's a residential home for the elderly … But something like this alters your whole view o' things. Makes you realise no one ever knows what's round the corner. Except the Lord, o' course.'

He checked his clipboard again; nothing about God.

'An' afterwards I promised myself, from now on, I'm making the most of every day. No more *I can do that tomorrow* – because how do you know? As my dear Ma used to say: *If a job's worth doin', it's worth doin' well* – an' that's true enough. But what I say is: *If it's worth doin' well, it's worth doin'* now!'

Raj was impressed, if not entirely following. 'So you, er, you apply that to your work, yeah?'

'To everythin' ... My home, my family and my work.' Glory paused. 'Though not for much longer.'

'Oh? Why's that, then?'

'Because I'm leavin' the Hall. I've handed in me notice.'

A chair squeaked at the back of the room as something substantial shifted in its seat.

Raj nodded politely. 'Cool. Moving onto parsons new, yeah?'

'*Antigua.*'

'Sorry?'

'I'm movin' to Antigua.'

He was back on his clipboard. 'I don't fink I've got that. Did you tell—?'

'No, I didn't tell your girls cos I haven't told anyone. But I'm tellin' you now.' Glory looked into the darkness; someone was sucking their teeth. 'You only got one life, an' the best you can hope for is findin' a good person to share it with.' She lifted her chin in a challenge. 'An' I have!'

Raj sensed the human-interest levels rising. Cameras whisked silently around him, lights flashing like dumbstruck Daleks. He went for broke:

'That's great, Glory! Who's the lucky fella?'

A shy smile. 'He's called Errol. He works with me. He's been very good to me since it happened – an' in four weeks we fly to Antigua!'

A yelp at the back of the studio; Glory ignored it.

'His cousin runs a hotel in St John's. So we gotta place to stay and jobs to go to, an' if this hadn't happened I wouldn't be goin'!'

'BITCH!'

The TV crew turned in unison. The other black woman was on her feet; one of her children was crying.

Raj tried to keep control. 'Sit down, love – this ain't *Jerry Springer*!'

'You bitch, Glory!' bawled Mercy. 'You tell me nothin'!'

Glory sat proud, her face defiant. This was never goin' to be easy … Two of the burlier T-shirts got ready to move in as another studio boy made rolling motions with his hands.

Raj ploughed on. 'So, Glory – in a sense, you could say that you and Earl were brought together – *bonded* – by tragedy!'

'His name's Errol.'

'Errol, yeah. Good! So now the future's beckoning and the sun's shining bright for you in, er, Antigua!' He smiled, quietly elated at his own riffing. 'Great ... Great story!' He shuffled his notes, then put a hand to his earpiece. 'OK, then – where do we go from here?'

'Well, I know where I'm goin'!' said Glory. But the rest of her words were lost to the studio as she unclipped her microphone and tossed it on the chair.

'I gotta date for lunch!'

*

On the back row, Ian viewed the scene with rising trepidation.

A knot of bodies was muttering at the monitors. Glory brushed past him, ignoring her sister's seething eyes, pausing only to pick up her belongings. Raj was in touch with the director again. With the hand that wasn't on his ear, he gesticulated at the gallery like a Tourette's-wracked Romeo.

At the back of the studio, the soundproof door swung shut. The rest of Glory's entourage was charging for the exit pursued by a worried-looking operative. The child who wasn't crying caught Ian's eye as he scampered out, face lit by an incongruous smile. The boy fluttered a tiny wave in his direction, with the air of one who took such friction in his stride. Something about his fortitude made Ian melt a little.

A hiatus: the gallery had called a halt to the interviews.

'Sorry, everyone,' said Raj. 'We're just gonna run frew the inserts ...'

Ian hadn't a clue what he was talking about, but he felt relief *and* regret at this postponement of the inevitable. The monitors flashed simultaneously and he, Carla and Mari watched in silence.

The first clip was a youngish man; a media type in designer specs, bit swishy-looking. The caption read: *GEOFF ROYLE – Friend*. He appeared to have been filmed in a pound shop, since the shelves behind him were festooned with plastic novelties, Spanish dolls and a wind-up penis on legs. The scenario was at odds with his expression.

'You never think something like this'll happen on your own doorstep, let alone to someone you know ... I was at work when I heard about the crash. I called Tony's mobile, but it went straight to voicemail. And when I got home there it was – sitting on top of his rucksack.'

Ian sighed. Carla slipped a hand through his arm as the

screen cut to the next interviewee. A woman, plumpish, with sad eyes and long dark hair.

GRETA DANIELS – Friend. She had filmed herself on a webcam.

'Tony was the greatest friend I ever had. We had the best times, from uni on. He was always part of my life, even when we were ten thousand miles apart. We were going to meet up in the US – we had other plans too, but ...' She looked away. *'Tony wanted to see the world. We both did. But in his heart of hearts, he knew he'd end up back home one day ... His ma used to say him and me should get married.'* She raised an eyebrow. *'That wasn't going to happen, either. But we used to talk about retiring to the same street – next-door houses, with yards opening onto the beach. I still catch myself thinking about that even now. Then I remember.'*

The clip cut as she began to cry.

'Yessss!'

Raj was by the monitors, nodding like he'd potted a tricky red. Ian bit down hard.

'That it, yeah?' asked Raj. 'Oh, sorry folks. One more …'

It was someone else at a computer. A youngish man, awkward in shirtsleeves and a tie, sitting at a kitchen table. Ian thought he looked familiar. Then he saw why: *BRAD TORRENCE – Brother*.

'Tony was the best big bro in the world, and good to his ma … Not what you'd call a daredevil. No adrenaline stuff, rafting and bungee and that – he always kept outta trouble. He liked his travel, though – specially business class!' He almost laughed. *'Guess none of us knows what we'd do till you find yourself in that situation, God forbid … You either run or you get stuck in. My brother got stuck in. Ma always worried when one of us went anywhere – could be Europe or taking a boat out to the islands, it's all the same to her. But when we heard about Tony, we couldn't believe it. London – so bloody far away … Then it was on telly, on*

the news. Weird. Like Princess Di, but a million times worse.'

The screens went dead. Ian closed his eyes.

Someone tapped him on the shoulder. It was the dragonfly tattoo.

'You're on, Ian!'

Carla squeezed his knee. She held him back a second to brush off fluff.

He took the seat in a daze. Hands fitted the microphone to the pocket of his shirt, and he wondered for the hundredth time why he'd let her talk him into this.

'Quiet, please!' barked someone needlessly.

'*Bonded By Tragedy: Chopper of Doom* – take SIX!'

Raj had perked up. All that despair had reignited his enthusiasm.

'Ian – how has your outlook on life changed since the tragedy?'

He really wasn't in the mood. 'It hasn't. I've always believed in fate. *Que sera sera* and all that.'

'OK ... But do you plan your days differently now? Fink twice about going places?'

'I probably should have thought twice about coming here!'

A cautious chuckle. 'Nice one! I suppose, in a sense, your life had already changed. Given that your wife, Carla, was involved in a hit TV show at the time – namely, Edinburgh TV Festival Golden Fistle-nominee *To Hell in a Houseboat ...*'

Cue tittering at the monitors.

'Don't knock it – lighting's lighting!' Raj ignored the option of another take. 'In fact, you could say you were already at the eye of the storm when fate dealt you the double whammy of a second bite at the cherry ... Does that make sense?'

'No.'

'Well, let me put it another way—'

Ian twitched warily. 'I wasn't looking for any cherries to bite, Raj. What I *am* saying is that things very often work out for the best. Not for that pilot, or the other poor chap. But they happen for a reason.' Raj opened his mouth but Ian ploughed on. 'Case in point: ten years ago I was working in the City. Hated everything about it except the salary, but it never occurred to me to get out. Then I got made redundant – out the door, just like that. I started my own gardening business and it's the best thing I ever did.'

His eyes were glistening under the lights.

'Lovely, Ian … But getting back to the crash—'

'I am, Raj. Because six months ago, my marriage was limping along in much the same way. My wife and I were on the verge of drifting apart. But as Glory said, something like this makes you realise what's important … Now, I'll level with you, I was dubious about Carla going on your show.'

Raj was bristling; Ian soldiered on.

'But I knew I couldn't stop her, and ultimately this whole bizarre chain of events has brought us closer together. Indeed, and I hope she'll forgive me for saying this—'

His interrogator sensed a hijack. *'You're dead right, Ian!* It was, indeed, a bizarre chain of events! In fact, your role in this tragedy is unique, cos of course the helicopter was on its way to pick *you* up when it crashed. Wasn't it?'

'May I finish my point, Raj?'

'No! You can answer my question!'

'I thought I was.'

Raj had had enough.

'Listen, mate, I've bust a bollock getting the *Bonded By Tragedy* team to buy into *Chopper of Doom*!' He struck his thigh with the clipboard. 'So if you fink you're gonna walk in here and take over, you got another fing coming!'

Ian lowered his head. Thumbs and forefingers pressed into the inner corners of his eyes; his voice dropped dangerously.

'*Chopper of Doom* ... Was that your idea?'

'Oh God,' murmured Carla.

Raj's pale-green shirt was darkening symmetrically like a Rorschach inkblot.

'Questions at the end, Ian, we need to—'

'I'm asking you a fucking question now! Was it your idea?'

Raj looked like he'd been slapped. 'Yeah. And *Whirlybird of Woe*, but that got shot down for being "*too passé*", apparently —'

His smirk and the speech-mark fingers brought Ian to his feet.

'Right, fuck you! *Fuck the lot of you ...*'

His arm did a hula manoeuvre as he extricated it from the tangle of flex around his elbow. Carla was up at the plinth, her hair glossy in the spotlight.

'Darling, it's all right – forget them! Let's go!'

Ian was still shaking. His neck was crimson. Once free of the swinging microphone, he held it to his lips and stepped back on the platform. His voice was underlined by a squeal of feedback as it boomed through the studio:

'And let me tell you, when this child is born, it will work in television over *my – dead – BODY!*'

*

Mari settled back in the passenger seat. She wound down the window an inch and lit a cigarette. Neither of them spoke as they watched the figures troop past the end of the alleyway.

First Glory, with her beau. They'd been in reception

when Mari came down in the lift ... Nice-looking lad, if a bit young. He'd brought her flowers.

They walked off hand in hand, and a minute later the rest of her family appeared. Her sister was on her mobile with the little girl balanced on her hip. The boy had his leather jacket hooked over his head, playing aeroplanes.

Mari took another drag as Mr and Mrs Gardening Business appeared. He was still limping. They hovered for a taxi, pretending not to see the others until the little boy collided with the backs of Ian's legs. He bent down and they started to talk.

Mari rested her cigarette on the ashtray and took the tiny box from the dashboard. The ring was gold plate; pink stones in a filigree setting, no attempt at sapphires. Raj's research was about as thorough as you would expect.

'Did you tell them about Adam?' asked Felix, beside her.

She aimed a jet of smoke through the gap in the window.

'No.' She snorted. 'I should have told them everything, really. You know — *loses future husband to the office slapper, then seduces colleague of her own away from his pregnant fiancée.* Probably would have got my own show ...'

Felix tutted. 'You really want to go into work?'

Mari took out the ring and tried it on. It almost fitted over two fingers.

'Why not? About time we faced the music. Mark-James and Melissa think I'm a bitch anyway, so what the hell.'

He leaned across the handbrake. Slipped a hand between her neck and the headrest, and kissed her.

'Lucky I know better.'

Mari smiled. She might have had a boyfriend ever since she was eight, but they didn't all kiss like this one. Whatever that was worth.

A shout rang out from the road, followed by a screech of brakes. The other black woman and her children were piling into a taxi with Ian's wife. He said something to the driver, then hobbled in after them.

Felix reached for the ignition. 'Come on. We don't want to get a ticket ...'

Mari took one last drag on her cigarette, before tossing it out to smoulder on the smooth-worn cobbles.

As they pulled out of the alley, she wound down the window a little further. Slid the brittle ring off her finger and laid it across her thumb. Then, with the ease of a Premier League referee, she flipped it into the street.

ABOUT THE AUTHOR

Chris Chalmers was born in Lancashire and lives in south-west London. He has visited forty countries, swum with marine iguanas and shared a pizza with Donnie Brasco. He has written a diary since 1976 and never missed a night.

Praise for *Light From Other Windows*

'Chalmers can bring tears to your eyes on one page and make you laugh on the next. He deftly skewers the pretensions of contemporary urban life, and his dialogue is unfailingly sharp and witty.'
Suzi Feay, literary journalist

'Once again, Chris Chalmers combines sensitivity and wit in his observation of human behaviour with a cracking storyline. Unputdownable.'
Penny Hancock, bestselling author of *Tideline*

What the bloggers say:

'This story is beautifully structured with a pace and flow that draws the reader effortlessly in. It is a powerful, thought-provoking read about modern family life that will challenge comfortable assumptions. Despite the difficult subject matter its message is life-affirming. I cannot recommend it highly enough.'
neverimitate.wordpress.com

'A wonderful examination of human nature and relationships … The timing of the writing pulled me into the lives of the Maitland family and kept me turning page after page. The use of description overflowed with similes, conjuring sparkling imagery that fitted perfectly with the tone of the novel. A completely absorbing and entertaining read.' livemanylives.wordpress.com

'Not a thriller, grip-lit or misery lit. It's a study of family, uncertainty and grief … Chris Chalmers is a man of words that blend together and convey emotion with a raw intensity. Some moments are dripping with sadness whilst others release silent sarcasm and wry wit. The end result is a novel of substance; slow, sensual and utterly mesmerising.' bleachouselibrary.ie

What the readers say:

'The characters are human and flawed, and the family dynamics rang true and resonated deeply. Towards the end a particularly poignant passage reduced me to tears, yet even that was not the final ace up the author's sleeve. I thoroughly recommend it.' John

'I thought I knew where things were going with each member of the Maitland family as they struggled with the loss of a son/ brother. But I was caught out at every turn including some juicy and sometimes shocking revelations. Our holiday mornings continued to be late starting as we all ended up reading the book and had a great time discussing it.' Amazon Customer

'Finished it. Loved it. Not my usual read but recommended by a friend. I loved all the characters and the effect the tragedy and blog had on their lives. Eyes were teary from page 35. Eyes watering page 216! And such a great way to end (and start) the book. I put it down then rang my mum.' Boo

COMING SOON from Chris Chalmers

Dinner at the Happy Skeleton

Warm, witty and serially promiscuous, Dan Lucas is the kind of gay guy whose heart melts at the sight of a chocolate-brown Labrador. But with men, it's a different matter. He's thirty-nine and as single as ever — not counting the couple he just met online. An arrangement that looks oddly like it might be going somewhere, until Dan gets fired from his job in advertising.

With time out from his career and a payoff in his pocket, the summer presents him with a world of possibilities – if he can just stay off the internet long enough to explore them. So when memories surface of the old flame Dan blames for the thinly-veiled chaos of his life, a need for closure sends him on the trail of his nemesis.

From London to Helsinki, Trieste to Ljubljana, *Dinner at the Happy Skeleton* follows the misadventures of a man for whom the Noughties might have been named. Through an eerie encounter at the home of the Olympiad and an unscheduled sleepover at the Dutch Embassy, run-ins with a fading porn star and the celestial manifestation of Margaret Thatcher, Dan ultimately confronts his past. Until, with his Big Four-Oh rapidly approaching, destiny beckons from where he least expects it.

Printed in Great Britain
by Amazon